CYBORGS IN LATIN AMERICA

Cyborgs in Latin America

J. Andrew Brown

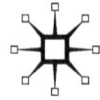

CYBORGS IN LATIN AMERICA
Copyright © J. Andrew Brown, 2010.
All rights reserved.
First published in 2010 by
PALGRAVE MACMILLAN®
in the United States—a division of St. Martin's Press LLC,
175 Fifth Avenue, New York, NY 10010.

Where this book is distributed in the UK, Europe and the rest of the world, this is by Palgrave Macmillan, a division of Macmillan Publishers Limited, registered in England, company number 785998, of Houndmills, Basingstoke, Hampshire RG21 6XS.

Palgrave Macmillan is the global academic imprint of the above companies and has companies and representatives throughout the world.

Palgrave® and Macmillan® are registered trademarks in the United States, the United Kingdom, Europe and other countries.

ISBN: 978–0–230–10390–0

Library of Congress Cataloging-in-Publication Data

Brown, J. Andrew, 1970–
   Cyborgs in Latin America / J. Andrew Brown.
     p. cm.
   Includes bibliographical references.
   ISBN 978–0–230–10390–0 (alk. paper)
    1. Spanish American fiction—20th century—History and criticism.
  2. Science fiction, Spanish American—History and criticism.
  3. Cyborgs in literature. 4. Cyborgs in mass media. 5. Cyborgs in motion pictures. 6. Literature and technology—Latin America—History—20th century. 7. Mass media and technology—Latin America—History—20th century. 8. Human beings—Philosophy.
  I. Title.

PQ7082.S34B76 2010
863'.087620998—dc22   2009047964

A catalogue record of the book is available from the British Library.

Design by Newgen Imaging Systems (P) Ltd., Chennai, India.

First edition: July 2010

For Amy

Contents

Acknowledgments   ix

Introduction   1

Chapter 1
Posthuman *Porteños*: Cyborg Survivors in
Argentine Narrative and Film   9

Chapter 2
Missing Gender: The Posthuman Feminine in Alicia
Borinsky, Carmen Boullosa, and Eugenia Prado   43

Chapter 3
Ripped Stitches: Mass Media and Televisual
Imaginaries in Rafael Courtoisie's Narrative   77

Chapter 4
Neoliberal Prosthetics in Postdictatorial Argentina and
Bolivia: Carlos Gamerro and Edmundo Paz Soldán   113

Chapter 5
Video Heads and Rewound Bodies: Cyborg Memories
in Rodrigo Fresán and Alberto Fuguet   145

Conclusion   175

Notes   179

Bibliography   185

Index   193

Acknowledgments

This book would not exist without the contributions and support from many friends, mentors, colleagues, and family throughout the years. I am grateful to my current and former colleagues at Washington University in St. Louis who have read and commented on various chapters at different stages of writing. I especially thank Elzbieta Sklodowska for her unflagging support as chair of the department and as my colleague and friend. I also thank my colleagues in the Spanish section: William Acree, Joe Barcroft, Cindy Brantmeier, Nina Davis, John Garganigo, Stephanie Kirk, María Fernanda Lander, Mabel Moraña, Eloisa Palafox, Ignacio Sánchez Prado, Joseph Schraibman, Claire Solomon, and Akiko Tsuchiya; all of whom have been very helpful with suggestions and encouragement throughout the evolution of the book. Indeed, the faculty from all the language sections and a wonderful staff (Rita Kuehler, Kathy Loepker, and Helene Abrams) have been a great support just by making the Department of Romance Languages and Literatures such a pleasant place to work. My many students who have taken graduate and undergraduate seminars over the past several years at Washington University and at Middlebury College have also been of great help. Those courses served as a wonderful testing ground for most of these ideas and my students' own excellent readings and comments on the various novels and films under discussion in the book have been very enriching. I also recognize the support of the Graduate School of Arts and Sciences that has supported much of the research involved in the book with a series of grants over the years.

There are many colleagues outside of my university who have also been extremely supportive and helpful over the years, sometimes reading pieces, sometimes with helpful comments at conferences and other places. Any list would be incomplete and I apologize in advance to anyone I neglect to mention, but I would like to recognize and thank especially Daniel Balderston, Alicia Borinsky, Catherine Boyle, Pablo Brescia, Raúl Bueno, Claudio Canaparo, Michelle Clayton, Rafael Courtoisie, Diamela Eltit, Genevieve Fabry, Alberto Fuguet, Libby Ginway, Jerry Hoeg, David Laraway, Rob Latham, Gastón Lillo, Dianna Niebylski, Patrick O'Connell, Edmundo Paz Soldán, Lois Parkinson Zamora, Gustavo Pellón, Eugenia Prado, Luis Rebaza Soraluz, Cristina Rivera Garza, and Mike Wilson Reginato for their comments and for the conversations that we have shared on this topic over the years.

Adria, Colin, Eva, and Liam have tolerated my fixations on cyborgs these last few years and have been so gracious as to show interest in these obsessions and share insights that I would not otherwise have encountered. Amy is a constant source of support and I dedicate this book, as I do all my work, to her.

I would also like to acknowledge that portions of this book have appeared in earlier forms in various articles.

Sections of chapter 1 appeared as "Sobrevivientes y cyborgs: Cine argentino al final de la dictadura." *Cine, Historia y Sociedad: Cine argentino y brasileño desde los años 80.* Ed. Gaston Lillo and Walter Moser. Ottawa: Legas, 2007, 37–46.

"Life Signs: Ricardo Piglia's Cyborgs." *Science, Literature, and Film in the Hispanic World.* Ed. Jerry Hoeg and Kevin Larsen. New York: Palgrave, 2006, 87–107.

In chapter 2, the section on Eugenia Prado appeared earlier as "Identidad poshumana en *Lóbulo* de Eugenia Prado." *Revista Iberoamericana* 73.221 (October–December 2007): 801–12.

Chapter 3 was expanded considerably from "Ripped Stitches: Consumerism, Technology, and Posthuman Identity in Rafael Courtoisie's *Tajos*." *Journal of Latin American Cultural Studies* 15.2 (August 2006): 127–42.

ACKNOWLEDGMENTS

Elements of chapter 4 appeared earlier as "Hacking the Past: Edmundo Paz Soldán's *El delirio de Turing* and Carlos Gamerro's *Las Islas*." *Arizona Journal of Hispanic Cultural Studies* 10 (December 2006): 115–29.

I express gratitude to the journals and presses that have granted permission for these sections to appear in this book.

Introduction

From the late nineteenth century, robots and artificial humans have gathered at the periphery of Latin American cultural production. Eduardo Holmberg's robots from his 1879 novella *Horacio Kalibang o los autómatas* took center stage in the work of an author who never arrived at the center of Argentina's literary circles. A couple of decades later, Horacio Quiroga, an author whose production has an important place in the Latin American literary canon, kept his novella *Hombre artificial* (1909) at the edge of his own oeuvre, publishing it as a serial under a pseudonym. While writers and artists have returned to the idea of technological life in a variety of venues since then, from Ernesto Sabato's scientific and technological paranoia (*Hombre y engranajes* 1951) to Julio Cortázar's fear of a cybernetic revolution (*Rayuela* 1963), only recently has a consideration of corporeal identity at the encounter of the mechanical and the organic occupied a central space in Latin American culture. These earlier works presented the various robots, artificial life forms, and technophilia as harbingers of a failing civilization, of the effects of scientific hubris and the uncritical acceptance of new technologies. Holmberg's robots were metaphors for the dangers he saw in uncontrolled immigration in nineteenth-century Argentina; Quiroga's artificial man was a retelling of the Frankenstein story. Even Sabato and Cortázar's more recent works held fast to the idea that the embrace of new technologies resulted in the loss of an essential identity.[1] Recent narratives from various countries in Latin America have simultaneously extended and problematized this vision of technological life, and done so with much greater frequency than we have seen in the past, with both established and new artists working through the implications of a culture increasingly impacted by new technology. *Cyborgs in Latin America* examines this meeting point in recent Latin American narrative, film, and cultural production where one increasingly finds cybernetic bodies and technological identity at the sociopolitical intersection of military dictatorship and neoliberal policy.

These developments in Latin American cultural expression occur simultaneous to the development of a theoretical vision of the posthuman by critics such as Donna Haraway, N. Katherine Hayles, and Chris Gray. Embracing the revolutionary potential of the figure, especially as it challenges patriarchal and heteronormative values, these theorizations often fail to transcend the North American and European contexts in which they are articulated. *Cyborgs in Latin America* theorizes a peculiarly Latin American vision of technological identity in the postdictatorial, neoliberal reality that is not the case in the situations where we find cyborg and posthuman theory most often cited. By including the narrative, cinematic, and cultural production of Argentina, Bolivia, Chile, Mexico, and Uruguay, this book examines an articulation of cultural identity that incorporates the technological and organic realities of cybernetic being in a way that extends and challenges current theories of cyborg life.

These theories have contributed in important ways to my thinking about the role of the posthuman in Latin American cultural production, and the dialogue that occurs when we put these theories in conversation with various Latin American countries I find particularly fruitful. While I include various forms of narrative in the book, from more traditional short stories, novels, and films to performance art and advertising, my focus is on narrative and each chapter has novels at its center. The decision to focus the study this way is conscious, and I am aware of the way that this study purports a cultural studies approach even as it is largely a literary study. Nevertheless, I would argue that literature, and especially narrative, is a particularly important place to think through the dynamics of culture, especially a dynamic that is so fully immersed in the symbolic language of technology and the body, where writing, computer code, and the technological brands that we associate with our identity produce signs that demand interpretation. I find myself also heavily influenced by Katherine Hayles's view of literature, especially as it relates to her own work on the development of posthuman identity in the United States and in Europe: "Literary texts are not, of course, merely passive conduits. They actively shape what the technologies mean and what the scientific theories signify in cultural contexts. They also embody assumptions similar to those that permeated the scientific theories at critical points" (1999: 21).

She then continues, "In this regard, the literary texts do more than explore the cultural implications of scientific theories and technological artifacts. Embedding ideas and artifacts in the situated specificities of narrative, the literary texts give these ideas and artifacts a local habitation and a name through discursive formulations whose effects are specific to that textual body" (22). Hayles's point is well taken; as we work through the technologies of state, of economy, of quotidian life, the literature that grapples with the formations of new kinds of hybrid subjectivities offers us a series of symbols and images that help us navigate the newly formed social realities of post-dictatorship and neoliberal Latin America. My project is, then, to understand how the literary cyborg figure helps us think through the various context-specific cultural realities that we see presented.

In so doing, I propose that we read texts presented as "realistic" alongside those from a more "science fiction" perspective. When one speaks of cyborgs and the posthuman, one usually thinks of works of speculative fiction that present future realities that have yet to occur. Indeed, much of the critical work undertaken on intersections of literature, culture, and the posthuman focuses on either cyberpunk literature (see, e.g., Thomas Foster's excellent *The Souls of Cyberfolk*) or new technologies still at the bleeding edge of development (if we can speak of the Transhumanist Society as part of culture, we must admit that it has yet to exercise a large presence in day-to-day life). In this book, I am interested in exploring how science fiction and fiction specifically coded as not science fiction run together in their consideration of human being as it appears in an increasingly technological world. Latin America serves as an especially important case study as it adds the prism of technological transfer, of the postdictatorships, and the neoliberal policies of the 1990s that have served as the backdrop to the rapid introduction of Internet technologies. This prism, especially, has been absent in the majority of studies of articulations of the posthuman. In so doing, I also want to distance this project from other critical efforts regarding Latin American literature and technology, especially as it relates to a so-called digital age or to the posthuman. In Borges studies, for example, we have recent books such as *Cy-Borges* (2009) or *Borges 2.0* (2007) that make great effort to position Borges as a kind of prophet or pioneer of technology and the posthuman. While such pursuits produce some fascinating readings of the Argentine author, in this project I am not as interested in how authors have anticipated the technological realities in which we live as I am in the ways in which cultural production uses the posthuman to make sense of social and political realities as they constitute themselves.

Chapter 1, "Posthuman *Porteños*: Cyborg Survivors in Argentine Narrative and Film," examines different expressions of technological identity in Raúl de la Torre's 1982 film adaptation of Manuel Puig's *Pubis angelical* [Angel Hair], Adolfo Aristarain's 1981 film *Tiempo de revancha* [Time for Revenge], and Ricardo Piglia's award-winning novels *Respiración artificial* [Artificial Respiration] (1980) and *La ciudad ausente* [The Absent City] (1993). The chapter examines the articulation of various political bodies whose prostheses and other technological appendages range from mechanical arms to artificial hearts to an entirely robotic existence. What joins all of these articulations is the vision of a cyborg whose existence stems from the moment in which the technology of torture is applied to the organic flesh of the victim, converting the surviving body into a living robot. In this case, Donna Haraway's cyborg that forgets and erases its capitalist father is replaced by one that cannot help but remember the father whose prosthetic phallus engendered the mechanical appendages that constitute its existence. At the same time, these scarred cyborgs maintain their subversive ability as their inability to forget their provenance is shared with all who see them and their mechanical scars. Hence, Puig's woman with an artificial heart, Piglia's mechanical narrator, and Aristarain's dumb protagonist whose mechanical "Speak and Spell" functions as his tongue all call attention to the crime that produced their altered bodies and in this way deny a culture of oblivion in postdictatorial Argentina.

Chapter 2, "Missing Gender: The Posthuman Feminine in Alicia Borinsky, Carmen Boullosa, and Eugenia Prado," examines a curious dynamic that appears in novels from Argentina, Mexico, and Chile. As noted earlier, much of cyborg theory concerns itself with the feminist and queer potential of posthuman theory. Cybernetic bodies escape the need for a nuclear, heteronormative family structure and, because of that, occupy an important part in what Haraway calls the "cyborg myth" of a world free of patriarchal limits and hierarchies. This chapter begins, then, with the Argentine writer Alicia Borinsky's conceptualization of just such a cybernetic character in her novel *Cine continuado* [All Night Movie] (1997) where the metal-skinned Noemí appears to spring directly from Harawayan myth. It then turns to Carmen Boullosa's *Cielos de la tierra* [Heavens of Earth] (1997) and Eugenia Prado's *Lóbulo* [Ear Lobe] (1998), both novels that employ either explicitly posthuman characters (as in the case of Boullosa) or characters whose own discourse identifies them as posthuman (as with Prado) and that present these posthumans as desirous of reclaiming the gender that their posthuman bodies have problematized. This chapter explores the discursive constitution of their posthuman bodies and the theoretical implications of that constitution, especially in the light of the North American and European theory that does not explain this particular conceptualization.

Chapter 3, "Ripped Stitches: Mass Media and Televisual Imaginaries in Rafael Courtoisie's Narrative," combines a consideration of the 2004 marketing campaign Metro 95.1, a Buenos Aires radio station, with an analysis of the novels *Tajos* [Cuts] (2000) and *Caras extrañas* [Strange Faces] (2001) by the Uruguayan writer Rafael Courtoisie. As media technology and neoliberalism have joined to reinforce the spread of each other, the artistic response to this spread has increasingly incorporated a technological discourse. While the radio station posted images around the streets of Buenos Aires of their personalities where half their faces were robotic in attempt to portray themselves as urban and hip, Courtoisie's *Tajos* marries robot identity and mass media in a much darker examination of human being in an age where psychological imaginaries arrive ready-made in the form of television programming and advertising. *Caras extrañas* then projects this cyborg imaginary into the postdictatorship, where television serves as the national memory of the trauma of dictatorship and the internal struggles between Marxist insurgents and the anticommunist military that set up the military coups and oppression of the 1970s. So, while Courtoisie does not include references to the cyborgs of science fiction that we saw in the radio campaign or in the characters that wander through the work of Puig and Piglia, we see realistically portrayed bodies that can only function as a synthesis of organic being and the technology that infuses it. As the media that is delivered in this technological form appears principally as a foreign import and product of neoliberal policy, the chapter also explores the creation of a "tele-borg" whose technological imaginary is not merely based in mass media but functions as a cyborg at a distance. This cyborg is one whose fundamental hybridity is born as various cultural identities are grafted together and are then generated as foreign technology, Latin American organicity, and blended televisual media interact.

Chapter 4, "Neoliberal Prosthetics in Postdictatorial Argentina and Bolivia: Carlos Gamerro and Edmundo Paz Soldán," focuses on the Bolivian novelist Edmundo Paz Soldán's technological exploration of the peculiar links between neoliberalism and dictatorship as evidenced in a country where a former military dictator was democratically elected in the 1990s to preside over the institution of neoliberal policy. In *Sueños digitales* [Digital Dreams] (1999) and *El delirio de Turing* [Turing's Delirium] (2003), Paz Soldán presents a series of technological bodies and posthuman subjects that inform a historically based critique of present-day Bolivia. This chapter also uses *Las Islas* [The Islands], the 1998 first novel by Argentine writer Carlos Gamerro, to compare a similar use of posthuman bodies to relate dictatorship and neoliberalism in Argentina. In the work of both novelists, we also see the introduction of the hacker figure as an important element in their explorations of posthuman bodies in the postdictatorship period.

The final chapter, "Video Heads and Rewound Bodies: Cyborg Memories in Rodrigo Fresán and Alberto Fuguet," explores the various representations of cyborg identity in *Por favor, rebobinar* [Be Kind, Rewind] (1996) by Alberto Fuguet and in *Mantra* (2001) by Rodrigo Fresán as well as in various short stories by both authors. In each narrative, we see attempts to re-form personal, national, and global mythologies that arise from the mass consumption of film and television. This chapter examines the cyborg as the conflicted hero of these mythologies, produced by the human's constant contact with film as a technological medium, simultaneously conflicted and liberated by its ambiguous, techno-organic body. The chapter includes both a theoretical exploration of film as a "cyberneticizing" agent, especially in the light of theories by Marshall McLuhan, Gilles Deleuze, and Kaja Silverman as well as a consideration of film's place in mass culture—drawing on Nestor García Canclini and Jesús Martín Barbero. Fuguet and Fresán, in complicated and contradictory manners, expose the posthuman imaginaries that reside at the meeting of film theory and Latin American cultural theory.

Posthuman and cyborg theory have received a great deal of critical attention of late, extending from the ground-breaking work of Hayles and Haraway to several refinings and applications of that theory. The theme of technology and culture in Latin America has similarly occupied the work of many of Latin America's leading cultural theorists, including Beatriz Sarlo, Jesús Martín Barbero, and Nestor García Canclini. *Cyborgs in Latin America* represents one of the first explorations of the articulation of the technological body in Latin American cultural production. As such, it aims to broaden the scope of posthuman and technology studies both inside and outside Latin America while it deepens our understanding of many of the most significant artists of the current generation of Latin American writers and directors.

Chapter 1

Posthuman *Porteños*: Cyborg Survivors in Argentine Narrative and Film

Manuel Puig's *Pubis angelical* creates a curious temporal frame around Argentina's Dirty War. The novel was published in 1976 as the Videla Junta took oppressive control of the chaos of Isabela de Perón's failed government, and Raúl Torres's film adaptation appeared in 1982 as the chaos of the junta's failed government drew the dictatorship to a close. The narrative centers on the body of a woman that is repeated through various points in time from 1970s Argentina backward through 1940s noir Hollywood and forward into a science fiction dystopic world. In all time periods and with each female character, the woman's body is presented as traumatized, ravaged by illness, by heartbreak, by surgery; all these traumas are represented symbolically in an artificial heart that ticks like a clock within her. The film draws especially upon science fiction tropes as it presents a series of scenes in which the mechanism of her heart is viewed in conjunction with larger machinery even as it rests on her incised flesh. What makes the appearance of the film in 1982 even more significant than its function as a bookend to the dictatorship is that it shares its debut with one of the most significant films in the history of science fiction cinema and a principal film in the corpus of posthuman studies, Ridley Scott's *Blade Runner*, the adaptation of Philip K. Dick's novel *Do Androids Dream of Electric Sheep?* The way in which Puig creates a cyborg woman who is a survivor of dictatorship as a person and as a text—the filmic text "surviving" the censorship of the dictatorship—heralds a meditation on cyborg identity in Argentina that extends from Puig to Ricardo Piglia to Alicia Borinsky to Carlos Gamerro as well as suggests a new way to read yet another film from 1982, Adolfo Aristarain's *Tiempo de revancha*.

Of all the literary and cinematic texts that have occupied the attention of theorists of cyborg and posthuman identity, *Blade Runner* is likely the most commented upon. It appears as an exemplary model in Donna Haraway's "A Cyborg Manifesto" and runs throughout the pages of N. Katherine Hayles's *How We Became Posthuman*. The cover of the excellent collection of posthuman feminist essays, *The Gendered Cyborg*, displays a picture of the character Pris (Daryl Hannah), an android, playing with a dismembered Barbie and the film figures prominently in many of the essays that the collection includes.[1] The film's representation of the android as menacing in its biological ambiguity and its centering of the ambiguity on female characters have provided excellent material for critical and theoretical attempts to plumb identity in the late twentieth century. Furthermore, the way in which cyborg identity challenges rigid patriarchal hierarchies, promising subversive hybridities and fusions where capitalism and sexism attempted separations and categorization, meant that the cyborg could become the champion of late feminism, especially in the theories of Donna Haraway. As she observed: "The cyborg appears in myth precisely where the boundary between human and animal is transgressed. Far from signaling a walling off of people from other living beings, cyborgs signal disturbingly and pleasurably tight coupling" (1991: 152). In that critical context, Pris and the more principal character Rachel suggest that disturbing power. But, as noted before, the early 1980s was a time rife with female androids and cyborgs in general, appearing in such unexpected places as late dictatorship Argentina.

At this point we should turn briefly to an analysis of cyborg and posthuman theory as it currently stands, and especially to cyborg identity as Haraway has imagined it. Her "Cyborg Manifesto" has been particularly influential in the cultural theory of the past decade. The revolutionary possibilities of the boundary-crossing cybernetic life forms that fuse organic body with mechanical prostheses, both real and metaphorical, have found an important place in much of postmodern thought where the rigid hierarchies of earlier systems of thinking have come under critique. Michael Hardt and Antonio Negri hold up her ideas as visionary and influential in their description of Empire, noting as follows: "Donna Haraway's cyborg fable, which resides at the ambiguous boundary between human, animal, and machine, introduces us today, much more effectively than deconstruction, to these new [revolutionary] terrains of possibility" (218). The hybridity she describes as central to cyborg identity has become emblematic of late twentieth-century postmodernity and her work has been extended and developed by many critics and theorists, especially by those who work on issues of posthuman identity. Hayles explains that this hybridity is essential to the conception of the posthuman: "[T]he posthuman view configures human being so that it can be seamlessly articulated with intelligent machines. In the posthuman, there are no essential differences or absolute demarcations between bodily existence and computer simulation, cybernetic mechanism and biological organism, robot teleology and human goals" (1999: 3).

It is important to note that posthuman identity includes both the physical reality of flesh fused to metal and the metaphorical combinations that occur with the daily interactions between organic body and technology. Posthumans can have artificial implants, but they can also have an identity based on the relationship between them and their machines. It is the seamlessness between organic and technological body—the absence of traditional boundaries that keep humans, machines, and animals in their previously assigned places—that identifies and empowers posthuman and cyborg identity.

Haraway specifically describes the cyborg as female, a machine-animal hybrid with important possibilities for the women's movement, well suited to challenge the hierarchies she sees as inherent in patriarchal capitalism. Haraway defines cyborg identity in the following manner:

> A cyborg is a cybernetic organism, a hybrid of machine and organism, a creature of social reality as well as a creature of fiction. Social reality is lived social relations, our most important

political construction, a world-changing fiction....The cyborg is a matter of fiction and lived experience that changes what counts as women's experience in the late twentieth century. This is a struggle over life and death, but the boundary between science fiction and social reality is an optical illusion. (1991: 149)

Haraway combines the hybridity, the seamlessness, of the posthuman identity that Hayles would later describe with the revolutionary role of feminist theory. In that sense, the cyborg ideal suggests an alternate societal construction that would afford, according to Haraway, a way to escape the oppression perpetuated in noncyborg societies.

In Haraway's view one of the sources of the cyborg's power lies in its avoidance of Western notions of origin and unity and subverting traditions that maintain these boundaries, despite the presence of machines that hark to the military-industrial complexes that first generated them. Again, Haraway explains:

> The cyborg skips the step of original unity, of identification with nature in the Western sense. This is its illegitimate promise that might lead to subversion of its teleology as star wars....The cyborg does not dream of community on the model of the organic family, this time without the Oedipal project. The cyborg would not recognize the Garden of Eden; it is not made of mud and cannot dream of returning to dust. The main trouble with cyborgs, of course, is that they are the illegitimate offspring of militarism and patriarchal capitalism, not to mention state socialism. But illegitimate offspring are often exceedingly unfaithful to their origins. Their fathers, after all, are inessential. (151)

Haraway's cyborg occupies, then, a central (if one can use such terminology while talking about cyborg theory) role in theories of gender and revolution against accepted power structures. Her cyborg views origin stories as immaterial to the struggle against "patriarchal capitalism" dismissing its provenance as inessential to the power of its myth. If cyborgs were first conceived within capitalism, their hybrid bodies erase the father as neatly as they avoid the familial structures that have provided the meaning for terms such as "father" and "mother." As theorists of the posthuman, Judith Halberstam and Ira Livingston, have argued the posthuman body is also a "postfamilial" body (10). It is also for this reason that Haraway's theories have been used persuasively in the analysis of texts that propose similar revolutions in the construction of gender.

The first scene of De la Torres's adaptation of Puig's novel displays an operation in which surgeons remove an artificial heart from a woman's body. The camera pans to show a group of men observing the surgery, contemplating the female body with a mix of medical detachment and sexual desire. The camera then shifts to a series of close-ups that alternate between the scalpel cutting the woman's skin, the sutures that circle the woman's chest, and the masculine gazes emanating from both the male observers as well as the angelic statues that fill the room. The collection of shots emphasizes the technological nature of the woman's body, not only in the clockwork heart that is removed from her chest but in the montage of scalpel, flesh, and statue. The scalpel, especially, functions as a phallic object, metallic and penetrating and in whose function we see the application of the mechanical to the organic as it acts as the prosthetic extension of the desiring male gaze. After the surgery the camera lingers on the sutures that help the body recover from the trauma of the surgery even as they act as markers of that invasion, announcing the presence of the artificial heart and archiving the physical pain and deformation that the surgery caused. The film then continues to recount the story of Ana, recuperating in a Mexican hospital while in exile from Argentina and the horrors that the nation experienced in the 1970s. Ana suffers from nightmares where she appears, alternately, as a 1940s Hollywood film star and a futuristic killer robot with both realities commenting on the themes of loss, deceit, trauma, and prosthesis.

The dreams in which Ana is a robot that can read men's minds and is, therefore, dangerous, situate this cyborg figure in a well-known science fiction trope. Just as in *Blade Runner*, where the existence of inorganic replicants who are indistinguishable from humans challenges existing power structures, Ana-Robot is pursued as an inorganic threat to the power men wield from their apparent ability to dissemble and conceal. The film follows Puig's novel in this representation, including various scenes in which she exercises her subversive power by killing her male antagonists before they are able to assassinate her. The fact that the film and the novel present Ana as robot and as 1940s film star creates a further connection with Ridley Scott's film. Mary Ann Doane argues as follows: "Yet, Rachel can be conceived only as a figure drawn from an earlier cinematic scene—1940s *film noir*—the dark and mysterious femme fatale with padded shoulders and 1940s hairdo" (119–20). This combination of female robot with female film archetype, both subversive figures, suggests that the protagonist of *Pubis angelical* participates in a cinematic tradition that not only includes the replicants of *Blade Runner* but the women of *film noir* as well as the classic Maria of Fritz Lang's 1927 *Metropolis*, yet another female robot that challenged male power hierarchies.[2]

At the same time, there is an important difference in the genesis of Puig's cyborg. If Rachel, and even Maria, appear as the results of economic forces and multinational corporations—Rachel and her fellow replicants are constructed by a corporation that then loses control of its products; Maria is the culmination of a desire to replace workers with machines in a Fordian vision of capitalism—Ana's cybernetic body is the result of the trauma caused by dictatorial oppression. Her body has no economic utility, it is not made for money, and consequently, she does not function as a cautionary tale of the dangers of capitalistic technophilia. Instead, the artificial heart that she bears functions as a necessary prosthetic for a woman who has, with the loss of her daughter, her country, and her health, developed the need for a new organ. In this way, the extraction of the future Ana's heart at the beginning of the film foreshadows the death of the 1970s Ana at the end.

In this sense we have in Ana a true cyborg body, a body whose continuing existence depends upon the fundamentally cybernetic relationship between organic flesh and technological prosthesis. Throughout the film, we see a strong semiotic connection between electronic apparatus and dictatorial trauma. By situating the plot on a series of flashbacks and dreams of the future that emanate from the hospital bed of a moribund woman, the cybernetic body that begins the film functions as the oneiric memory of trauma that was suffered as a consequence of dictatorship. The painful experiences that produced the figurative loss of her heart occasion, then, the need for an artificial replacement. What this establishes is the idea of the cybernetic body as an emblem of trauma; the prosthesis that the cyborg carries bears testimony of the violence that caused the need for its presence. In this semiotic function, we see an important contribution to the cyborg theory that has sprung from *Blade Runner* and other U.S. and European science fiction. In fact, this articulation of the cybernetic body extends through several works of the postdictatorship, as we shall see, and suggests a reading of the decidedly nonscience fiction film, *Tiempo de revancha* by Adolfo Aristarain.

Upon first (and even subsequent) consideration, *Tiempo de revancha* does not present any kind of cyborg body—no science fiction robot as was so central to *Pubis angelical*. The film recounts the story of Federico Bengoa, an ex-montonero who has erased his past with his ties to leftist terrorism and now begins a new life as a demolitionist with Tulsaco—a multinational corporation that has hired him to oversee the explosives they use to mine copper in Patagonia. At the beginning of his employment he runs into an old friend from his leftist days who tells him of the safety violations at Tulsaco's mining operation and of his plan to take legal advantage of those abuses. The plan consists of provoking an avalanche in one of the explosions, hiding in a cave, and, when rescued, feigning muteness as a psychological reaction to the trauma of being buried alive. Bengoa decides to participate; but when they carry out the plan the friend is killed, and Bengoa is left to carry out the silent charade. The rest of the film follows Bengoa's legal battle against Tulsaco and ends with Bengoa having won a judgment but condemned to never speak again lest his deception be discovered. To assure his continued silence, he cuts out his tongue.

The image of prosthetic technology functions much more subtly in *Tiempo de revancha* than the artificial heart in *Pubis angelical*. At the same time, it fills a much more central role in the main themes of the film than did the clockwork heart that mostly disappears after the opening sequence. From the beginning of the film, Aristarain creates the idea of an oppressive capitalistic apparatus whose nature is based upon the fusion of human body and mechanical prosthesis. One of the initial sequences shows Bengoa's arrival at the Tulsaco office building for the final interview pursuant to his receiving employment. Aristarain begins the sequence with an establishing shot that presents images of a modern city, Tulsaco appearing first in a metonymical identification between the corporation and the skyscraper that serves as Tulsaco's headquarters as well as the elevator that allows Bengoa's entrance. In the moment that Bengoa approaches the Tulsaco building Aristarain changes the shot from an establishing panoramic view to one that looks up at Bengoa from below, juxtaposing Bengoa and the building and associating their upright figures visually while emphasizing simultaneously Bengoa's smallness compared to the immensity of the corporation. In a literal sense, Tulsaco *is* the building and Bengoa is, then, swallowed by Tulsaco when he enters its body through the doors—an idea that Aristarain emphasizes with a series of shots that show Bengoa in the elevator and waiting in the corridors. Aristarain intercuts this series with close-ups of the gears, pulleys, and cables that drive the elevators as well as typewriters and other office equipment, all images that emphasize the mechanical and technological nature of the corporation within which Bengoa finds himself. This long sequence of shots, all situating Bengoa as one more cog in a series of Tulsaco components, further strengthens this swallowing idea; Tulsaco digests the human Bengoa and converts him figuratively into a part of its mechanical existence.

When the interview finally begins, the interviewer activates a large tape recorder that occupies an important place in the office as well as in the cinematic frame. The machine acts as the interviewer's superior, permitting the beginning of the interview only after it has been activated. The movement of the camera in this scene contributes to this idea as it moves from the interviewer to the machine and then to the photograph of the CEO of Tulsaco, creating visual relationships between the three as it simultaneously suggests a hierarchy of power. In this sense, the organic representation of the corporate power that is situated in the interviewer's body is subjugated to the machine's ability to discipline the bodies of the people in the room. The recorder's ability to subject them to electronic surveillance controls the communicative options that the humans have. Here the organization of images is of particular importance as Aristarain places the recorder at the head of the table, establishing its presence as the head executive of the corporation while also functioning as the prosthetic ears of the photographic reproduction of the "human" CEO, Don Guido Ventura. The interaction between the interviewer and the recorder emphasizes this interpretation as it is only through the act of manually pressing a button that the human interviewer receives the permission he needs to begin the interview; physical contact with the machine serves as the conduit for the transfer of corporate authority. This recording is the first of a series of scenes in which Tulsaco maintains a prosthetic presence through a tape recorder that has, by now, become a fundamental extension of the biomechanical corporate body. This image is separate from one that is exclusively associated with a corrupt corporation, an image that merely attests to the dehumanizing effect of capitalism. While it certainly could include that view, it also determines the exercise of different kinds of power in the film. In the scenes that comprise the court case that Bengoa brings against Tulsaco after the accident and that he supposedly wins, we see a final image of a recorder—continuing to function in the presence of the different emblems of state power (the national seal and flag) while in the absence of the humans who have left the chambers. The fact that Tulsaco later produces these recordings apparently captured by the government merely underlines the connection between corporation and dictatorship that Aristarain suggests with the image of the tape recorder.

For this reason, when Tulsaco begins its persecution of Bengoa, it exercises its power through the recordings that the surveillance machine has produced. The tapes that the corporation sends him remind him of the ubiquitous presence of the tape recorders and, therefore, the ubiquitous presence of the corporation itself. Here we see the idea of a huge surveillance machine that functions because of its mix of organic body and technological apparatus; that is, its power stems from the direct effect that the technology exercises on the body of those it surveys. The series of scenes in which Bengoa attempts to escape this surveillance, to make himself invisible to the sound-capturing devices that Tulsaco uses to construct its presence, emphasizes the creation of a kind of feedback loop between technological *recorder* and biological *recorded*. What I propose with this interpretation is the cybernetic body interpreted as the product of the process that Michel Foucault described in his analysis of the Panopticon. Foucault postulated the internationalization of surveillance, the idea that the presence of an agent of surveillance produces fundamental and internal changes in the body of the observed subject. He claims:

> Hence the major effect of the Panopticon: to induce in the inmate a state of conscious and permanent visibility that assures the automatic functioning of power. So to arrange things that the surveillance is permanent in its effects, even if it is discontinuous in its action; that the perfection of power should tend to render its actual exercise unnecessary; that this architectural apparatus should be a machine for creating and sustaining a power relation independent of the person who exercises it; in short, that the inmates should be caught up in a power situation of which they are themselves the bearers. (201)

The language Foucault employs suggests the cyborg nature of surveillance; its agent is described as a machine that exists within the bodies of those subjected to surveillance. The explicit use of a machine as Panopticon in *Tiempo de revancha* suggests, then, that the body that is subjected to modern surveillance is necessarily a cyborg body; that is, a body whose behavior depends on the relationship between electronic prosthesis and organic flesh and whose genesis proceeds from the application of mechanical prosthesis to the victim's organic body.

Following this idea, the strategy of feigning dumbness as a way to attack the company has an important semiotic value. Deciding not to speak is the logical product of a body under surveillance attempting to resist the tape recorder that effects that supervision. It is for that reason that Bengoa's body converts itself into a subversive entity and escapes from mechanical control by refusing to produce the sounds that the recorder is designed to control. In this way, his body becomes a paradox. It is simultaneously the silenced body of the victim of oppression; its trauma, supposedly organic, is the result of the abuses that have been visited upon that body. At the same time, it is a subversive body that resists further surveillance, a body made possible, ironically, by the very oppression that it now resists. It is, therefore, the absolute victim of surveillance and an emblem of resistance to that surveillance at the same time. It is in this paradox that Bengoa achieves his own personal power against Tulsaco. Being mute denies him the ability to tell his story, to vocalize the abuses that he suffered as a representative of the victims of the corporation. At the same time, being mute distinguishes him and, through this difference, converts him into evidence of those abuses—evidence that resists being silenced and forgotten.

Aristarain develops the paradox of the victim whose voice has been silenced and magnified simultaneously with a series of images that once again emphasize the cybernetic nature of the oppressed body. Upon losing his voice, Bengoa begins to acquire several prosthetic devices to resolve his newfound inability to communicate. He first uses a small chalkboard, employing the written word to replace the spoken. While we can interpret this image as a representation of the role of writing in resisting political and economic power, we can also see the chalkboard as a prosthetic extension of Bengoa's body—an artificial tongue that accomplishes what his organic tongue no longer can. Later, Bengoa's son-in-law gives him a "Speak and Spell" that he can use to speak and thus communicate orally with others. This machine extends the cybernetic nature of Bengoa's body much further than the chalkboard. The machine is not only a prosthetic tongue; it is his artificial voice, a voice that replaces the organic voice of the victim who has been traumatized by the violence that the victim has suffered. It is, at the same time, the hybrid production of written and pronounced word as the machine appears as a keyboard and only speaks the words that are typed into it—fusing, in a sense, the Derridean possibilities of the written word with those of the spoken word. Once again, the hybrid body of the cyborg becomes a particularly appropriate symbol of the hybrid body of the victim of surveillance and dictatorial oppression. The "Speak and Spell" is the machine that fuses the cyborg body with Bengoa's victimized body. Its machine state accompanies him; he wears it as a kind of necklace and, therefore, participates in the production of a body that is both organic and mechanic. The electronic voice that it emits is at once his voice, an aural representation of his intent, and a completely artificial voice of a machine, so computerized that it could never be mistaken as organic. In this contradiction we see once again the paradox to which I referred earlier. The machine restores the lost voice while it makes it impossible to cover up the trauma that caused the loss of speech in the first place. In that way, the electronic voice that the cyborg body uses with its mechanical tongue will always remind its hearers of the trauma that made its presence necessary.

The negotiation scene between Bengoa, his lawyer Dr. Larsen, and the CEO of Tulsaco Don Guido Ventura emphasizes this aspect of the Bengoa cyborg. Once again we see a sequence of shots that displays Bengoa's entrance into a large building, but this time the machinery is explicitly associated with Bengoa's body rather than with the building. Bengoa first appears in a long shot, his face set off by double necklace of chalkboard and "Speak and Spell"—two objects that have converted into extensions of his body, an image Aristarain perpetuates in a series of long and medium shots that always include Bengoa's prosthetics. The moment when Bengoa rejects the offer is centered on the repeated electronic response, "no gracias" [no thank you], a response that marks a fundamental scene in the film. Aristarain accents this moment with a series of electronic beeps and chirps that accompany the computerized phrase, relating Bengoa's resistance to his prosthetic tongue. The moment is climactic, then, on several levels. In terms of plot, it is the point at which Bengoa decides to eschew a monetary reward that a private settlement would bestow for the social justice that a public trial could achieve, a decision that affirms his father's anarchist ideals. At the same time, this moment marks the revenge of the cyborg, a figure who is, after all, the product of the corrupt machinery of the corporation. If his association with Tulsaco provoked his literal transformation in cybernetic body, then the power of this prosthetic body to speak without words of, and to testify to, the violence that brought it into being is the power that reveals Tulsaco's corruption.

The film ends with the unforgettable scene in which Bengoa shaves, puts on a shirt and tie, and then carefully cuts out his tongue. While this act can be interpreted persuasively as an extreme act of autocensorship, the reading that I have proposed of Bengoa and his cyborg body suggests an alternate understanding. In a literal way, Bengoa makes his conversion into a literal cyborg complete, his prosthetics are now a biological necessity rather than an aid to help him in his deception. That is, his mechanical tongues now testify to the true violence and the painful absence of flesh. In this sense, Bengoa accepts his new cybernetic status completely and violently, with all the possibilities and restrictions that this new identity offers just as we have seen throughout the film. Aristarain develops this version of Bengoa's identity, emphasizing the hybrid status of Bengoa's body with the cinematic cliché of the broken mirror that fractures Bengoa's reflection as he cuts out his tongue. In the case of Bengoa, the fissures in the mirror extend beyond the standard connection between a broken mirror and a schizophrenic subject that one generally sees in film. Here the cracks in the mirror foreshadow the cracks that will open in Bengoa's body, principally his mouth. At the same time they function as a cybernetic suture that opens and closes flesh simultaneously, multiplying images of Bengoa's face while they also fuse to create a reflection of an entire body that is made up of disparate pieces—both organic and mechanical. The victory of a cyborg Bengoa strengthens the persuasive interpretation that Juan Poblete has advanced in emphasizing Bengoa's subaltern situation.

> La posición cabal del sujeto subalterno que se caracteriza por la resistencia (a menudo la burla) y la dislocación mimética que muchas veces el poder deja como único espacio de una respuesta posible, no se abre para Bengoa sino en el momento en que pierde el habla. La re-presentación del primer grado acaba cuando la segunda se instala. Desde el momento, Bengoa representa al subalterno y su cuerpo constituido y atravesado por el

poder, es a la vez el espacio en que la burla y la subversión se manifiestan. (117–18)

The consummate position of the subaltern subject that is characterized by resistance (and mockery) and the mimetic dislocation that power many times leaves as the only space for a possible answer is not opened for Bengoa except in the moment in which he loses his ability to speak. From that moment, Bengoa represents the subaltern figure and his body is constituted and crossed by power, it is at one the space in which mockery and subversion are manifested.[3]

The authentically cybernetic nature of Bengoa at the end of the film also suggests one of the possible sources of the subversive power accessible to the subaltern subject that ends up as the product of power as well as a threat to it.[4]

Bengoa's cyborged body with his prosthetic tongue acquires a subversive power that is based on the story that his silent body can tell because of the prostheses that he carries. The chalkboard and the "Speak and Spell" are scars that function to heal a mortal wound and testify to the trauma that opened that wound. *Tiempo de revancha* and *Pubis angelical* both present a species of wounded cyborg that has experienced the trauma of dictatorship and political violence, a species that is a cyborg because of that experience and that can then use its new identity to survive and resist the threatening political reality that has birthed it. If this new cyborg exercises a subversive power similar to that of *Blade Runner*'s androids, its new power stems not from a "pleasurably tight coupling" of flesh and metal but from the horrible loss that necessitated that fusion. Bengoa and Ana also serve as a pattern for the Argentine cyborg that would find its most complete expression in Ricardo Piglia's narrative work.

Ricardo Piglia's *La ciudad ausente* (1992) has received a considerable amount of critical attention in the years following its publication, from journal articles to chapters and sections in many of the recent books on Latin American culture and narrative.[5] This attention has confirmed Piglia's prominent position in Argentina's and Latin America's contemporary narrative landscape, first begun with his 1980 novel *Respiración artificial* [Artificial Respiration] and continuing with his most recent novel *Plata quemada* [Burnt Money] (1997). *La ciudad ausente*'s combination of science fiction and exploration of the aftermath of dictatorship, along with its innovative use of a mechanical female narrator, has served as one of the principal focal points in Piglia criticism to date. Francine Masiello opens her analysis of intellectuals and cultural minorities in Argentina with Piglia's image, commenting that "Piglia, who otherwise has earned considerable respect as one of Argentina's main intellectual forces, obliges us in this recent novel to think of the ways in which women are transformed by a technological culture in order to serve the political and esthetic projects of men" (1997: 239). Masiello's characterization of the machine's technology as a masculine tool for the transformation of women is contested somewhat by Eva-Lynn Jagoe's article in which she reads the image in a much more positive light: "The gendered machine's role is powerful, a symbol of possibility, of resistance. Stories create identities. To speak the horror is to resist, to create languages that deconstruct ideas of individuality.... She is all the stories, and she is the teller of all the stories. Technology is the storyteller" (7).[6] Other critics, while not focusing on the image of the female machine, always include reference to it as evidence of Piglia's ongoing interest in science fiction.[7] The power of the image, especially when understood in the light of Donna Haraway's influential articulation of a feminist cyborg myth, would seem to extend Masiello's initial reaction along the lines Jagoe suggests. While such is indeed the case, I would argue that the presentation of Piglia's mechanical narrator simultaneously excludes and alters other essential aspects of current cyborg theory. That is, the focus on the machine narrator and its connections with Haraway's cyborg myth, while enlightening in many respects, is also somewhat problematic when one considers the other real and metaphorical cyborgs, male and female, that populate the novel as well as an accompanying meditation on the cybernetic nature of narrative. If Piglia's use of a female machine to narrate his novel activates both the gender-focused analysis Jagoe suggests as well as the criticism Masiello argues, the image of the cybernetic organism he develops is one that, following Puig and Aristarain, also explores the nature of the traumatized body within an oppressive political state. When examined from this perspective, *Pubis angelical*, *Tiempo de revancha*, and *La ciudad ausente* suggest a reading of the possible cyborgs that populate Piglia's earlier work, principally his novel *Respiración artificial*. In all cases we see an articulation of cyborg and posthuman identity that, while participating in (and anticipating) much of the theoretical work undertaken by U.S. and European thinkers, proposes new and different directions in our understanding of the mechanized body especially in a Latin American context.

La ciudad ausente begins with Junior, an Argentine journalist of English descent, who is drawn into investigating a mysterious museum purported to hide an equally mysterious machine. As he does so, he encounters several characters that tell him stories that branch out from the narrative line of Junior's inquiry. When he arrives at the museum he continues in that mode, able now to combine his reading of the various stories with the exhibits that complement and expand the written texts that Junior discovers. As the investigation develops, he learns that the museum does indeed house a storytelling machine inhabited by the consciousness of one Elena, the deceased wife of the Argentine writer Macedonio Fernández. This Elena, now a machine, turns out to be the narrator of many of the stories that Junior has come across along the way as well as the novel itself. The novel concludes with a monologue explicitly evocative of Molly Bloom's meditations at the end of James Joyce's *Ulysses*.

One of the stories she tells, "Los nudos blancos" [The White Nodes] works in counterpoint to the main narrative. The story is that of a woman also named Elena interred in a mental institution who believes that she is a machine. She and the other patients in the clinic suffer interrogation and torture disguised as therapy at the hands of the doctors there in a thinly veiled allusion to the human rights violations of Argentina's most recent military dictatorship. Elena resists the torture but is forced to observe as friends and associates also undergo both the torture and the ubiquitous mechanical surveillance that defines the hospital where she is trapped. The story functions as both a microcosm for the rest of the novel as well as a possible alternate explanation for the Elena-machine that Junior finds in the museum. If the machine Elena is not the narrator the patient Elena may well be, which is a possibility that is never ruled out.

In addition to the very central image of the Elena/Machine enclosed in the museum and who also exists either literally or figuratively in the clinic, the novel provides several examples of what cyborg theorists might term posthuman identity. Many of the characters in the intercalated stories appear as bodies not easily defined separately from the machines and technology that surround them. In one story, "La nena," [The Girl], a girl who possibly suffers from autism perceives the world through her experience with the spinning fans in her room and is described as "una máquina lógica conectada a una interfase equivocada" (54) [She was a logic machine connected to the incorrect interface] (48). In the previously mentioned story "Los nudos blancos," the women in the clinic describe themselves as indistinguishable from the tubes and medical machinery that substantially alter their sense of being. Nor are the cyborgs all women. A Russian friend of Macedonio Fernández who appears near the end of the novel is described as more metal than flesh as a result of his many battle wounds. He functions as a kind of walking robot whose prostheses keep his body functioning while they simultaneously serve as medals of honor commemorating his several battles. The novel itself appears as a kind of mechanism akin to the cyborgs that inhabit it; a network of stories, intertextual references, and mirrored events and images that exists not in a single textual "body" but in the relationships between the different narrative lines.

At first consideration, the machine Elena appears to fulfill Haraway's characterization of cyborg identity—confirming Jagoe's observation that "*La ciudad ausente*, is, in some senses, the postmodern text that Haraway invokes, and with that label comes the problematic of politics, of deciding the use-value of this text, whether it is liberating or repressive, both or neither" (8). Elena's double existence, as either a woman interned in a mental clinic who believes that she is a machine or the actual machine in the heart of the "museo," contributes to a sense of the cyborg that Haraway suggests. Her hybrid nature functions as a threat to the masculinized hierarchies suggested by the doctors in the clinic and the officials of the state. The experience of the clinic in "Los nudos blancos" strongly reinforces on several levels the connection between the cyborgs proposed by Piglia and Haraway.

In the clinic, Elena not only constructs herself as a machine but is also presented as a kind of medicalized cyborg—the patient whose continued life depends upon the artificial support of various medical devices. In both cases, the machine woman is viewed as dangerous and is contained and questioned within a clinic that bears a close resemblance to the Argentine police state of the 1970s and early 1980s. On one occasion, Doctor Arana, the psychiatrist, interrogates Elena in such a way as to make the historical reference clear:

—Hay que operar—dijo—. Tenemos que desactivar neurológicamente.

—Arregla televisores—dijo Elena.

—Ya sé—dijo Arana—. Quiero nombres y direcciones.

Hubo una pausa, en el consultorio los vidrios blancos del armario reflejaban el vaivén del ventilador.

—Hay un telépata—dijo Elena—. Me sigue y me lee los pensamientos. Se llama Luca Lombardo, viene de Rosario, todos le dicen el Tano. Si digo lo que usted me pregunta, va a hacer estallar las microesferas que tengo implantadas en el corazón.

—No sea imbécil—dijo Arana—. Se ha vuelto psicótica y tiene un delirio paranoico. Estamos en una clínica de Belgrano, esto es una sesión prologada con drogas, usted es Elena Fernández.—Se detuvo y leyó la ficha:—Trabaja en el Archivo Nacional, tiene dos hijos.

—Estoy muerta, él me trasladó aquí, soy una máquina.

—Vamos a tener que aplicarle un electroshock—le dijo Arana al médico que tenía cara de bebé. (79)

"We have to operate," he said. "We have to deactivate her neurologically."

"He repairs television sets," Elena said.

"I know," Arana said. "I want names and addresses."

There was a pause. The white glass of the cabinet in the consulting room reflected the spinning fan.

"There's this telepath," Elena said. "He follows me around and reads my thoughts. His name is Luca Lombardo, he's from Rosario, everyone calls him the Tano. If I tell you what you are asking me for, he is going to blow up the microspheres implanted in my heart."

"Don't be stupid," Arana said. "You have become psychotic and are in the middle of a paranoid delirium. We are in a Clinic in the neighborhood of Belgrano, this is an extended drug session, you are Elena Fernández." He stopped and read her chart. "You work in the National Archives, you have two children."

"I am dead, he moved me here, I am a machine."

"We are going to have to use electric shock treatment on her," Arana said to the doctor with the baby face. (69)[8]

Throughout the questioning the woman's body is described as machine-like, not merely in her own protestations where she identifies herself as machine but in the reference to deactivating her brain as doublespeak for the questioning that would follow. The electroshock therapy is especially disturbing, a clear reference to the use of the *picana* as a central element in the Argentine military's torture machine. Elena's stay in the clinic, combined with her interrogation and the figurative (perhaps real) torture implied by the electric therapy, presents her as emblematic of the body of the *desaparecido/a* [disappeared] in Argentine history in addition to her cyborg characteristics.[9] The combination of the cybernetic images that construct Elena's identity with her role as symbol of the so-called subversive element in 1970s Argentina further strengthens the representation of Elena as an example of Haraway's cyborg myth. She functions as the feminized hybrid figure whose existence contests the categories imposed by a masculine society. Furthermore, Elena's continued existence suggests the kind of resistance that Haraway identifies as essential to the cyborg and that theorists such as Hardt and Negri have championed in their consideration of cyborg identity.

Piglia unites the physical imagery of the cyborg that characterizes Elena in both her guises as machine and patient with a consideration of the cybernetic language as used in the novel and even of the nature of narrative itself, a strategy that Nicolás

Bratosevich has called an "estética cibernética" (215) [cybernetic aesthetic]. *La ciudad ausente* contains at least seven different stories that Junior encounters, as well as several more told by Elena to herself that exist both as separate narratives and as thematically and situationally related stories. The web-like structure of the novel suggests an almost hypertextual experience of reading—an idea suggested by the image of Junior in the museum, seeing the paintings and exhibits that reproduce the images of the stories he reads. Note, for instance, Junior's observations of the museum after emerging from "Una mujer" [A Woman]; a story that tells of a woman who abandons her family and commits suicide in a hotel:

> En el Museo estaba la reproducción de la pieza del hotel donde se había matado la mujer. En la mesa de luz vio la foto del hijo apoyada contra el velador. No recordaba ese detalle en el relato. La serie de los cuartos de hotel aparecía reproducida en salas sucesivas. [...] Lo asombraba la fidelidad de la reconstrucción. Parecía un sueño. Pero los sueños eran relatos falsos. Y éstas eran historias verdaderas. Cada uno aislado en un rincón del Museo, construyendo la historia de su vida. (49)

> The room in which the woman committed suicide was reproduced in the Museum. Junior saw the picture of the son against the lamp on the night table. He did not remember this detail from the story. The series of hotel rooms was reproduced in successive halls.... He was astonished by the precision of the reconstruction. It seemed like a dream. But dreams were false stories. And these were true stories. Each one isolated in a corner of the Museum, building the story of their lives. (43)

The series of exhibits that provide a visual confirmation of the story suggests a vision of writing where meaning appears at the juncture of image and text; Junior sees, for example, a photo in the exhibit that forces him to rethink his reading of the story. We see this character negotiate potential meanings between image and text, as provided by a device designed to deliver content in accordance with that reader's decisions. Junior receives the narrations as related by a machine (museum) that encloses both the texts and the apparatus that permits their reading. Junior becomes a kind of hypertextual reader, to whom the stories are told by a truly cyborg narrator, even as he participates as a kind of writer/reader (or "wreader" as some hypertext theorists would have it) as he moves from story to story and makes connections between his physical location (the museum) and the stories that he encounters.[10] In that same sense, Elena as a biomechanical narrator also becomes the mechanical element of a kind of cyborg "wreader" that also incorporates an organic Junior and the mechanical museum/textual repository within her own biomechanical body. Mark Amerika has argued that hypertext opens a space for a "cyborg-narrator" whose creation of "discourse networks" serves as the basis for the new narrative form (qtd. in Ryan 2001: 9). Piglia not only describes a figurative hypertextual situation but he provides the literal cyborg-narrator.

In that sense, Junior's experience as a reader becomes that of Jean Baudrillard's museum visitor. This critic observes as follows:

> For example some museums, following a sort of Disneyland processing, try to put people not so much in front of the painting—which is not interactive enough and even suspect as pure spectacular consumption—but into the painting. Insinuated audiovisually into the virtual reality of the Déjeuner sur l'herbe, people will enjoy it in real time, feeling and tasting the whole Impressionist context, and eventually interacting with the picture. (22)

Junior's insertion in the museum and the stories it exhibits produces a situation in which text is presented as a kind of virtual reality, a reality made all the more virtual by Junior's own position as a character within the novel that Elena narrates. If Baudrillard saw such a virtual reality as negative, as a kind of device designed to imprison the masses, Junior's experience as a reader is even more ambiguous, caught within the text, but not necessarily forced into submission by a controlling state.[11] In that sense, Junior appears to benefit from what hypertext theorists have identified as the narrative form's liberating potential. George Landow has argued: "As long as any reader has the power to enter the system and leave his or her mark, neither the tyranny of the center nor that of the majority can impose itself" (281).[12] Junior's discovery of narratives that the state has attempted to suppress suggests that his hypertextual reading experience promises similar revolutionary possibilities.

While Junior's position as reader within the museum suggests the hypertextual nature of his reading experience and the weblike structure of the novel, Piglia reinforces the image of mechanical language with many of the stories that Junior examines. The cyborg girl in "La nena" speaks like a machine, "canturreando y cloqueando, una máquina triste, musical" her limited linguistic abilities revealing the mechanical sounds at the foundation of language (58) [singing softly, clucking, a sad music machine] (51). The section called "La isla" [The Island] is especially indicative of this characteristic, a story about an island where languages change from day to day and the only reliably decipherable book is James Joyce's *Finnegans Wake* (since it is written in all languages at once). The inhabitants attempt to read the book biblically, using what they can glean from it to form belief systems and scientific approaches to language. In all their attempts, the idea of language appears as a fake, mechanical construct that is at once impossible to control and hopelessly artificial. The language of the island is described as follows:

> El carácter inestable del lenguaje define la vida en la isla. Nunca se sabe con qué palabras serán nombrados en le futuro los estados presentes. A veces llegan cartas escritas con signos que ya no se comprenden. A veces un hombre y una mujer son amantes apasionados en una lengua y en otra son hostiles y casi desconocidos. Grandes poetas dejan de serlo y se convierten en nada....(121)

> The unstable character of language defines life on the island. One never knows what words will be used in the future to name present states. Sometimes letters arrive addressed with symbols that are no longer understood. Sometimes a man and a woman are passionate lovers in one language, and in another they are hostile and barely know each other. Great poets cease being so....(102)

The unstable meanings of the constantly shifting languages accentuate the tenuous relationship between sign and meaning and by so doing create a sense of artificiality, one that we see in the conceptualizations of narrative proposed by Junior the cyborg "wreader" and Elena his narrator. The island narrative serves, then, as a microcosm of the novel, contrasting the linguistic systems of the island-dwellers with the narratives produced by the cyborg narrator. This section of the novel also emphasizes once again the revolutionary potential of language when situated against the state. As Francine Masiello has observed in her more recent analysis of *La ciudad ausente*: "Insofar as the machines always translate from language to language, they facilitate a subversive communication that eludes the market-run state" (2001: 165).

With the novel's attention to cybernetic themes and, more importantly, with its attention to the idea of language as cybernetically organized, *La ciudad ausente* functions as what David Porush calls "cybernetic fiction." This critic explains:

> Therefore, not only do these authors confront technology—and in particular cybernetics—thematically, they also focus on the *machinery or technology of their fiction*, remaining uniquely conscious that their texts are constructed of words, that words are part of the larger machinery of language, and that language is shaped by the still larger machinery of their own consciousness and experience. Yet paradoxically, each of these texts calls attention to itself not merely as a machine but as a fictional work.... Because both the theme and form of this sub-class derive from cybernetics, I call it *cybernetic fiction*. (19, italics in original)

In turn Hayles has examined the impact of cybernetic theory on literature to an even greater extent, arguing that the mechanical form of the text is inseparable from the meaning that a reader infers. In her book *Writing Machines*, this critic shows how the materiality of the text, be it a book, a hypertext, or something else entirely, combines with the text's theme to challenge notions of human and textual identity. Essentially, the physical presence of the text recasts the work in terms of the reader's relationships with the textual and technological machinery that delivers the language. With its combination of an apparently Haraway-inspired cyborg narrator and a hypertextual "wreader," *La ciudad ausente* would appear to propose just such a rethinking of narrative theory. In that sense, Piglia's novel seems to present itself as a poster-child for contemporary cultural theory, at least if it were really that easy to fit literary texts within already established cultural theory.

However, cultural production precedes theory much more effectively than the production incorporates that theory. In fact, it is precisely at the point at which a machine literally narrates his novel that we begin to observe a marked tension between literary cyber-theorists and the Argentine novelist's project. *La ciudad ausente* is still a traditional book; it does not allow the actual reader options like a hypertext narrative would, nor does it create for him or her a virtual reality. What Piglia's novel does do is provide those tools for the reader trapped inside the novel. It is Junior who becomes a "virtual" reader that acts out the implications of hypertext; the "real" reader of *La ciudad ausente* cannot access these same opportunities or possibilities. The book is, then, a paradoxically virtual novel, one in which the technological experience described is "virtual" only because it is not. In a fashion Baudrillard would have enjoyed, virtuality, like everything else in the work, is a simulacrum and the novel remains a traditional, paperbound volume that only pretends to offer hypertextual possibilities.

This surprising ambiguity in the narrative's own hypertextual possibilities suggests similar wrinkles in the novel's exploration of cyborg identity through the bodies that populate the text. While Piglia develops an image of the cyborg consistent with many of Haraway's ideas, a closer look at *La ciudad ausente* reveals an expression of cyborg identity that is peculiarly Argentine. Jagoe claims that "[i]n this novel, women are cyborgs: they are dolls, statues, figures in mirrors, machines. Their easily programmable identities invoke a postmodern ideal of heterogeneity and fluidity of identity, yet it is always up to the men whether this retelling of the woman will be an act of love or an act of torture" (8). While such a statement is generally accurate, it tends to exclude the implications of the male cyborgs that also populate the novel. If we include the male-gendered cyborgs in Piglia's novel in our examination, we better perceive the theory of an Argentine cyborg that Piglia attempts to present, not only in *La ciudad ausente*, but in his earlier *Respiración artificial*. Near the end of the novel, Junior discovers the story of the conversion of Elena the human being into Elena-cyborg. Upon her death, Macedonio both relates and relates to the story of an anarchist who had sacrificed himself during a bombing in order to save an innocent family, an event his friend Rajzarov witnessed firsthand. The bomb had left the Russian alive, but horribly disfigured. Macedonio sees the pain of that series of events as akin to the suffering he felt at the death of his wife. The narrator notes: "El que ha perdido a la mujer amada queda como el hombre al que le estalla una bomba en el cuerpo y no muere" (152) [When a man loses the woman he loves he is like the man who has a bomb blow up on his body and does not die] (126). As he undergoes such trauma, Macedonio begins to experience a transformation in his identity, which the narrator describes immediately after relating the tale of the anarchist:

> Macedonio se sentía un hermano del impetuoso Rajzarov, que estaba hecho de metal más que de vida. Su dentadura de acero centelleaba al hablar, bajo su peinado había una placa de plata, un enrejado de oro entretejía un tatuaje tridimensional en medio de los leves despojos de cartílago y hueso que le quedaban en la articulación de la rodilla derecha, un sello de dolor hecho a mano, cuya forma siempre sentiría como un recuerdo doloroso y a la vez el círculo de fuego libertario, una condecoración de combate que llevaba con el máximo orgullo por ser invisible y estar grabada en su cuerpo.... Macedonio había quedado así, metálico, maltrecho, sostenido con operaciones y prótesis, el mismo dolor, el mismo cuerpo rehecho artificialmente, porque Elena de golpe estaba ausente. Congelado, de aluminio, caminaba con los brazos y las piernas separados del cuerpo, como un muñeco de metal, no podía sonreír ni alzar la voz. (152–53)

> Macedonio thought that the impetuous Rajzarov was like his brother, that Russian who was made more of metal than life. His steel teeth sparkled when he spoke, he had a silver plate in his head, a gold lattice interwoven like a three-dimensional tattoo held together the few strands of cartilage and bone that were left in his right knee—a man-made badge of pain that he would always recall simultaneously as a painful memory and as

a circle of liberating fire, a medal of honor that he carried about with the utmost pride.... That is how Macedonio had ended up, metallic, impaired, held together by operations and prostheses, the same pain and the same body artificially reconstructed, because Elena was suddenly absent. Frozen, made out of aluminum, walking as if his arms and legs did not belong to his body, like a metal doll, he was unable to smile, he could not raise his voice. (126)

Rajzarov becomes the visual manifestation of Macedonio's grief; the former man's scars, steel teeth, and silver plate in his head not only serve as reminders of the violence the Russian suffered, but also of the trauma that Elena's death caused Macedonio. Rajzarov's literal prostheses transform into Macedonio's figurative artificial body, a body made cyborg not by physical violence but by the emotional injury of grief. In both cases, the posthuman body comes into being because of trauma, be it physical or psychological or both. Pain becomes the defining characteristic of the birth of the cybernetic organism.

The presentation of Rajzarov as cyborg and as a model for the identity that Macedonio begins to construct in a post-Elena reality contributes to a vision of the cyborg that extends and transforms Haraway and Hayles's ideas in an Argentine context. Rajzarov functions as a cyborg whose amalgamated body works against its own hybrid nature. All of the metal prostheses, instead of fusing with his flesh to produce a new identity, merely testify to the violence of their origins. That is, the mechanical prosthetics act as grotesque replicas of the human body and constantly remind the human beings, in this case both Rajzarov and Macedonio, of the trauma that brought this hybrid body into existence. Cyborg identity for Piglia becomes the identity of the violated and injured body whose mechanical appendages merely signal the absence of living tissue rather than the presence of a new kind of cybernetic life. If Rajzarov views his injured body with pride, the artificial parts functioning as war medals, Macedonio's psychological conversion into a figurative cyborg suggests a negative interpretation of the prosthetics. Despite the difference in reaction, both see the metallic components as symbols of violence and suffering. Macedonio's sense of self as artificial is grounded completely in the trauma of his being separated from his wife. His survival is compared with the prosthetic arm that always fails to replace the real one, whose mere presence constantly signifies the traumatic experience that caused the loss of the still-preferred living arm.

The cyborg bodies of Rajzarov and Macedonio are complemented and contrasted with the description of Doctor Arana, the psychiatrist in "Los nudos blancos" who is responsible for the care of Elena in the clinic. Elena describes him as he enters her room:

> Sabía que la Clínica era siniestra, pero cuando vio aparecer al doctor Arana se le confirmaron las premoniciones; parecía estar ahí para hacer reales todos los delirios paranoicos. Cráneo de vidrio, las venas rojas al aire, los huesos blancos brillando bajo la luz interna. Elena pensó que el hombre era un imán donde se incrustaban las limaduras de hierro del alma. (66)
>
> She knew the Clinic was a sinister place. When Doctor Arana came in, he confirmed her worst fears. He seemed to be there just to make every single paranoid delirium come true. A glass skull, the red windows facing out, white bones shining in the artificial light. Elena thought the man was a magnet that attracted and drew the iron shavings of the soul to itself. (58)

Arana appears as a kind of medical robot, his parts disassociated from any kind of living body and transformed into a monstrous magnetic machine. She later remarks on his aluminum teeth, a comment that further distances Arana from any kind of organicity (72). If Elena, Rajzarov, and Macedonio appear as truly cybernetic organisms, hybrids of human being and machine, Arana is a kind of pure robot that embodies only the mechanical side of their, and especially Elena's, cyborg nature. He is, then, firmly associated with the exercise of political power in his interrogations of Elena; his complicity with state terror clearly linked with his mechanical nature. Furthermore, Arana highlights the connection Piglia forges between mechanical imagery and the police state.

The suggestion provided by these three male examples, Rajzarov, Macedonio, and Arana, is that the subversive power of cyborg identity does not necessarily lie in the boundary-challenging hybridity of its body, but in the fact that the cyborg body inherently testifies of trauma. The cyborg becomes a re-membering figure that can never forget the dismembering reasons for its prosthetic grafts and metallic replacements. Indeed, it views those apparatuses as the by-products of torture. Haraway's characterization of the fusion of flesh and technology as "pleasurably tight coupling" seems wildly inappropriate here (152). The power of the cyborgs' hybridity that Piglia creates comes because their undead bodies cannot be buried and forgotten. Their artificial lives continuously reveal their violent origins and, for that reason, they continue to threaten the cultures and regimes of silence that have plagued Argentina. They also suggest a different way of reading Elena's cyborg body; one that engages Haraway's ideas and then extends them within a view of cybernetic identity that is specific to its Argentine context.

Understood in that sense, the electroshock therapy that Elena receives in the clinic and that represents the torture suffered by the victims of the dictatorship gains further significance. While "Los nudos blancos" makes reference to that therapy, the novel also refers to the actual acts of electroshock torture that had become commonplace in twentieth-century Argentina. Toward the end of the novel, Junior encounters a museum exhibit dedicated to the son of the poet Leopoldo Lugones. Named after his father, he achieved notoriety as a police chief who "pioneered" the use of the cattle prod in police questioning and torture. The narrator reports:

> En el Museo Policial había una sala dedicada a la vida del comisario Lugones, llamado igual que su padre, Leopoldo Lugones (hijo) que fundó la Sección Especial e introdujo una mejora sustancial en las técnicas argentinas de tortura, usó la picana eléctrica, que tradicionalmente se había empleado con las vacas para embarcar el ganado en los trenes ingleses, meterlas en los bretes, la usó en el cuerpo desnudo de los anarquistas encadenados de los que quería obtener información. (160)
>
> In the Police Museum there was a room dedicated to the life of Lugones, the chief of police, whose name was the same as his father's, Leopoldo Lugones. He founded the Special Division and introduced a substantial improvement to the torture

techniques utilized in Argentina: he took the electric prod, which was traditionally used with cows to direct the cattle up the short ramps and into the English trains, and used it on the naked bodies of the shackled anarchists from whom he wanted to get information. (131–32)

The exhibit recalls the electroshock therapy suffered by Elena and the other patients in "Los nudos blancos," strengthening the already established connection between the psychiatric clinic and the Argentine police state. It simultaneously anticipates a remark made by Elena a few pages later in the Molly Bloomesque monologue that concludes the novel, where she has completely revealed her mechanical nature:

> ¿Y ahora quién está ahí? ¿Fuyita? ¿Russo? No, quién va a venir a esta hora, sos loca, por qué esperás, te morís de cáncer, sos otra loca más, una loca cualquiera al borde de la muerte y ahora siento como un golpe de corriente, el suave refucilo en las vértebras, el electroshock que hacía empalidecer de terror a mi hermana María. (167)

> And now who's there? Fuyita? The Russian? No, who would come around here at this time of day, you're crazy, what are you waiting for, you're dying of cancer, you're just another crazy woman, a crazy nobody waiting at the edge of death. Now I feel like there's a current blowing, the soft flash of lightning in my vertebrae, the electric shock that used to make my sister María turn white with fear. (137)

These apparent ramblings ambiguously position Elena's voice both within the clinic of "Los nudos blancos" and near the point at which Elena, wife of Macedonio, would succumb to disease.

In the latter position we find Elena at the moment that would convert Macedonio into the sort of cyborg described earlier, with her death from cancer figuring as the traumatic experience that linked Macedonio's robot feelings with Rajzarov's metallic scars and gave birth to the novel's specific brand of cyborg identity. Furthermore, the inclusion of the electric shocks in these ramblings associates the police torture with the moment of cyborg birth. That is, the traumatic events that caused

Macedonio to become posthuman and, in turn, to create a cyborg Elena are, through a kind of textual metonymic, made equal to the trauma of torture on the victim's body. The electricity that tortures and scars the flesh simultaneously converts that body into a cybernetic organism. The *picana* [electric cattle prod] serves, then, as the sexual prosthesis of the mechanized state, one that begets the cyborg body on the feminized (though not necessarily female) organic body of the victim. With that kind of horror present at the inception of the cybernetic body, the mechanical appendages and prosthetics, those elements that make Piglia's cyborg a cyborg, become the scars of torture and the testimonies of the violence that brought it into being.

It is because of the testimonial nature of Piglia's cyborg body that it is so subversive, a kind of Frankenstein's monster whose presence continually reminds the viewer of the artificial experiments performed on violated flesh that gave the creature its existence.[13] The mechanized police state must attempt to contain the body, not because the cyborg challenges limits or boundaries of what is human and what is machine—the state already did that in the torture chamber; it must contain the cyborg body because it is a continual witness to the horrors of the past and the crimes of the mechanical father. It is in that representation of the subversive nature of the cyborg body that we see most clearly a theorization that extends beyond the ideas presented by Haraway and others. That is, the illegitimate cyborg is unfaithful to its militaristic father not because it makes the father unnecessary, but because it refuses to let that father disappear into postdictatorship oblivion. The cyborg is the traumatized storyteller, whose re-membered and re-membering body recalls the trauma and horror of dictatorship and state-sponsored terror in the face of national attempts to forget the past. At the same time, the machine half of the hybrid is constructed as the remnant of the mechanical father, a horrible grafted emblem of pain that the living body suffers as a continual reminder of the living tissue that was destroyed by that father. The posthuman body's hybridity is not embraced as inherently positive; it merely exists as the inevitable result of pain of state-induced trauma. In this light, the origin stories that Haraway rejects are, for Piglia, an essential element of cyborg identity. It should not surprise us, then, that Piglia names Villiers de l'Isle Adam's *L'Ève future* as an important source for *La ciudad ausente*, a text whose use of a female robot reinscribes Western origins rather than erasing them.[14]

Additionally, this theorization of the Argentine cyborg invites a reevaluation of one of the characters of Piglia's earlier novel, *Respiración artificial*, as well as of the title of that novel. *Respiración artificial* has been regarded as one of the principal novels of the Dirty War period: its combination of investigation of fear and oppression with a decidedly postmodern textual aesthetic marks it as one of the principal novels of late twentieth-century Argentine narrative. Brett Levinson calls the book "one of the most profound literary meditations on nationalism and dictatorship in the Latin American Southern Cone" (91). The novel details, roughly, an investigation conducted by Piglia's alter ego Renzi, an intellectual character who appears throughout much of Piglia's narrative. Renzi's investigation into Argentina's past is accompanied by letters and diaries that include episodes from the nineteenth century, a strategy that emphasizes the hybrid nature of a text moving constantly between the 1830s and 1970s. The first page begins with the phrase, "¿Hay una historia?," and Renzi's subsequent search mirrors the search for those individuals and their histories that were made absent during the most recent military dictatorship in Argentina. The novel's publication at the lowest point of the dictatorship makes its critique of intellectual life and history during the Dirty War all the more powerful.

At one point in his investigation Renzi is hired by a man named "El Senador," a former politician who has played an active role in many of the Argentine governments of the twentieth century. The description of the Senator anticipates many of the details of the cyborg identity Piglia would describe more fully in *La ciudad ausente*.

> Y uno de sus entretenimientos, dijo, «es pasear con mi carrito, mi carricoche, mi berlina, de un lado a otro, de una pared a otra, en mi silla de ruedas, por este cuarto vacío. Porque ¿en qué se ha convertido mi cuerpo sino en esta máquina de metal, ruedas, rajos, llantas, tubos niquelados, que me transporta de

un lado a otro por esta estancia vacía? A veces, aquí donde reina el silencio, no hay otra cosa que el suave ruido metálico que acompaña mis paseos, de un lado a otro, de un lado a otro. El vacío es total: he logrado ya despojarme de todo. Y sin embargo es preciso estar hecho a este aire, de lo contrario se corre el riesgo de congelarse en él. El hielo está cerca, la soledad es inmensa: sólo quien ha logrado, como yo, hacer de su cuerpo un objeto metálico puede arriesgarse a convivir a estas alturas. El frío, o mejor», dijo el senador, «la *frialdad* es, para mí, la condición del pensamiento. Una prolongada experiencia, la voluntad de deslizarme sobre los rayos niquelados de mi cuerpo, me ha permitido vislumbrar el orden que legisla la gran máquina poliédrica de la historia. (53–54)

And one of his diversions, he said, was "to wander around in my wheelchair, my rattletrap, my stagecoach, from one place to another, from one wall to the opposite one, in my wheelchair in this empty room. Because my body is now no more than a machine made of metal, wheels, spokes, tires, nickel-covered tubes, which transports me from one end of this empty room to the other. Sometimes here in this kingdom of silence there is no noise other than the smooth metallic hum that keeps me company on my excursions, back and forth. The emptiness is absolute: by now I have managed to give up everything. And yet one must be prepared for the thin air, otherwise one runs the risk of *freezing* in it. The ice is close by, the solitude is immense: only someone who has managed, as I have, to turn his body into a metallic object can risk living at these altitudes. The cold, or rather," said the Senator, "*coldness* is for me propitious for thought. Prolonged experience and the desire to slip between the nickel spokes of my body have granted me the possibility of glimpsing the order that rules the polyhedral machine of history." (51)

The Senator's metallic body appears in conjunction with the emptiness to which this figure aspires, while the mechanical nature of his identity is inextricably linked with the solitary nature of power and the great machine of history that he claims to understand. The Senator has achieved a sense of identity not unlike that described by Hayles, where the body is considered as just another prosthetic device. At the same time, this process of cyborg conversion is one in which the flesh is slowly eliminated and replaced by metal. In this case, the positive, or even neutral, fusion of elements Haraway and others ascribe to posthuman identity does not occur and the flesh/technology hybrid remains, rather, a failed, unreconciled dialectic. If we read *Respiración artificial* from the anachronistic vantage point of *La ciudad ausente*, we see a similar kind of cyborg in the identity of the Senator. In this case, the character's wheelchair continually reminds both the Senator and those who view him of the assassination attempt that put him there. The Senator appears as one whose mechanical parts signify his close association with the historical power structures that have dominated Argentine politics during the twentieth century. The clear and important difference between the Senator as cyborg and Elena as cyborg is that the mechanical testimony that the Senator's cybernetic body gives is of his own political crimes, while Elena's body testifies to the crimes committed by the state against the body of the oppressed. That said, the testifying function of the cyborg body is the same. In *Respiración artificial* we see the beginnings of a posthuman theory that adds an Argentine perspective to the work being conducted in the United States and Europe, while anticipating much of the writing on cyborg identity that would appear more than a decade later.[15]

Piglia's cyborg senator additionally suggests an alternate interpretation to the title of Piglia's first novel. Most critics have, justifiably, read the title as a reference to the state of Argentina under dictatorship, a nation in such bad shape that it needed artificial respiration in order to continue breathing. The cyborg theory that these two novels propose suggests a complementary reading of the title, one in which breathing persists in the presence of the artificial. In that sense, the cybernetic combination of breath and artificiality suggests a cyborg Argentina whose respiration tells the stories of hybrid life created by the aggression of the artificial state. Levinson notes that the Senator's voice "is his only movement, the very sign that he is alive" (111). The cyborg's continued breath manifests signs of life in the face of the violence that has given birth to its prosthetic existence.

This emphasis on the signs of life that emanate from the cyborg embodies the earlier paradox we noted in the development of the virtual hypertext. The human figures that are at once caught within the hypertextual machine, yet are essential to its function, complement the living breath of the cyborgs that use their bodies to testify of the violence of their creation. Idelber Avelar has described convincingly the role of mourning in Latin American fiction and specifically in Piglia's first two novels. This critic notes: "Restitution depends on the survival of storytelling because that which is to be restituted belongs in the order of memory. Only in this terrain, *La ciudad ausente* claims, can the tasks of mourning work be posed to thought" (135). In the end, we see a conceptualization of posthuman identity that both embraces its revolutionary potential while refusing to recognize any pleasure in the couplings that join their organic and mechanical bodies. Piglia's cyborgs are breathing, speaking machines that carry grafted onto them the commemorative prosthetic emblems of the horrors of Argentine history.

Furthermore, they echo the traumatized bodies of the earlier films as Elena reinscribes and reembodies Ana and Bengoa from the earlier films. What we see form in this constellation of films and novel is a class of cyborg that can be called peculiarly Argentine, one whose prosthetics respond specifically to its national context. As the clockwork hearts, the speak-and-spell tongues, the machines that preserve consciousness combine, they create a corporeal space in which national mourning and survivorship can be processed. This type of cybernetic body continues on—we see it in *La sonámbula*, the film Piglia cowrote in which survivors of an unknown trauma are identified by the scars and stains they bear. They will not be the only way that posthumans' bodies are used to explore new realities, but they exercise an important influence in those imaginaries that help a people re-member the dictatorship from the postdictatorship as they focus on the tortured couplings of prosthetics and scarred flesh.

Chapter 2

Missing Gender: The Posthuman Feminine in Alicia Borinsky, Carmen Boullosa, and Eugenia Prado

Both Puig and Piglia use cyborg women as the sites upon which their dictatorial and postdictatorial narratives are enacted, the altered female bodies functioning simultaneously as a storyteller and text. When we turn to those relatively few Latin American women writers who have explored posthuman identity, we find a disparate collection of narratives that strengthen, challenge, and reinvent theories of posthuman subjectivity and cyborg representation. While North American and European theorists have adopted the cyborg figure as a powerful element of feminist thinking, Latin American narratives with explicitly feminist perspectives have problematized the posthuman subject on several levels. Indeed, three novels in particular examine the cyborg figure from a variety of perspectives, some upholding the tenets of North American and European posthuman theory as in the case of Alicia Borinsky's *Cine continuado* (1998), some providing very different views of cyborg identity as in the case of Carmen Boullosa's *Cielos de la tierra* (1997) or Eugenia Prado's *Lóbulo* (1998). In all cases we see a clear exploration of gender identity and posthuman being that is absent from much of the work we have studied or will study in male-authored narratives.

Alicia Borinsky's *Cine continuado* (1998) is the most recent of a series of novels that she refers to as "novelas de espectáculo" (qtd. in Niebylski 2001: 54–55). Dianna Niebylski has argued persuasively that Borinsky's presentation of "moveable and unstable female subjects" in these novels (especially in *Mina cruel* [1989, Cruel Girl] and *Cine continuado*) allows Borinsky to emphasize the subversive possibilities of this continually morphing, continually moving (or nomadic) feminine figure (2001: 55).[1] In *Cine continuado*, we see Borinsky's leveraging of the inherent instability and hybridity of the female cyborg figure in her ongoing exploration of feminine identity. The novel displays the fragmented tale of several women, including Felipa, a prostitute whose preferred workspace is a telephone booth, and Noemí, a stripper who was kidnapped by a lesbian couple unhappy with her act and with her prostitution. Felipa is presented as a protean figure that adapts her body (and her name) dynamically to the various men that appear in her life. In the case of Noemí, her kidnappers glue a uniform on her skin with an impossibly strong adhesive as a way to force her to change professions. She later escapes and finds help from any number of men willing to help her off with her sticky clothes only to find that the adhesive has caused her skin to change from flesh to metal, leading the national media to name her "La llagada" [The wounded girl]. Borinsky accompanies this tale of technological magical realism with a series of technical and structural gestures that emphasize the slippery identities and mutative subjectivities that emphasize the formation of a new feminine presence.

From the beginning, Borinsky associates the rebellious female figure with important cyborg tropes. Felipa gains her experience as a prostitute in a telephone booth in a series of scenes that suggest an intimate knowledge with the logic of prosthetics. The narrator remarks:

> Para Felipa, el corazón trinando de sabiduría, la cabina era la cámara nupcial. Con cada Felipe que traía su cuerpo se adaptaba más a las esquinas, los accidentes de terreno, las distancias entre el tubo telefónico y su espalda. Después de varios meses de práctica con el camarero aprendió un oficio pero dejó una pasión. (14)
>
> For Felipa, her heart beating with wisdom, the booth was a nuptial chamber. With each Felipe she lured in, her body got

better attuned to the corners, the uneven surfaces, and the distance between the receiver and her back. After several months of practice with the waiter she gained a skill but lost a passion. (10)

Not only does Felipa learn a trade as she conducts her affairs in the phone booth, her body learns a new state of being. As the "cabina" shifts from phone booth to marriage bed, we see that this space dominated by communication technology begins to affect changes in Felipa's body. In addition to the more figurative heart that begins to fill with the erotic knowledge that her new trade imparts, Borinsky adds that Felipa's body communicates with the phone booth, molding itself to the contours of the space and learning the proximity of the telephone receiver. Indeed, the paragraph focuses exclusively on the communication between Felipa's body and the telephone, eschewing completely the apparent erotic communication between Felipa and her various Felipes—an erasure that suggests the conversion of the "tubo telefónico" into a sexual prosthetic device that replaces an organic, masculine presence. The lack of a specifying comma in the phrase "Con cada Felipe que atraía su cuerpo se adaptaba más a las esquinas" strengthens this sense of shifting and slippery signifiers. The noun "cuerpo" floats between two possible verbs, possibly attracting, possibly adapting. The more logical reading suggests that Felipa is the subject of "atraía" and "su cuerpo" is the subject of "se adaptaba," but the lack of the comma makes it possible to exchange subject and verb, a possibility that suggests a kind of posthuman cleavage where Felipa is simultaneously separated from her body and inextricably intertwined in it as she becomes one with the telephone booth.[2]

Borinsky, in a way that we have not seen so far, follows Haraway and many other cyborg theorists by linking posthuman being and issues of gender. Felipa, while an extremely sexual being, is also ambiguously gendered from the very beginning of the novel. Her first sexual experience is with a more mature woman, one who bids her goodbye by exclaiming how much pleasure they had shared while noting that she will make some man very happy. Borinsky then emphasizes Felipa's bisexuality with this initial name, one that springs from her encounter with the waiter Felipe, Felipa then occupying a hermaphroditic role, one that could certainly carry out Haraway's vision of the cyborg free from heteronormative restraints. Indeed, it is Felipa's status as sexual outsider, as threat to the nuclear family, that makes her a force that must be contained. Her blatant use of sexuality as a bisexual prostitute with an office in a telephone booth makes her a presence that is simultaneously the object of desire and fear. The fact that this subject is continually situated within the apparatus of the telephone booth and that her body intersects and is intersected by a technology whose function is to disembody voices establishes clearly the couplings the novel joins between cyborg identity, ambiguous sexuality, and feminine subjectivity.

Turning to the other principal feminine character in the novel, Noemí/La llagada, we see a series of related dynamics. The sticky attempt to control her exhibitionism suggests a similar desire to possess and deny that we see played out in Felipa's many transformations. Nevertheless, the adhesive becomes counterproductive and Noemí's metal skin endows with further disruptive power.

> Todos pueden ser rotadas menos ella. Hecha un trompo da vueltas, se para por un instante, les da el latigazo de sus pestañas perfectas y cuando todos se han ido sigue por sí misma. Magnífica muñeca de hierro. Ya no la pobrecita. Ni rastro de las llagas.
>
> Están solos y el Dr. Gutiérrez rendido de amor a sus pies la sueña de día y de noche, la canoniza. (124)
>
> They can all be rotated except for her. Spinning she whirls, pauses an instant, gives them the whip of her perfect eyelashes and when everybody has gone she keeps going for herself alone. Magnificent iron doll. No longer a poor little girl. Not a trace of the scars. They're alone and Dr. Gutiérrez at her feet exhausted by love dreams of her day and night canonizes her. (118–19)

The phrase "magnífica muñeca de hierro" fuses concepts that would be contradictory within traditional constructions of gender, endowing the feminine doll with the not-so-feminine hardness of iron. Borinsky here makes literal the figurative power that Felipa had exercised earlier as bisexual prostitute and uses, significantly, a cyborg image to express that fusion. Additionally, the cyborg nature of the iron body suggests a healing image, one that overcomes the fissures that her paradoxical nature suffered when confined to an entirely organic matrix. She is no longer the poor little thing, but a worshipped being, described later as "una diosa de acero inoxidable" an image that reminds one of the android photographs of Naomi Campbell that are mentioned in Edmundo Paz Soldán's *Sueños digitales* and that will be discussed in a later chapter. Ultimately, her metal body serves as the ultimate threatening subject/object. She remarks, near the end of the novel, as follows:

—El aluminio tiene estar muy brilloso.

—Queda mejor un poco opaco. Da categoría. Acordáte del museo Metropolitano en Nueva York, por ejemplo ¿las armaduras medievales brillan? No. Porque tienen la autoridad de los años y la gente fascinada pasa a verlas pero qué te vas a acordar si vos, pobrecita, nunca fuiste a ningún lado seguro que nadie te llevó, falta de guita, de interés.

—Basta que esto me está aburriendo y lustre bien que tiene que quedar como un espejo.

—¿Como un espejo?

—Para que cuando me miren a mí se vean a sí mismos. Un espejo. De aumento. Que se vean, depilen y acicalen. (169–70)

—The aluminum has to be very shiny.

—It looks better a little dark. It lends class. Think of the Metropolitan Museum in New York, for example, does the medieval armor shine? No, because it has the authenticity of years, and the people are fascinated and go to look at it, but how are you going to remember, poor girl, if you've never gone anywhere, I'm sure no one ever took you, lack of wherewithal, or interest.

—That's enough because I'm getting bored, now polish it well so it looks like a mirror.

—Like a mirror?

—So when they look at me they'll see themselves. A mirror. It enlarges. Let them see, let them get a body wax and makeup. (163–64)

The mirroring aspect of her body creates, then, the possibility for societal change as her presentation as the object of erotic, voyeuristic desire then reflects her ambiguous sexual and corporeal nature back on the voyeur. At that point, she is able to share her fusion of subjectivity and objectivity with those that gaze at her.

When Chela Sandoval argues, "Haraway's cyborg textual machine represents a politics that runs parallel to those of U.S. third world feminism" (412), she could find no better narrative support than Borinsky's exploration of feminine spectacle and subjectivity. Indeed, Dianna Niebylski has used Haraway's work specifically to contextualize Borinsky's presentation of the rebellious female figure to great effect. In *Cine continuado* we see the first text that we have considered so far that embraces those elements of cyborg identity that appeal to many contemporary posthuman theorists. While Borinsky's own female subjectivity could be argued as the source for this difference in approach to the posthuman figure, she also happens to be the first female writer that we have considered in this study, we should not make that argument too quickly. If Felipa "missed" her gender by using her cyborg body to reject the traditionally constructed and imposed definition of the female, we see posthuman women in other female-authored texts who "miss" their gender in very different ways.

The publication of Carmen Boullosa's 1997 novel *Cielos de la tierra* was both preceded and accompanied by a great deal of interest, due in part to the critical and popular success of her previous work, in part to the novel's remarkable narrative structure, and in part to an interview Boullosa granted in 1995 where she announced that her next novel would include a "posthuman" character. The Mexican novelist remarked that her forthcoming novel "begins with a third voice and it's a voice of a woman of the future.... They are post-humans...she has no father, no mother, they have artificial parents, they are another kind of human" (qtd. in Hoeg, 151). Jerry Hoeg, in particular, includes this interview as proof of what he calls "the beginnings of a Latin American hybrid fusion of the posthuman and the mestiza into a sort of cybermestiza" (99), a position he develops with several references to North American and European theorists on posthuman and cyborg identity and then uses to advance his argument that

> [t]he ultimate stage of Latin American narrative, if it can still be called narrative, follows the pattern of previous Latin American narrative. It is mediated by the discourse of technoscience and searches for a resolution to the question of the impact of the dominating uses of technology in Latin America. What is new is that it now embraces technology rather than rejecting it as foreign and imposed. (107)

Boullosa's novel, by comfortably including Lear and her/his posthuman community within the narrative, certainly carries through on that promise. However, the work of subsequent theorists that suggests that Boullosa uses Lear to include ideas that mirror contemporary posthuman theory does not enjoy the same support. While the novel does include a well-developed posthuman community, it appears in such a way as to problematize current theories on posthuman and cyborg identity. The novel becomes an excellent opportunity to explore the implications of a Mexican novel whose curious depiction of the posthuman can be seen as more of a nostalgic gesture than one that looks forward to a new technological reality in Latin American writing.

Cielos de la Tierra is an ambitious novel that intertwines three narrative voices: Lear, a member of a postapocalyptic, utopian community L'Atlàntide, Estela, a Mexican woman from the 1990s who studies and translates colonial literature, and Hernando de Rivas, a sixteenth-century indigenous Mexican living in a Franciscan utopian project. The novel moves between their three texts, narrating the lives and experiences of the three outsiders who attempt to live and resist within their respective dominant cultures. Estela and Lear are also able to use the writings of Hernando as a part of that resistance, a strategy that Boullosa emphasizes as essential. The characters are constantly reading, writing, and reflecting on those acts, from Hernando and his journals to Estela's fond recollection and critical evaluation of her generation's reading of *Cien años de soledad* to Lear's attempt to preserve historical writings and language in general. While the entire novel is certainly worthy of and has received a great deal of critical attention, it is Lear, our futuristic posthuman, who serves as the focus of this section. Indeed, as Claire Taylor has argued, "it is in Boullosa's configuration of the science fiction scenario that the most pressing issues of the novel arise" (477). Just as Boullosa claimed Lear is presented as a posthuman, another kind of human. The self-description on the first page of her narrative establishes the context of her identity.

> Porque no sé quién fue mi padre ni quién mi madre, porque fui gestada en un engendrador y pasé los años de crecimiento en la Conformación (la primera estaba en La Cuna, la segunda en El Receptor de Imágenes), porque aunque polvo eres, Lear, en polvo no te convertirás, no puedo echar mano de gran parte de las interpretaciones que en el tiempo de la Historia usaron los hombres para desentrañar lo que soy. (15)

> Because I don't know my father or my mother, because I was gestated in a machine and was raised in the Conformation (the first was in the Cradle, the second in the Image Receptor), because though you are dust, Lear, you shall not return to dust, I cannot use many of the interpretations that men used in the time of History to work out what I am.

This description emphasizes several of the key attributes many North American theorists have ascribed to the posthuman condition, that is, the ectogenetic pregnancy that produces the posthuman body, the concomitant destabilization of the traditional family structure that its existence causes, the heavy emphasis of the role of technology in its generation, and its abandonment of traditional origin stories, evident in both the machines that constituted the formation of her body and her physical and societal detachment from History—a word Lear emphasizes with a capital "H." In fact, Lear's comments evoke quite clearly Donna Haraway's definition of the cyborg that was mentioned earlier: "The cyborg does not dream of community on the model of the organic family,... The cyborg would not recognize the Garden of Eden; it is not made of mud and cannot dream of returning to dust" (151). Judith Halberstam and Ira Livingston emphasize the rejection of reproduction within the organic family model as an essential characteristic of the posthuman body, noting that "[p]osthuman bodies were never in the womb. Bodies are determined and operated by systems whose reproduction is—sometimes partially but always irreducibly—asexual" (17). This dismissal of procreative sex serves as the idealized sociopolitical state in posthuman theory. Haraway concludes her Cyborg Manifesto, observing the following:

> [H]olistic politics depend on metaphors of rebirth and invariably call on the resources of reproductive sex. I would suggest that cyborgs have to do with regeneration and are suspicious of the reproductive matrix and of most birthing....We have all been injured, profoundly. We require regeneration, not rebirth, and the possibilities for our reconstitution include the utopian dream of the hope for a monstrous world without gender. (181)

Lear's initial presentation appears to fulfill all the characteristics of posthuman identity described here as well as it appears to invoke the utopian ideal Haraway advances. In that sense, Hoeg's suggestion that Boullosa occupies a principal role in his characterization of a new, more technologically friendly Latin American narrative is well supported. Claire Taylor, whose study of cyborg identity in *Cielos de la tierra* misses Hoeg's previous work, attempts to extend the technological comfort level of the novel with the idea that Boullosa leverages Haraway's vision of the subversive cyborg in her own technologically enhanced critique of gender and language.

And yet, as I suggested earlier, *Cielos de la tierra* may not be an entirely appropriate candidate for this theory. While Lear is clearly posthuman, her subsequent experiences and comments tend toward a dismantling of the cyborg model. Indeed, Lear's interest in the uncovering of History suggests a cyborg uneasy with its theoretical definition. Lear comments: "Con mi trabajo, urgo en nuestros orígenes, en el tiempo de la Historia. Ah, pero aquí empezaría un problema serio. Porque nadie en L'Atlàntide querrá reconocer en los hombres de la Historia a nuestros padres, ni fincar en ellos nuestros orígenes" (15) [With my work I delve into our origins, in the time of History. Ah, but here is where a serious problem begins. Because no one in L'Atlàntide wants to recognize the men of History as our parents, nor place our origins in them]. If Lear belongs to a community that embodies the cyborg utopias to which theorists such as Donna Haraway aspire, Lear herself appears at the margin of such a society—nostalgic for precisely what her community forbids and what cyborg theorists have rejected.

In fact, Lear's linking of History with origin further distances her from L'Atlàntide's posthuman ideals. Haraway explains the rejection of origin in cyborg thought: "An origin story in the 'Western,' humanist sense depends on the myth of original unity, fullness, bliss and terror, represented by the phallic mother from whom all humans must separate.... The cyborg skips the step of original unity" (1991: 151). Haraway dismisses the importance of origin as unnecessary to the cyborgs who are, after all, "exceedingly unfaithful to their origins. Their fathers, after all, are inessential" (1991: 151). Lear, in her obsession with history and origin, appears to stumble as she skips the step of origin that Haraway's cyborg leaves behind. In that sense Lear appears to be more like Star Trek's Data, the android who dreams, like Pinocchio, of being human, of having and knowing parents, and of feeling organically based sensations.

Boullosa develops the idea of the posthuman who, contrary to her nature, dreams of origins throughout the novel. Lear continually emphasizes the contrary nature of her historical work, one that opposes the utopian project of the rest of the community. "Mientras me inclino hacia el pasado, los demás habitantes de L'Atlàntide se empinan hacia un presente perpetuo y se utilizan para reconstruir lo que los hombres de la Historia se empeñaron en destruir, la sublime Naturaleza. Yo sí recuerdo al hombre de la Historia, y dialogo con él" (16) [While I'm drawn in by the past, the rest of the inhabitants of L'Atlàntide look toward a perpetual present and dedicate themselves to reconstructing what the men of History worked so hard to destroy, sublime Nature]. If L'Atlàntide serves a space in which gender and nuclear family structures are eliminated as the cause of the ecological apocalypse that has nearly destroyed the planet, Lear attempts once and again to recoup not only the origin stories that the cyborg rejects but the familial structures that have been replaced by the machines in which Lear and her companions are grown. Furthermore, Lear attempts to resituate L'Atlàntide within Western origin stories. At one point in her description of the community she remarks: "En nuestra casa el Paraíso Terrenal (como el del primer hombre y su primera mujer en la leyenda que retoma la Biblia), es un paraíso sin vegetación, suspendido en el medio del cielo" (18) [In our house, Earthly Paradise (like that of the first man and the first woman in the legend that the Bible retells) is a paradise without vegetation, suspended in the middle of the sky]. She later remarks in the same vein: "¿Han creado un jardín donde pasean evas y adanes inmaculados, sin haber aún pecado, porque no han reconstruido a su serpiente?" [Have they created a garden where immaculate eves and adams walk around, not yet having sinned because they have not reconstructed the serpent?] (25). In both cases Lear uses the biblical creation story to recontextualize the utopian project of L'Atlàntide, effectively reinserting a very clearly cyborg utopia within the origin myths that cyborgs and posthumans supposedly subvert. While one could certainly argue that such a recontextualization upsets the "original" origin story, Lear's position as rebel suggests one in which the Garden of Eden undercuts the posthuman project. Indeed, the origin story becomes the subversive element, recasting the attempt to create a new utopian project as merely the repetition of the already-told Judeo-Christian tale. In fact, the original unity that Lear seeks is made dystopic by the posthuman society's inability to reproduce completely the biblical origin as they leave out the serpent. The flaw that will ultimately destroy the society is that they apparently embrace Haraway's rejection of the Garden of Eden.

This cyborg utopia that cannot be, a clearly dystopian civilization that merely falls apart rather than present a new subversive possibility, is what the novel leaves us. While L'Atlàntide appears to reenact the description of a hopeful possibility of a cyborg mythology, its subsequent fall affirms Lear's critical position as a marginal member of the community. As a function of the desire to eliminate reference to and memory of the destructive culture that occasioned the apocalypse language is forbidden, a law whose enforcement emphasizes the authoritarian nature of this technological posthuman community. Lear recounts one episode in which the totalitarian tendencies of the community become clear.

> Sentimos la alarma contra el palabrerío palpitar en nuestros pies. Sin darnos cuenta, Rosete y yo nos habíamos puesto a conversar. Ya lo dije, no se debe conversar adentro de L'Atlàntide. Pero ahí estábamos otra vez Rosete y yo, platicando, irresponsables. Qué vergüenza. Sentida la alarma, nos callamos. De inmediato la Central nos trasmitió, a cada uno, en silencio, la retahíla de recomendaciones pertinentes: N41, N42, N43, 087 y Y1. (92)
>
> We heard the alarm against word use vibrate in our feet. Without realizing it, Rosete and I had begun to converse. I've said it before, one cannot speak in L'Atlantide. But there we were once again, Rosete and I, speaking irresponsibly. How embarrassing. Once we heard the alarm, we were quiet. Immediately the Central office transmitted to each of us, silently, the list of pertinent recommendations: N41, N42, N43, 087 and Y1.

The community projects a sense of constant, omnipresent vigilance that is enforced electronically through a series of alarms. The already posthuman bodies of Rosete and Lear are subjected to further artificial alteration and control as the technology of discipline modifies and regulates their behavior. The codes at the end of the quotation act as a final silencing mechanism, not merely replacing language but suggesting the idea of Lear and Rosete as parts of a large computer that sends code back and forth as it functions. L'Atlàntide appears, then, as the science fiction cliché of the evil cybernetic empire that uses technology as a part of its repression of the human body. It is at this point where we see both the importance of Taylor's argument that the science fiction (SF) nature of the novel is its most salient feature and the flaw in the critic's argument that Boullosa's use of the SF genre is subversive along the lines of Donna Haraway. Boullosa's rather straightforward condemnation of the dehumanizing effects of technological society situates it among much of traditional science fiction, well before cyberpunk destabilized an anticyborg tendency that can be traced as far back as *Frankenstein*.[3]

The process of events set in motion by the abolition of language results in the destruction of the society. The posthumans begin to procreate once again, to reproduce, but without a familial context. Lear looks on in horror as her friends sacrifice and eat the children that are born organically rather than created. The monstrosity of the event only underscores for Lear the depraved cyborg nature of the community while affirming her own anti-posthuman sentiments. She remarks at the sight of the dissolution of the society:

> ¿Tengo también el cuerpo lleno de cosas? Estoy convencida de que no. Yo no estoy rellena de cosas. Respiro. Estoy viva. Mi cuerpo es de carne y no de tiesa materia artificial. Pienso con las vísceras. Deseo. Me llena de horror el corazón saber que no podré jamás cruzar palabra alguna con nadie, que nunca más podré conversar, pero más todavía saber que nunca más podré practicar con nadie las artes amatorias. Nunca más, Lear, sábelo bien. Los atlántidos son ahora remedos de carne, son moblaje relleno de cosas. Eres la única carne y el único apetito que restan vivos sobre la Tierra. (359)

> Is my body full of things? I am convinced that it is not. I am not full of things. I breathe. I am alive. My body is of flesh and not of artificial material. I think with my guts. I desire. My heart is filled with horror as I contemplate no longer being able to cross words with anyone, to never again converse with anyone, but even more so as I realize that I will never again practice the arts of love with anyone. Never again, Lear, know if well. The Atlanteans are now artificial flesh, furniture filled with things. You are the only flesh and the only appetite that remains alive on Earth.

Lear's rejection of the artificial nature of the *atlántidos* as well as her reassertion of organicity very clearly suggests a vision of technology and the posthuman that runs counter to those views suggested by the majority of North American and European theorists as well as by Hoeg's ideas on a Latin American acceptance of technology within narrative. In that sense, Boullosa has proposed the cyborg utopia as yet another dystopia; the posthuman ideal of the dissolution of an organic family structure results, for Lear, in a technological nightmare. When combined with the images of a repressive cybernetic state we observed earlier, Boullosa suggests that posthuman bodies merely reconstitute an oppressive social order rather than subvert it. The implications of such a position are certainly curious, especially considering the source. It was Boullosa's novel *Duerme* [Sleep], with its inherently hybrid main character who, very appropriately, inspired Hoeg's idea of cybermestizaje. Indeed, the novel does not completely eschew the hybridity inherent both to posthuman nature as well as to her earlier theorizations of feminine identity. The denouement of the novel finds a place within literature where the boundaries of time and space are erased, where Hernando, Estela, and Lear's textualized bodies can enter into contact with one another in the pages of the novel—existing within a kind of idealized space that endures and overcomes the broken utopias that populate the rest of the novel. Lear remarks in the final pages:

> Me uniré a Estela y a Hernando hasta el fin de los tiempos. Desdeciré la muerte anunciada de Hernando, quitaré el párrafo en que se la menciona, no le permitiré llegar a su fin. A Estela tampoco la dejaré alcanzar su muerte propia, la que tendría con el gran estallido. A los dos los traeré a mí, compartiremos un kesto común que nadie sabrá cerrar. Los tres viviremos en un mismo territorio.... ganaremos un espacio común en el que nos miraremos a los ojos y formaremos una nueva comunidad. (368–69)
>
> I will join with Estela and Hernando until the end of time. I will contradict Hernando's announced death, I will remove the paragraph where it is mentioned, I will not allow him to come to his end. I won't let Estela reach her own death either, the one she would suffer in the great explosion. I will bring them both to me, we will share a common kesto that no one will know how to close. The three will live in a same territory... we will gain a common space in which we will look one another in the eye and will form a new community.

Literature serves as the last space in which hybrid utopias can exist, one whose pages allow the textualized bodies of the characters to transcend boundaries set by history, race, or gender that Boullosa's posthumans are unable to challenge despite their nature. In fact, it is precisely in that idea of literature as an archive, as a place of origin, that the novel finds its possible utopia, one that appears in stark contrast to the failed social projects of colonial Mexico and the equally problematic posthuman L'Atlàntide. Writing becomes the place where true connection can exist, one that achieves the posthuman ideals that the cyborgs themselves apparently cannot. In a sense, Lear is able to achieve the subversive and revolutionary goals of the posthuman precisely because she rejects her own posthuman nature.

In his study of utopia and heterotopia in *Cielos de la tierra*, Javier Durán concludes as follows:

> It seems to me that Carmen Boullosa echoes García Márquez's comment that it is not too late to write a new and devastating utopia of life, where no one can decide anything for others—not even the way in which they should die—and where, as the Colombian Nobel laureate has said, the lineages condemned to one hundred years of solitude may at last have a second opportunity on earth...precisely in those heavens of the earth written by Boullosa. (63)

Seen from this perspective, Carmen Boullosa's subversion and inversion of the posthuman condition can be seen as part of a larger nostalgic gesture in which Lear's defiant attempts to recuperate an historical origin mirror Boullosa's radical reconfiguration of García Márquez's "devastating utopia(s) of life." Instead, then, of a novel that looks toward some new technological embrace in Latin American narrative, we find a glance back at its History, where the posthuman writer seeks to reconstruct the origins and fathers that her existence made unnecessary. Rather than a Latin American example of contemporary cyborg theory, *Cielos de la tierra* suggests a literary space where the subversive voice joins in an unharmonious chorus with the echoes of the past.

This "missing" of the nuclear family, this attempt to recreate a gender made unnecessary by posthuman dynamics, finds further development in the work of the Chilean writer Eugenia Prado. In 2004, she formed a part of a collective group of artists who staged the performance piece *Hembros* in Santiago, Chile.[4] The work explores the changing identities that have emerged from the relations between flesh and technology that are depicted as omnipresent in Chilean and Latin American culture. In the piece, the audience contemplates a seminude female actor who appears in several roles as Hembro, a being whose name consists of the confusion of *Hombre* [Man] and *Hembra* [Female] while evoking *Hambre* [Hunger] and who occupies the posthuman space where prosthetic and flesh are similarly confused. The character is duplicated on three separate screens, at times with a camera strapped to his/her head, but always in that peripheral place where one finds bodies that challenge the definitions and limits of corporality that certain societies attempt to enforce. The installation was a great success, with plans (as yet unrealized) to take it to other, larger, venues. Prado has developed this theme throughout her career, and in *Lóbulo* (1998) Prado presented a thorough examination of the female body and consciousness caught at the passage from human to posthuman. The novel presents the life and strange death of Sofía, narrating the main character's obsession with a disembodied voice that calls her for phone sex throughout the novel. While *Lóbulo* does not contain the explicit posthuman imagery we saw in *Cine continuado* and *Cielos de la tierra* or in the literal cyborgs of science fiction, it does present a vision of posthuman identity that incorporates and challenges much of contemporary theory. What we find in Prado's text is a rich, idiosyncratic vision of the implications of posthuman life in contemporary culture that suggests new theoretical possibilities for the understanding of gender and identity at the meeting point of flesh and machine.

Not only can we continue our dialogue with the work of Katherine Hayles and Donna Haraway in our discussion of Prado's novel, but we also see an important place for Gilles Deleuze and Felix Guattari's theories on the schizophrenic body. We recall from the earlier chapter that Haraway emphasizes the cyborg's ability to harness hybridity in the construction of a patriarchal structure-resisting identity who can sidestep origin mythologies as it exults in the "pleasurably tight couplings" that come from transgressing the societally prescribed boundaries that separate human from machine. The cyborg suggests a symbol of the subject that escapes the oppressive capitalist systems that depend on the aforementioned limits. In that sense we see the definition of the posthuman following Boullosa's articulation, specifically as that body that is generated outside of heterosexual procreation, outside of the nuclear family, and, subsequently, without the mother and father of what Haraway has called the "organic family." As I mentioned in the discussion of *Tiempo de revancha*, Katherine Hayles's exploration of posthuman identity is important for its expansion of posthuman identity from that of literal cyborg bodies and the cyborg as physical symbol of the possibilities that those literal bodies suggest to a more general state of consciousness in which the human imaginary extends to one in which the organic and the artificial are conceptualized as interchangeable prostheses of a disembodied mind. Cyborgs are not merely science fiction monsters or even people with prosthetic arms or pacemakers, but anyone whose identity no longer resides exclusively within the organic body. These posthuman identities locate themselves in the exchange of information between organic body and technology, a computer perhaps, or, in the case of *Lóbulo*, a telephone. Hayles's work, in particular, allows us to follow Prado's articulation of a theory of posthuman identity that, with Boullosa's, challenges and reworks those couplings that Haraway forges between gender liberation and cyborg mythology.

Lóbulo is Eugenia Prado's third novel, one of several in which the Chilean writer explores issues of female identity and subjectivity. She tends to describe the psychological realities of her female protagonists in texts that challenge both definitions of gender identity as well as the traditions of literary genre. Her previous work, *Cierta femeninidad oscura* [A Certain Dark Femininity], vacillates structurally between theatrical play and novel, confusing deliberately any kind of hierarchical limit. *Lóbulo* initially appears as a novel, only to morph relatively quickly into another kind of text in which blank pages are included with an invitation for the reader to collaborate in the writing of the text and narratorial asides question the interpretations that the novel presents as reality. In that sense *Lóbulo* can be seen to fulfill the iconoclastic role that Haraway describes as inherent to cyborg hybridity, the novel's fusion of disparate literary elements mirroring the cyborg's fusion of similarly disparate organic and mechanical prostheses.[5] Prado starts the novel with a presentation of an unstable female body, in search of both corporeal and psychological definition. The beginning evokes a cinematic opening shot in which the camera alternates images of the protagonist with the space that the protagonist inhabits. From the first page in which a description appears of the character's bedroom, the street that can be seen from the bedroom's window, and the protagonist's body within that room, the narrative focuses on close-ups of the protagonist that emphasize her fleshy existence and anticipates the events that will determine the development of the novel:

> Se acuesta, con la certeza de un acto inútil, ni siquiera la oscuridad más absoluta permite el sueño reposado. La veo acurrucada entre las ropas de la cama, la veo abandonada al recorrido de las sábanas. Hurgando en los espacios más alejados se busca, ella abre las piernas, luego los dedos de los pies, una forma de sentir más plenamente cada espacio de su carne. Bastaría con relajar el cuerpo, bastaría eso apenas para estar tranquila, piensa. (16)

> She lies down, certain that it was useless, not even absolute darkness would allow restful sleep. I see her curled up in the bedclothes, I see her abandoned to the flow of the sheets. Twisting in the farthest spaces, she searches, she opens her legs, then her toes as way to feel each part of her flesh more fully. It would be enough to relax my body, just that would be enough to be at peace, she thinks.

The attempt to open up, to experience her surroundings on a corporeal level, activates the idea of carnal sensuality on various levels. Not only does the importance of sensorial experience appear prominently, but so too does the preeminence of the sensual invitation to fusion, an attempt to enter into contact with foreign elements that will produce new sensations and forge the "couplings" that Haraway emphasizes. In this scene, we see an extended meditation on the ideas of Deleuze and Guattari with the presentation of a body that desires, that seeks to open itself up to the distinct flows that surround it. Note the

MISSING GENDER 61

language they employ in their description of Lenz's stroll at the beginning of *Anti-Oedipus*,

> To be a chlorophyll- or a photosynthesis machine, or at least slip his body into such machines as one part among the others. Lenz has projected himself back to a time before the man-nature dichotomy, before all the co-ordinates based on this fundamental dichotomy have been laid down. He does not live nature as nature, but as a process of production. There is no such thing as either man or nature now, only a process that produces the one within the other and couples the machines together. (2)

The mechanical language that Deleuze and Guattari use in their vision of schizophrenia will appear later in *Lóbulo*, but their vision of the body as a site where sensorial flows intersect appears from the beginning. We witness in these first pages, then, the articulation of a permeable flesh that does not respect the boundaries that preserve a closed human identity.

This moment of opening establishes the context for the series of events that will penetrate Sofía's imaginary. As she wanders through her apartment, still attempting to open herself up, she pauses:

> Sofía retrocede. Camina inquieta. Una vez más el pequeño espacio. Necesita algo que la mantenga lejos de aquel estado incompleto, busca insistente en los recuerdos, alguno en especial. Puedo verla confusa, sólo imágenes desordenadas, y en aquel desorden de ideas, la mujer buscará una imagen única, una imagen de su padre, un recuerdo difuso, un único recuerdo, una fotografía que Carmen, su madre, le entregara al cumplir los nueve años. (17)

> Sofía retreats. She walks uncertainly. Once again, the small space. She needs something that will keep her far from that incomplete state, she looks insistently in her memories, one in particular. I can see her confused, disarranged images and in that disorder of ideas, the woman looks for a single image, an image of her father, a blurry memory, an only memory, a photograph that Carmen, her mother, gave her when she turned nine.

The experience emphasizes the ideas of lack and necessity, already implicit in her previous attempt to open up where her organic flesh does not satisfy the desires that she appears to suffer. The first object of that previously diffuse desire is the photograph of her unknown father, an object whose semiotic possibilities contribute to the formation of an incipient posthuman identity. The language used to present this idea vacillates between memory and photographic image, combining Sofía's organic memory of her absent father with the chemical process that encloses the image of that father. The photograph appears as a signifier stripped from its signified object as it no longer refers to a memory of a specific event or experience but exists merely as a memory of itself. That is, when Sofía views the photo, she remembers only the image of her father's body, not the actual organic body itself. The fact that this picture displaces the event that it should represent, erasing any referent of a separate "real" experience, indicates a process in which the technology responsible for the creation of that memory has begun to integrate itself with the organic system that attempts to preserve the memory of that father. Moreover, by representing the object of desire as one of avoiding "that incomplete state," the photograph appears as a prosthetic memory that completes Sofía's incomplete organic recollections serving much the same function as a prosthetic limb.

At the same time, it marks Sofía as a body that exists outside of the traditional family structure. If she is not presented as the result of a medical operation that made unnecessary the presence of a father, she does occupy the space of the body that does not find a place within the definition of the nuclear family. Prado emphasizes this interpretation with the conversion of the father's organic body in photograph where the image of him replaces not only the memory of him that we have already mentioned but also his own corporeal presence. Sofía seeks the photograph as a way to satisfy her craving for paternal contact. In this sense we again see how the photo continues to function as a signifier that promises a physical referent but that is, after all, the only body that exists. We can intuit, then, the presence of a posthuman consciousness in Sofía where her own sense of self comes from the fact that she is the product of an organic mother and a photographic father. At the same time, we can also infer a marked difference between Haraway's cyborg and the posthuman figure we see rising from Sofía's imaginary. If Haraway's cyborg makes its father unnecessary, nullifying the paternal presence with the cyborg's illegitimate existence, Sofía feels her father's organic absence and attempts to fill the hole with the artificial image that remains of him. She is the cyborg that does not forget her origin and does, to a certain extent, still dream of the Garden of Eden.

This first indication of prosthesis sets the stage for the telephone call that ends the first chapter of the novel. As Sofía looks for the photograph of her father the telephone rings, surprising Sofía:

> Un sonido que en fracción de segundos se transforma en algo incierto que completa su angustia. Como si intentara detener el tiempo, Sofía se abalanza sobre el reloj. El teléfono sigue sonando.
>
> —¿Quién se atreve...tan tarde? —dice.
>
> Descuelga el auricular sobreponiéndose al miedo, sin embargo, recorriéndola, un temblor la envuelve.
>
> —¿A l ó?...—insinúa con esfuerzo.
>
> Al otro lado de la línea telefónica aparece un susurro apenas perceptible. Un susurro leve.
>
> —¿Q u i é n?—insiste Sofía, tratando de mantener la calma, mientras los latidos sagitados de su corazón se desplazan rápidamente, transformándose en pulsaciones que la recorren completa, para rebotar en la parte de atrás, la más cóncava de su cabeza.
>
> —Sólo alguien que espera por ti...—responde un hombre del otro lado, precipitándose.
>
> —¿C ó m o?...—agrega Sofía, imaginando apenas su respiración.
>
> De inmediato cuelga el teléfono. Rápidamente esconde la fotografía en el clóset y corre, como una niña corre a meterse en la cama, esperando quizás, que el sueño interfiera su angustia. (19–20)
>
> A sound that, in a fraction of a second, transforms into something uncertain that completes her anguish. As if she were trying to stop time, Sofía throws herself on the watch. The telephone keeps ringing.
>
> —Who would dare to call...so late?—she says.

She lifts the receiver, overcoming her fear and yet reviewing it, a tremor envelops her.
—Hello?...—She insinuates with effort.
On the other end of the telephone line a barely perceptible whisper appears. A light whisper.
Who?—Sofía insists, trying to maintain her calm, while the beats of her heart quickly come, transforming in pulses that run through her entire body, to echo in the back part, the most concave of her head.
Just someone who waits for you...—responds a man on the other end, anticipating.
What?...—asks Sofía, barely imagining her breathing. She immediately hangs up the phone. She quickly hides the photograph in the closet and runs, like a little girl runs to get in bed, waiting, perhaps, that sleep stop her anguish.

The interruption of her search for the photograph situates the call within the context of the organic body that combines with artificial elements as it attempts to constitute a whole identity. At the same time, it accentuates the search as a hybridizing process. When the phone rings, Sofía tries to use the clock as an extension of her desire to stop time. When she is unable to achieve that desire, she lifts the phone and, when she hears the voice at the other end of the line, she enters into a world of cables and machines in a way that anticipated the popular film *The Matrix*'s use of the telephone. That is, just as the characters of that science fiction film could enter and exit a technological, virtual world by means of telephone calls, Sofía enters a world mediated by technology where masculine voices are able to affect important alterations in Sofía's corporeal reactions. The passage emphasizes the change in Sofía's breathing, her quickened pulse, a direct result of the fear she feels as she enters into contact with the voice that awaits her on the other end. Prado reinforces this interpretation by suggesting that the whisper that travels through the telephone line is then translated into the heartbeats and pulses that run through Sofía's entire body. The description suggests the image of Sofía plugged into the telephone line through the earpiece that she has connected to her own ear. In that sense, we see articulated the situation that

Hayles describes when she speaks of the dynamic connection between organic and technological bodies. The organic Sofía, attempting to leave behind her incomplete state, opens herself to the telephone and thus creates a new system in which her body responds physically to the electronic impulses that come through the telephone line.

Using this as a point of departure, Prado begins a series of scenes and images, centered generally on the erotic, that extend, develop, and challenge contemporary theories on posthuman identity. In one of the many such telephone calls that Sofía receives, Prado employs images and references that posit Sofía's transformation from organic entity to a body that cannot be separated from the telephone that now constitutes an integral part of its identity.

> Algunos minutos después de las doce, como empieza a ser habitual, el teléfono. Sofía levanta el aparato con tranquilidad. Al empuñarlo su mano se humedece, puede sentir que todo es exacto, hasta en el largo de los dedos al acariciarse las palmas. Se queda un tiempo conectada a esa forma, que a la altura del lóbulo de la oreja encaja de una manera casi perfecta. Al otro lado de la línea telefónica, el hombre la succiona desde aquella profundidad. Ella lame la parte de abajo del auricular. Él sigue estando en el otro extremo de la línea. Su lengua, simultáneamente resbala por los pequeños orificios. (37–38)

> A few minutes after twelve, as has become habit, the telephone. Sofía lifts the receiver calmly. As she touches it, her hand moistens, she can feel that everything is exact, even in the length of her fingers as she caresses her palms. She remains connected to this forma for a time, that at the point of her earlobe it fits almost perfectly. At the other end of the line, a man sucks her from that depth. She licks the lower part of the receiver. He continues on the other extreme of the line. His tongue simultaneously slips over the tiny holes.

Throughout the narration of the experience, we see elements that emphasize the interaction of the organic and the mechanical. Sofía's hand moistens when it touches the telephone, an object that has now become a prosthesis, one with her body as it fits "exactly" in her hands, and the earpiece of the phone a "perfect" extension of her own ear. In this moment, the technology of the telephone has become inseparable from her organic body, and Sofía is now a cybernetic body whose senses are not situated within her flesh but within a system of telephone, wires, ears, and consciousness. Prado continues in this vein, suggesting that the virtual contact between Sofía and "Él" that occurs when they lick each other through the phone is now physical as their ears include the telephone receivers that transmit voices and sexual desires. The sucking that Sofía's lover is able to perform at long distance creates the very sensual feeling of intimate contact, made possible by Sofía's now posthuman body.

In a subsequent scene, we can appreciate the extent of Sofía's transformation:

> Con esas palabras, la mujer casi no puede sostenerse y cae, como rebotando en el tiempo. De inmediato aparecen nuevas imágenes en su cabeza. Él está frente a mí y todo se nubla al contacto con sus murmullos de manos. No puedo pensar en él de otro modo sin alcanzar la distancia que existe entre ambos a través de la línea telefónica. Una parte de su cuerpo se talla como metal, un frío intenso en la superficie lisa de los brazos se resiste a negar su propia permanencia. Desde el torso hasta la espalda, un naufragio. Toda la piel escurriéndose es aceite, una mutación. Las gotas que me empapan se atoran en la plástica armonía del teléfono, preciso cercarlo en una reunión furtiva. Ambos cuelgan el aparato y sus cuerpos se ahogan entre los quejidos sin llegar hasta el final del cable, en un último suspiro en que no hay tono, como una forma de grabar los sonidos en su memoria. Preciso hacerlo fotográficamente estático, detenerlo instantáneo y anular su fuerza. (66–67)

> With those words, the woman can no longer support herself and she falls, as if she were slipping in time. New images immediately appear in her head. He is in front of me and everything goes cloudy at the touch of his murmuring hands. I cannot think of him in any other way without reaching across the distance that there is between the both of us over the phone line. A part of his body is like metal, an intense cold in the smooth surface of his arms that won't deny its own permanence. From his torso to his back, a shipwreck. All of the skin that is

flowing out is oil, a mutation. The drops that soak me are stuck in the plastic harmony of the telephone, I have to surround it in a furtive meeting. Both hang up the phone and their bodies drown among the complaints without making it to the end of the cable, in a final sigh in which there is no tone, like a way to record the sounds in their memory. I need to make it photographically static, stop it instantly, and annul its strength.

The fusion of bodies that occurs in the erotic act is here accompanied by a series of images that suggest other types of fusion more in line with the hybridity of the cyborg body. The telephone line not only serves as a means for human contact it contaminates Sofía's organic body with its technological nature, causing it to begin to convert into metal and oil. Sofía finds herself in a situation in which she is obliged to become machine in order to continue with the relationship. Just as the telephone has facilitated her relationship with her lover it also emphasizes the distance between them, the prosthetic resisting the posthuman fusion of prosthesis and consciousness. For that reason, the process that we saw begin with the telephone as a figurative prosthetic auditory and sexual organ now culminates in Sofía's conversion into oil so that she can become one with telephone and, hence, enter into direct physical contact with her lover. Where before Sofía's palms would moisten when she handled the telephone, now her perspiration has become oil and the cyborg aspect of her body occupies center stage. Prado further emphasizes this by commenting explicitly on the formation of an erotic circuit between the two lovers in which a kind of cybernetic feedback loop is created by means of the telephone cable that transmits pleasure between the two bodies as it simultaneously records the experience in the memories of each of them.

It is at this point where we see an important meditation on the ideas of Deleuze and Guattari mentioned earlier. Prado not only presents the image of a body that seeks contact, that attempts to combine with the flows of the world, she also makes Deleuze and Guattari's mechanical discourse literal by situating it within a telephone cable. If we turn to their description of the machine body, we can appreciate better the way in which Prado plumbs their machine metaphor in her exploration of Sofía's psychological reality.

> In a word, every machine functions as a break in the flow in relation to the machine to which it is connected, but at the same time is also a flow itself, or the production of a flow, in relation to the machine connected to it. This is the law of the production of production. That is why, at the limit point all the transverse or transfinite connections, the partial object and continuous flux, the interruption and the connection, fuse into one. (36–37)

Deleuze and Guattari's semiotic system depends on the establishment of cybernetic systems between bodies, food, social forces, and so on whose behavior is determined by the feedback loops that run between them. In this, they do not differ much from early cyberneticists such as Norbert Weiner, although they employ this language within very different ideologies. What is important to note here is the ubiquitous use of the mechanical metaphor in Deleuze and Guattari's work, a metaphor that Prado makes real by proposing a schizophrenic body (i.e., a body that continually attempts to enter into contact with the flows of the world) that achieves that contact through literal machines. That is, in *Lóbulo*'s narrative world, it is not sufficient to describe Sofía's body and its contact with the world with machine images; these relationships occur because of machines and, therefore, create posthuman identities that are more literal than figurative.

The erotic relationship that Sofía maintains over the telephone with her lover's voice begins, then, to alter the constitution of her body. At the end of another, earlier, telephone call,

> Sofía permanece en silencio algunos segundos, sabe que de un momento a otro, él colgará el aparato telefónico. Lo hace. Entonces relajo los brazos, hasta que mis dedos caen resbalando como gotas de agua, luego los aprieto con fuerza contra las palmas. Descubro que la belleza no atrapa los días. Quiero ser belleza. Quiere ser belleza, pero imposible, se mantiene misteriosamente atada al aparato telefónico. Enciende la lámpara, todo en ella se detiene. En el estómago, un dolor como de

máquinas me hostiga. Continúa inmóvil y hunde sus huesos en la cama, esperando el cuerpo, que de viva dé calor. (39)

Sofía sits in silence for a few seconds, she knows that any moment he will hang up the phone. He does. Then I relax my arms, until my fingers fall sliding like drops of water, then I press them hard against my palms. I discover that beauty does not trap days. I want to be beauty. She wants to be beauty, but it's impossible, she stays mysteriously tied to the telephone. She turns on the lamp, everything in her stops. In her stomach, there's a pain like machines that pursues me. She stays still and buries her bones in the bed, waiting for the body to bring heat from its life.

As she disconnects from the telephone Sofía loses energy, the relaxation of her arms and fingers create the impression of a robot that has suddenly been unplugged from its energy source. As she turns on the light we see an attempt to reestablish contact with the electricity that had fueled Sofía's body earlier, the visual image of electric light suggesting a connection between the literal electricity of the lamp with the erotic electricity of the phone sex that Sofía had just experienced and that has converted her into a mechanical body that depends on that electricity. Prado emphasizes those electrical (and metaphorical) changes in Sofía's body with a split in her narrative voice as it shifts between third and first person, as if the cessation of electrical power has also caused abrupt changes in the narration itself.

At the same time, there is a loss of control that, as depicted in the passage, ascribes a negative connotation to an experience that could be seen as an excellent example of the "pleasurably tight coupling" that Haraway sees as integral to cyborg identity. Sofía begins to associate her telephone conversations with images of death: "Con palabras misteriosas él tiñe sus intenciones y destruye algo que estaba quieto. Atrapados los huesos blanquecinos que muertos han, de carne pútrida, sido violentamente removidos" (42) [He tinges his intentions with mysterious words and destroys something that was still. The trapped bleached bones that, dead, have been from putrid flesh been violently removed].[6] At this point, the organic body decays in the face of the electronic relationship that Sofía maintains with the man, an act that evokes the typical cyberpunk description of the body as "meat" and of its insistence on the superiority of the virtual, disembodied condition. The transition from corporeal reality to virtual existence culminates a few pages later in a previously quoted passage when we see Sofía's visceral reaction to one of the conversations ("Con esas palabras...anular su fuerza" [66–67]). The transformation of Sofía's skin in oil, her experience of self as robotic, the telephone line that connects both their voices and their bodies, all create a cybernetic existence that, at first, satisfies the lack that Sofía expressed at the beginning of the novel. Nevertheless, the erotic experience exercises a profound impact on the bodies of those involved and Prado does not permit any kind of return to a purely organic state. The cables continue as extensions of desire, the sighs retain a technological aspect in the simile that compares them to a recording. The fact that Sofía "needs" a photographic state at the end of the passage underlines this continuing technological existence, even after the call is over. She is now so much a part of the technological that she prefers the artificial existence of the photograph to any kind of organic existence.

And yet, capturing a moment in a photograph suggests a static state that imprisons the subject. The relationship, instead of liberating Sofía from a life restricted by systems of control, subjects her to further insanity and eventual death. Her fingers lose themselves in the machine and she similarly loses the ability to distinguish between body and apparatus. She explains, "Siete son los números, uno a uno puedo rasguñarlos desde mi memoria, siete veces mi dedo en los orificios, como si nada pudiese detenerlos, mi mano va perdiéndose entre los giros en un gesto mecánico" (65) [There are seven numbers, one by one I can scratch them from memory, seven times my finger in the holes, as if nothing could stop them, my hand loses itself in the whirls of a mechanical gesture]. It is not just that her hand makes mechanical gestures; it is that it is lost within the machine itself. In fact the erotic act here occurs not so much between the voices of the lovers as it does between Sofía's fingers and the orifices in the face of the telephone, the contact between flesh and plastic resulting in a union in which the organic and the artificial blend so profoundly as to be indistinguishable. At this point the masculine voice becomes menacing, whispering that the conversion into machine is now her inescapable obligation—a fact of evolution: "Aquel que no evolucione con el tiempo hace inevitable el camino a la extinción" (59) [That which does not evolve with time makes the path to extinction inevitable]. Later, with an even more aggressive tone, he says: "—Todo ha sido programado, tarde o en algún momento, serás parte de esto— insiste él" [Everything has been programmed, later or at some point, you will be part of this, he insists], a threat to which Sofía responds with the following, "—Terminamos desistiendo— dice Sofía. Sus pies no pueden moverse, vuelve a la inquietud, desespera. No logra contener sus movimientos. No obedece su cuerpo a las órdenes de la cabeza, como si estuviesen totalmente separados uno de otro" (69) [We will end up surrendering, Sofía says. Her feet cannot move, and restlessness returns, she grows desperate. She cannot contain her movements. Her body does not obey the orders her head gives, as if they were completely separate]. Sofía now begins to reject the posthuman experience, finding the schism that now exists between consciousness and body a disquieting sensation—the result of an invasion that she will describe as similar to a serpent that has contaminated and impregnated her.

Her resulting posthuman body is, therefore, very different from Haraway's cyborg. Sofía does not challenge the structure of the nuclear family that oppresses her, she does not threaten the society in which she live, she only experiences a madness that has grown worse as her posthuman condition has developed. The narrator observes:

> Ausente como el equívoco de muchas otras llamadas telefónicas. El teléfono es un mero instrumento para hacerle participar de un proceso de comunicatransacción que he imaginado. Pero acaso... ¿Podría soportar por más tiempo a la madre de Sofía en un escenario delimitado por alucinaciones, un personaje inconexo, anacrónico, hasta con algunos efectos de descalce? Somos intentos intervenidos por llamadas retocadas usted y yo en un acto extremo de incomunicatransacción. (72)
>
> Absent like the wrong number from many other phone calls. The telephone is merely an instrument to make her participate

in a process of communicatransaction that I have imagined. But maybe, could one put up longer with Sofía's mother in a scene defined by hallucinations, a disconnected, anachronistic character, to the effects of this mismatch? We are intervening attempts by calls touched by you and me in an extreme act of incommunicatransaction.

By narrating the path to Sofía's individual madness, Prado establishes a vision of posthuman identity specific to one woman's particular reality. At the same time, and through this vision, Prado advances an antitechnological theme that would be profoundly conservative were it not for the challenging imagery that she employs in the articulation of that theme. Moreover, her inversion of the well-used plotline of the man who makes a female robot for sexual satisfaction produces an exploration of female desire, technology, and identity that extends far beyond the science fiction cliché. In terms of the meditation that we have seen on the work of Deleuze and Guattari throughout the novel, the end of the relationship suggests two possibilities. On one level, the destruction of Sofía's world suggests her conversion into "body without organs," the closed body that the two philosophers describe. The implications for the production of that body are even more illuminating. The fact that Sofía desires opening, an entrance into contact with the world, makes literal Deleuze and Guattari's body/desire machine with the telephonic relationship. However, Sofía's desire cannot be realized, and when we see Sofía shut down and close off we witness the failure of the mechanical metaphor as well as the promise of connection that the description of the body as a system of nodes of communication offers but cannot fulfill.

In the final section of the novel we find a Sofía who can no longer communicate with the bodies that surround her, whether it be an ex-lover or her own mother. Her paranoia, present since the beginning of the novel, has grown till the point at which she dies during the birth of her child/text.

La mujer se acercó con cautela al cuerpo de Sofía que permanecía inmóvil sobre la cama. Más cerca vio su rostro, tenía el color de la muerte. Sus ojos estaban abiertos. Se quedó unos segundos mirando su sonrisa plácida. Cerca de los labios algo extraño llamó su atención, una materia de color blanquecino asomaba por la boca aquello no parecía fluido, se veía como algo sólido. La mujer se acercó más para abrir la boca de la muchacha. Al rozar lo que había dentro, un escalofrío la recorrió de pies a cabeza. Se volvió para mirar a la madre que estaba acurrucada de rodillas junto a la cama de su hija, mientras gemidos cortos y secos salían de su garganta. Armándose de valor empezó a sacar lentamente lo que había dentro de la boca de la muerta, primero despacio, luego empezó a tirar con más fuerza... eso parecía no tener fin.

Pronto fue descubriendo papeles arrugados con inscripciones ilegibles, como si hubiesen estado mucho tiempo dentro del estómago diluyendo parte de la tinta.

Sofía descansaba para siempre, con el cuerpo taponeado de papeles. (212–13)

The women approached Sofía's body carefully, the body was still on the bed. Up close she saw that her face was the color of death. Her eyes were open. She looked at her calm smile for a couple of seconds. Near her lips, something strange caught her eye, some kind of bleached material that came out of her mouth that was not fluid but looked like it was solid. The woman got closer so that she could open the girl's mouth. As she brushed what was inside, a shiver ran through her from feet to head. She turned to look at the mother who was on her knees next to her daughter's bed, while short dry moans left her throat. Gathering her courage, she began to remove slowly what was in the dead woman's mouth, slowly at first and then she began to pull with more effort. It seemed to never end. She quickly discovered wrinkled papers with illegible inscriptions, as if they had been in her stomach for a long time, with the ink diluting. Sofía rested forever, her body plugged with papers.

Sofía's cybernetic body is converted, at the end of the novel, in a kind of organic printer whose production is also the cause of its death. The implications of such an image in the light of post-human theory proposes another way to interpret what has been for much of contemporary theory a principal feminist figure. What Prado suggests is a much more complex body than that of a revolutionary figure whose ambiguity challenges the patriarchal systems and societies that created it. Prado elaborates the body of a victim at one level, a victim made cyborg by a mechanical, masculine presence that left her contaminated and dead. Instead of resisting that masculinized force this figurative cybernetic body carries its technological prosthesis as emblems of its violation, much as we saw in chapter 1, albeit on an extremely individualized level in which governmental oppression does not figure. On another level the power of the cyborg body lies in its textual production, the ability it has to articulate experiences with its own peculiar language. The telephone that was Sofía's prosthetic auditory and sexual organ during her erotic relationship is now revealed as the technological means through which language entered her body to then be born from it. Sofía's cadaver that was once cyborg is now the mother of texts that reveal the hybrid experience that she suffered.

If Haraway celebrated the ambiguity of the cyborg, signaling its ability to transgress limits and produce hybridity and Deleuze and Guattari suggest the intriguing possibilities of combining organic body and mechanical semiotics, Prado invents a new cyborg whose own ambiguity extends and frustrates Haraway's "cyborg myth" as it critically explores the metaphorical systems created by Deleuze and Guattari. Sofía seeks connection with her absent father and present mother rather than seeking to embrace the escape from the nuclear family that her posthuman identity seems to promise. Her death in childbirth suggests a rejection of heterosexual procreation that many posthuman theorists celebrate as central, but this procreation is presented as an artificial product of the contact between a machine father and an organic mother. Sofía's mechanical body with its conversion into printer could be connected with the idea of the subversive body whose ability to write, to produce language, threatens systems of control, much as we saw in the figure of Elena in *La ciudad ausente*. However, the organic body's fluids have rendered the text illegible and, while Elena is able to continue her testimony after her death thanks to her cyborg body, Sofía is dead because of that body and her language has been destroyed by the conflict between the organic and the mechanical. What Prado achieves with her exploration of posthuman life and Sofía's individual experience is the knowledge that Sofía's very name promises of an unknowable life, or the possibilities of connection in a technological reality opposed to the alienation that that same technology engenders. In that sense, Prado articulates the fundamental ambiguity of the posthuman figure in an even more fundamental way than what we have seen in earlier analyses of cyborg identity. While Haraway celebrates the cyborgs' ambiguous hybridity and Hayles critically and comprehensively explores the history of the posthuman as a concept as well as its function in contemporary culture, for both of them (and for many others) the posthuman is something that can be known, understood, and appreciated. In Haraway's myth, the cyborg body draws its power from its ability to function as the bearer of knowledge; that is, the knowledge that there is a powerful alternative to male-centered society. For Hayles, the posthuman body occupies a clearly defined place in the evolution of the human body. Indeed, knowledge and the cyborg body are inextricable in the articulations of cyborg identity in Argentina that we have studied for therein is found their subversive threat. What Prado creates is a body that does participate in all the fusions between organic flesh and technology from the erotic to the prosthetic that we see described in contemporary posthuman theory while resisting any attempt to situate it within that theory, any attempt to define what it is or, more importantly, what it could do.

While Borinsky's cyborgs inhabit a space well within Haraway's manifesto, the uncontrollable woman whose peripheral existence relative to the norms of conservative society threatens the continuation of the society, the posthumans that occupy the work of Boullosa and Prado suggest a very different vision. Borinsky's stripper, an expression of female sexuality ambiguously unencumbered by the strictures of the nuclear family, would, with her metallic skin and her irrepressible presence, act out the feminist promise of the cyborg. However, the frustrated quests of Lear and Sofía create both a future and a present world in which the gender roles that the posthuman so effectively destroys are retroactively seen as valuable. Lear witnesses the destruction of a society because of their lack and Sofía obsessively tries to recuperate hers, only to find that not only can she never find it but that motherhood will ultimately destroy her as well. Both, however, find some kind of relief in writing, though with very different implications. Boullosa seems to propose some kind of utopian view of literature, of life in words. Sofía's writing can never be read—illegible papers that were previously a fetus and/or a snake. In both cases, though, the answer to the posthuman condition is an escape from it.

Chapter 3

Ripped Stitches: Mass Media and Televisual Imaginaries in Rafael Courtoisie's Narrative

In the winter (June–August) of 2004, the Buenos Aires radio station 95.1 Metro ran an advertising campaign that covered the city in photographs of their on-air personalities altered so as to present them as half-human, half-robot. The advertisements, found throughout the streets of Capital Federal on phone booths and subway billboards, used the image of the cyborg to enhance the "cool" factor of the station, associating cyborg identity with urban sound, technology with the "hip." Indeed, the campaign fit precisely within the image that the radio station continues to project, both on-air and on its website http://www.metro951.com: that is, a radio station whose emphasis on contemporary, electronic (techno) music places it among the most current, most up-to-date of the radio stations in the Greater Buenos Aires market (whether that image is accurate is, of course, debatable).

The campaign's use of cyborg imagery is of particular interest, both as presented in the advertisement as well as within the cultural and societal context of the imagery of technological identity traced in this book. The advertisement itself displays the pictures of its cyborg DJs in an appropriately paradoxical fashion. The station is presented as being wholly urban with its slogan "100% SONIDO URBANO," only to disrupt a sense of totality with the split photographs of men whose faces are evenly divided between organic and robotic. Furthermore, despite appearing above the pictures, the visual construction of the advertisement places the slogan after the images. That is, the cyborg images catch the eye of the passer-by who then proceeds to read the text that explains it. One is presented, then, with an apparently fractured self that is then stitched together by the text that claims that the cyborg DJ is the visual representation of a radio station that is "100% SONIDO URBANO." The tension of the dichotomous photographs turns dialectic as the declaration of 100 percent purity synthesizes the organic and the technological in a single, sonic-based cybernetic identity. The naming of the cyborgs beneath each picture adds another level to this display of a media-based posthuman identity. Each photograph functions as not only a symbolic figure that endows an Argentine radio station with the futuristic implications of science fiction but also as the representation of real people, people whose apparently cybernetic voices one will be able to hear if one tunes in to 95.1.

The image at the top of the advertisement, one that 95.1 uses as its symbol in all of its advertising, represents a digital equalizer, a computeristic representation of sound and the measures and limits that we place on sound with technology (on the website this particular image is animated). At the same time, the form—a circle with a long line, short line, long line inside—suggests the shape of a human head with two ears, or more likely, two headphones, a suggestion that links digital music technology with human identity as it draws on the explicit cyborg photographs below to make that linkage. It also reaches out to the passer-by in a gesture that extends its series of posthuman combinations. If the three personalities are cybernetic DJs, producers of the aural information that the listener will experience in their quest for the urban and the modern, this headphone/equalizer cyborg provides a space for the insertion of the listener within the technological imaginary of the radio station. That is, the three cyborgs whose technological selves promise the most current of the current also offer their hip identity to anyone who will plug themselves into their message. Cyborg identity becomes a welcome virus, one that anyone with the proper taste can contract if they will but expose themselves. Indeed, the advertisement placement on phone booths seemed to suggest a *Matrix*-inspired access point to the digital system even as the Telefónica reminds the potential cyborg citizen of the neoliberal reality that underlies the various technological connections.

This campaign taps into a technophilia that we have not seen in the works considered thus far. One might be tempted to dismiss the campaign as not authentic; the music the station plays is almost exclusively foreign. Indeed, this particular marketing strategy would serve as an example of the hotly debated claims made in the now notorious prologue to Alberto Fuguet and Sergio Gómez's *McOndo* anthology where Latin American culture is argued to be more global than local. Of most interest for this study is the way that cybernetic identity is portrayed as a desirable aspect of contemporary identity and as a by-product of the consumption of popular culture as delivered by the technology of mass media. This image, this gesture, serves as the focal point for two novels by the Uruguayan writer Rafael Courtoisie, where mass media, posthuman identity, and global culture develop, collide, fuse, and founder in neoliberal Latin America.

In his 2000 novella *Tajos*, Courtoisie describes a scene that combines the ridiculous with a studied meditation on posthuman and consumerist identity in turn-of-the-millennium Latin America. Raúl, a fledgling psycho killer whose crimes include the slashing of supermarket foodstuffs, teddy bears, and a Mickey Mouse doll, calls into a television variety show. He wins a chance to play a game in which he uses his remote control to shoot down airplanes that fly across the television screen as a part of the program. Raúl is ultimately unsuccessful, and while he proceeds to more heinous crimes over the course of the novel the image of the young man waving his remote control at the television set while plugged into the program via his telephone remains as a focal point for the events that transpire. Courtoisie uses this and other related images to examine the articulation of a consumerist identity constantly mediated by the combinations of technological and organic bodies. By so doing, the Uruguayan writer suggests a nuanced vision of the connections between global capitalism, posthuman bodies, and televisual media that engages and critiques contemporary theoretical examinations of these issues. I would argue that in *Tajos*, and in his more recent *Caras extrañas* (2001), Courtoisie articulates a "cleaving" of posthuman identity where the *tajos* perform both contradictory meanings of the verb as they sever bodies and fuse disparate elements simultaneously. That is, neither the slice nor the suture completes the transformation of identity that exists at the crossing of organic, technological, and consumerist bodies in postdictatorship Latin America.

The novella *Tajos* represents an intriguing narrative addition to an oeuvre known principally for its contributions to Latin American poetry. The Uruguayan writer recently won the 2002 Jaime Sabines award in Mexico, one of several such international literary prizes he has received. His prose texts have also earned him acclaim, from the curious *Vida de perro* [A dog's life], a dog's history of the world, to his several collections of short stories, *Tajos* and his most recent novel, *Caras extrañas*, a meditation on postdictatorship Latin America. *Tajos* enjoyed a moderate amount of success in Latin America in an Alfaguara edition and was reedited in Spain with Lengua de Trapo where it continues in print. Mario Benedetti has identified Courtoisie as "uno de los nombres más descollantes y de más merecido prestigio" [one of the most outstanding names and of most deserved prestige], agreeing with those that place Courtoisie at the forefront of Uruguayan letters. In *Tajos*, and later in *Caras extrañas*, Courtoisie develops realities where technology, television, consumerism, and dictatorship intersect and interact in the construction of corporeal identity. If *Tajos* tackles this technologically and televisually mediated reality on an individual level, *Caras extrañas* contextualizes it within the postdictatorial aftermath of political violence.

In the earlier novella, Courtoisie presents a protagonist whose ability to interact with reality has been severely eroded by his obsession with knives, television, and his grandmother's death. Raúl's forays out of his apartment follow a repeating sequence where Raúl acquires a knife, cuts a series of absurd objects, loses the knife, and returns to his apartment to watch more television. The titular *tajos* become a series of figurative and literal cuts that metonymically represent Raúl's divided sense of self as they simultaneously represent what could be thought of as cinematic "cuts" that fuse the disparate scenes and identities that compete within Raúl's divided self. The resultant body, one that fuses flesh, knife, television, and commodity even as it exists "cut off" from the society it inhabits becomes Courtoisie's image of a frustrated posthuman body paradoxically unable to find union within a hybridized conglomeration of organic, prosthetic, and video components.

In keeping with the paradoxical fissures and fusions that such a body suggests, the vision of the posthuman that emerges from Courtoisie's novel both extends and rejects the articulations of posthuman and cyborg identity we have discussed earlier from theorists such as Haraway and Hayles. Certainly the hybridized combinations of technology and flesh, both literal and figurative that these theorists describe, appear as centerpieces in this work. We can return to Haraway's insistence on the cyborg's subversive power as grounded in its ability to transgress boundaries and limits: "There is much room for radical political people to contest the meanings of the breached boundary. The cyborg appears in myth precisely where the boundary between human and animal is transgressed. Far from signaling a walling off of people from other living beings, cyborgs signal disturbingly and pleasurably tight coupling" (1991: 152). As we examine the scenes Courtoisie uses in his meditation on consumerism, television, and technology we will appreciate an alternate conceptualization of the effects of boundary transgression in a world where the blurry demarcations between machine, human, and consumerism dictate the construction of identity.[1]

The initial scene of the novel, Raúl's attack on a supermarket, develops this idea of posthuman cleavage, where his literal knife cuts are accompanied by fusions of meaning and erosions of limits. The description of the mutilated vegetables begins a series of imagery that blends human being with the materials that surround it.

> Entro a un supermercado.
> Tajeo las bolsas de azúcar. Me alejo. Viene un supervisor. No se explica el desastre. Voy impertérrito. Parezco manso.
> El peso del contenido empuja los labios del tajo. Salta el azúcar sólido, la hemorragia blanca en el piso.

Sigo inmaculado. Como un doctor. Sigo con la navaja.
La clavo.
Sigo.
Clavo la navaja otra vez.
Sigo sin prisa.
Los tomates sangran.
Malogré un racimo, castré una sandía. Apuñalé tubérculos, perforé huevos. (11–12)

I enter a supermarket.

I slice the sacks of sugar. I move away. A supervisor approaches, he doesn't understand the disaster. I leave, unperturbed. I seem tame.

The weight of the contents presses on the lips of the cut. The solid sugar jumps out, the white hemorrhage on the floor.

I continue, immaculate. Like a doctor. I continue with the knife.

I stick it in.

I continue.

I stick the knife in again.

I continue, without hurry.

The tomatoes bleed.

I destroy a bunch of grapes, I castrate a watermelon, I stab roots, I perforate eggs.

The castrated watermelon, the lipped sugar, and the bloody tomatoes combine to create a literary space where the once-unique qualities of human embodiment expand to include the food that nourishes that body. The effect of this metaphorical system is a destabilization of the boundaries of human being. Instead of maintaining control over the images that describe humans exclusively Courtoisie creates a situation in which food functions as the body, at least from the perspective of the first-person attacker who makes his way through the supermarket. The idiosyncrasies that make Raúl see packages of sugar as human bodies suggests an aesthetic in which the human being does not occupy a separate, hallowed sphere. While bleeding tomatoes and castrated watermelons are a far cry from the metaphorical cyborgs that move through Hayles and Haraway's theoretical writings, the decay of the boundaries that delineate human identity sets the stage for a further erosion of boundaries between the organic and the mechanical. If Haraway's cyborg appears at the transgressed boundary between animal and human, Courtoisie situates his creation at a place where vegetable and human merge in semiotic hybridity.

The reaction of the police and the media to Raúl's attack on the supermarket strengthens this confusion of human identity. As the police arrive on the scene, they encounter a woman whose young son is still inside the supermarket. Her hysterical screams draw repeated blows from the police who claim to be attempting to calm her (*Tajos*, 15). The result of this scene of institutional violence is the woman's bloodied mouth, a red-stained image that repeats the vegetable gore of the mutilated tomatoes and castrated watermelons. The blood from the woman's mouth then flows into the next section where Raúl describes another aspect of his supermarket assault:

> Yo había lanzado las botellas de salsa ketchup sobre los automóviles y los carteles del estacionamiento, había estrellado botellas de salsa de tomate en las casas cercanas, había derramado salsa ketchup en la garganta de los inodoros, dentro de los toilettes, había salpicado espejos y alfombras.
>
> También había desparramado un cargamento de calabazas. Parecían cabezas sueltas, sin dueño, cabezas solas de una masacre. La realidad estaba ensangrentada. La salsa de tomate parece humana.
>
> Parece sangre.
>
> Luce como sangre humana.
>
> Yo no tengo la culpa.
>
> La ropa se mancha. Los líquidos son semejantes.
>
> La policía se confundió. (16–17)
>
> I had hurled ketchup bottles over the cars and the parking signs, I had plastered the nearby houses with bottles of tomato sauce, I had spilled ketchup in the throats of the toilets, inside the restrooms, I had sprayed mirrors and carpets. I had also scattered a load of pumpkins. They looked like loose heads, without

owners, the solitary heads of a massacre. The reality was bloody.
The tomato sauce looked human.
It looked like blood.
It shone like blood.
It's not my fault.
The clothing was stained, the liquids are similar.
The police were confused.

The novel moves from an aesthetic that confuses human beings with vegetables to a situation in which the main character deliberately manipulates signs so as to produce chaos. The characters that attempt to read the scene are unable to arrive at accurate interpretations, precisely because they depend upon definitions of human bodies that Raúl has destabilized through his careful mix of human metaphor and vegetable reality. The ketchup that imitates blood and the pumpkins that mimic severed heads strengthen the previous moves that fudge the outlines of human identity as they simultaneously underscore the artificial quality of the image. That is, the scene describes the creation of a particular image as an exercise in deceit. At the same time, the similarities between ketchup and blood, round pumpkins and round heads, all suggest a metaphorical union of images that also fuses human body with vegetable body.

In a related, more cinematic move, the color red as an image of blood serves as a unifying logic for the scene progression from woman's mouth, to staged explosion, to the overall scene that deceives the police into identifying the mess as a terrorist attack. By ending on the three images I mention, the chapters I refer to in this section present a series of what can be seen as match cuts that use blood to bridge the gap between female victim of police aggression, spilled ketchup, and police confusion. Just as a film editor will use similarly shaped objects to provide a visual logic to the change in scenes in a movie, the red liquid that flows from the woman's mouth and the mutilated ketchup bottles mix to link the otherwise unrelated images. This strategy further strengthens the metaphorical mixing of human and vegetable bodies. This use of cinematic logic underscores the slippery nature of the markers we use to define human identity and sets the stage for the literal hybridity of the cyborg body. It also provides an alternate interpretation for the novel's title. If "Tajos" refers explicitly to the cuts that Raúl's knife will make on his psychotic journey, it also suggests the cuts in film that, paradoxically, unite the film's logic as much as dissect it. The media's arrival at the end of the sequence, asking the police's interpretation of what happened, functions as a culminating moment where these different strategies result in the transmission of a carefully constructed televisual scene (*Tajos*, 19).

The idea of a cinematic cut that joins as much as it separates helps explain the subsequent situations in which Raúl's relationship with his television suggests the genesis of a media cyborg where the main character's identity appears as an amalgamation of organic body, television set, and televised program. The following scene provides an example of Raúl's television watching experience.

En el Canal 3 dan Batman. Cambio. Es un murciélago estúpido. Robin es puto.
En el 11 dan Viva Minerva.
LLAME, LLAME, LLAME YA
49067 49072
PARTICIPE Y GANE CON MINERVA
Llamo al canal.
—¿Sí?
—¡VIVA MINERVA!—grito.
—¿Cómo es tu nombre?
Dudo.
—Raúl. Me llamo Raúl.
...
Podés jugar al avión.
El juego del avión es peor. Aparece un avión en la pantalla y hay que derribarlo tecleando al azar en el control remoto. El avión da vueltas muy rápidas en un cielo a lunares y hay que acertarle de lleno.
Cada tecla es un proyectil. El participante tiene cuarenta segundos. Si logra derribar el avión gana el automóvil y el viaje a París.

El avión ruge. Pulso el cero. Erré el tiro.

El ocho. Casi, casi.

Ahora el tres, le pego en el ala, pero no cae.

El cuatro, muy lejos.

El cinco. Se acabó.

Chau premio. (38–39)

Batman's on channel 3. I change it. He's a stupid bat. Robin is gay.

Viva Minerva is on 11.

CALL, CALL, CALL NOW
49067 49072
PARTICIPATE AND WIN WITH MINERVA

I call the station.

—Yes?

—VIVA MINERVA! —I yell.

—What's your name?

I hesitate.

—I'm Raúl, my name is Raúl.

You can play airplane.

The airplane game is the worst. An airplane appears on the screen and you have to shoot it down by pressing random buttons on the remote control. The plane flies around very quickly in the polka dot sky and you have to fit it full on.

Each button is a projectile. The player has forty seconds. If he's able to shoot down the plan he wins a car and a trip to Paris.

The plane roars, I push the zero. I miss the shot.

Eight. Almost, almost.

Now the three, I hit it in the wing, but it doesn't fall.

Four, way off.

Five, it's over.

Goodbye prize.

On one level, Courtoisie presents the zapping culture that Beatriz Sarlo has studied so carefully in *Escenas de la vida posmoderna* [Scenes of the Postmodern Life]. The initial scene of Raúl sliding past programs, creating his own hybridized televisual experience, suggests the monstrous television programs Sarlo describes as the irreproducible sequences of scenes produced by zapping through the various channels.² As the scene progresses, however, we see that Courtoisie is exploring the implications of zapping on a series of complementary levels that demand a closer analysis based on the implications of posthuman theory.

The situation suggests a complex exchange of information across technological and organic boundaries. The scene begins with a typical television-watching scene in which Raúl uses his remote control to find a show, even as his inner monologue suggests the beginning of a looping motion between the programs on the television, Raúl's commentary, and organic/mechanical contact between his hand and the remote control. He then happens upon Viva Minerva, a variety show whose unstable name suggests the odd combinations to come. On one level it expresses the idea of a live program, one that paradoxically combines the presence of the moment with the distance of the space between the organic bodies of the viewed and the viewer. On another level, the name becomes a cry of support for Minerva who is at once a ridiculous blonde and the goddess of wisdom. Raúl's arrival at Viva Minerva marks a second invitation into the technological loop already begun with the exchange between Batman and his remote control. In this instance Raúl uses the telephone to plug into the program, splitting into both viewer and viewed as his voice forms a part of the variety show he watches. At this point interactive television is at its most complicated. Raúl watches himself playing a game that responds to his choices as viewer, one that is at the same time analogous to his initial relationship with his remote control. Just as Raúl rejects Batman with a "Cambio," he attempts to use the buttons of the device to shoot down an airplane. In this instance, "Cambio" refers not merely to Raúl's decision to change the channel but to the action that is produced when Raúl sees the program option and presses the appropriate button to affect the change. In a similar process, the hit on the wing is represented with a verb (*pego*) whose singular first-person conjugation incorporates Raúl's consciousness within the technological action of the remote control/missile launcher. Courtoisie complements this fusion of human and machine with a telegraphic style that emphasizes Raúl's dialogue with the television, resorting to single words and short phrases that display the immediacy of the communication between Raúl, remote control, and television. In this communication, one can appreciate a situation in which Hayles's description of posthuman nature is applicable.

> The user's sensory-motor apparatus is being trained to accommodate the computer's responses. Working with a VR simulation, the user learns to move his or her hand in stylized gestures that the computer can accommodate. In the process, the neural configuration of the user's brain experiences changes, some of which can be long lasting. The computer molds the human even as the human builds the computer. (1999: 47)

We can see this process especially clearly in Raúl's repeated attempts to use the remote control to shoot down the plane. The blurring of identity that we saw in the metaphors and manipulation of images that we saw in the beginning of the novel now find a concrete example of organic and technological blending in Raúl's combination with his remote control and television. We also find that Raúl's molding of the supermarket scene finds a repetition here where Raúl's idiosyncratic viewing style results in a complementary molding of his own identity.

The prominence of the remote control in this scene connects zapping with video game playing, extending two of Sarlo's prominent themes. Raúl's running commentary emphasizes his control over the television medium, creating a dialogue with the programs that result in the creation of a hybridized Batman/Variety Show program fused together by the "cambios" that simultaneously cut them off. Courtoisie's incorporation of the remote control in the televised video game takes zapping one step further. Not only do viewers control the sequence of programming, they directly affect the course of the images shown—shooting down the airplanes that fly across the screen and providing feedback upon which the announcers will comment. If Sarlo anticipated a situation where human and television would merge in the creation of televisual art, Courtoisie presents it as reality.

Courtoisie strengthens this televisual blurring of identity throughout the novel. A subsequent episode, one that results in Raúl destroying his television, further develops this idea. Raúl calls into a television psychic with the hopes of finding out why his grandmother died.

> En la televisión hay un parapsicólogo.
> LLAME AL 22608 PARA CONSULTAR
> 22608
> TELEVIDA A SU ALCANCE
> 22608
> EL NÚMERO DE LA TELEVISIÓN
>
> El mentalista le adivina la suerte a una mujer. El marido la engaña con la hermana. La mujer grita. Conviene viajar. Olvide a su marido. Su hermana es perversa. Muy mala. Aléjese. Su marido no va a volver. Rehaga su vida.
>
> La mujer insulta, respira, solloza.
>
> —Rehaga su vida.
>
> Corta. Otra consulta. (47–48)

> There's a parapsychologist on the television.
> CALL 22608 TO CONSULT
> 22608
> TELELIFE WITHIN YOUR REACH
> 22608
> THE NUMBER ON THE TELEVISION
>
> The mentalist tells the fortune of a woman. Her husband is cheating on her with her sister. The woman screams. It's better to travel. Forget about her husband. Her sister is perverse. Very bad. Get away. Her husband won't return. Remake your life.
>
> The woman curses, breathes, sobs.
>
> Remake your life.
>
> He hangs up, another consult.

The introductory section to Raúl's experience with the parapsychologist illustrates a more generalized vision of televisual posthuman identity. The episode begins in the same way as his encounter with the game show; the television presents him with a point of entry into the televised world through his telephone. Raúl observes a woman already within the imaginary, whose previous life has fallen apart because of the statement of the psychic. What is of particular importance here is the process by which the woman's life is remade. Her entry into the television world through her phone line produces a situation in which she must rethink the assumptions that rule her life. Courtoisie emphasizes the "humanity" of the situation with her responses to the news: the sobs, the deep breath, and the curses. At the same time, these very human responses are both played out on television and are framed by the descriptions of the episode that begin with the television announcement and end with the click of the telephone. That is, the woman's apparently real life story both begins and ends mediated by machines and played out on a technological stage. She has become both viewer and character on a television show and, furthermore, has been caught up in that same feedback loop between television, telephone, and organic human body that we saw first in Raúl.

Raúl's experience with the psychic runs a similar course that reconfirms what we saw with the woman as well as with his experiences on the game show.

> Llamo yo.
> —Usted ha perdido un familiar muy amado—explica.
> Doy un salto.
> —Falleció su abuela.
> ¿Cómo sabe?
> —Sufrió un ataque al corazón.
> Hijo de puta. ¿Cómo lo sabe?
> —Lo voy a matar—amenazo—. Estafador. Farsante.
> Se corta.
> Llamo otra vez: 22608
> —¿Canal 20?
> —Sí. Canal 20. Estamos al aire.

—Quiero hablar con el parapsicólogo.
—Hable.
Respiro. Pregunto.
—¿Cómo lo sabe? ¿Cómo mierda lo sabe?
No contesta.
Insulto. Bramo. Corta.
¿Cómo adivinó la muerte de mi abuela? (48–49)
I call.
—You have lost a beloved family member—he explains.
I jump.
—Your grandmother died.
How does he know?
—She had a heart attack.
Son of a bitch. How does he know?
—I'm going to kill you—I threaten—. Fake, Crook.
He hangs up.
I call again.
—Channel 20?
—Yes, channel 20, we're on the air.
—I want to speak with the parapsychologist.
—Go ahead.
—How do you know? How the hell do you know?
—He doesn't answer.
I curse, I yell. He hangs up.
How did he guess how my grandmother died?

Courtoisie overloads the description of the conversation with references to the technological mediation of the encounter between Raúl and the psychic. The "llamo" and "corta" that frame both calls function in much the same way as we saw previously in the case of the woman, but in this case the television station reminds Raúl of their "on air" status—a remark that simultaneously reminds the viewer of the now televised life of Raúl who is living out his search on television. Just as with the previous caller and with his experience on the game show

Raúl's identity and reactions to life are determined by his relationship with his television, a relationship made all the more technologically based by the use of the telephone.[3] In the two most striking illustrations of Raúl's relationship with his television, we see the grafting of apparatus and organic body in a process that accentuates Raúl's inability to function in either sphere. Sarlo's description of the successful video game player seems to anticipate and explain Raúl's failure:

> ¿cuánto puedo acelerar mis reflejos corporales para lograr vencer la velocidad de los chip? ¿Qué nivel de dificultad admite, no mi previsión abstracta, sino mi capacidad física de transformarla en acciones que aparezcan en pantalla? Estas son las preguntas cruciales de todo buen jugador de video-game. Los malos jugadores... no intentan responder a estas preguntas. Se los descubre enseguida porque mueven la palanca como sonámbulos, aprietan los botones todo el tiempo, no se sujetan a la rapidísima lógica de efectos y consecuencias, no cambian de táctica. (50–51)

> How much can I accelerate my corporeal reflexes so that I can beat the speed of the chip? What level of difficulty allows, not my abstract foresight but my physical capability, to transform that foresight in actions that appear on the screen? These are the crucial questions of every good video game player. The bad players never try to answer those questions. They are discovered quickly as they move the control as if they were sleepwalking, pressing the buttons all the time without subjecting themselves to the very quick logic of cause and effect, they don't change their tactics.

Here Sarlo anticipates Hayles's description of posthuman identity already mentioned, describing the competent player as one who adapts his or her body to the reality of the chip, forming a kind of biomechanical feedback loop with the technology of the game. Raúl is the bad player who does not understand that process, who cannot adapt. This failure to achieve his goals, be they prizes or psychic knowledge and hence the objectives that bring Raúl the metaphorical cyborg into being, suggests a similar frustration of desire at the seat of a newly articulated posthuman identity. Courtoisie combines this failure with an omnipresent consumerism that constantly mediates the exchange of information between organism and television. Raúl's desire for commodity is what spurs the birth of the telehuman, a desire that the resulting cyborg is unable to satisfy. Raúl ends up frustrated both by his posthuman nature and by his inability to operate his technological appendages successfully. The condemnation of consumerism is obvious in the first example; Raúl's desire for the material prizes, the status symbols that European travel and new cars provide, all represent the desire for commodity with all that that desire entails.[4] The second example is subtler. Here we have the commoditization of emotion in the blending of biography, the promise of inner knowledge through psychic insight, and the televisual medium that presents the psychic life as an object of consumption. Raúl's fusion with the television, both metaphorical and real, both accentuates the commoditization of the individual and underscores its inherent failure. It is at this point where Courtoisie's challenge to Haraway's "cyborg myth" is most clear. Raúl as cyborg only ever functions within the capitalistic framework that provided the technological components of his identity.[5]

The resulting implications of both the video game and the conversation with the psychic form a commentary on the posthuman relationship that emerges from the interaction between organic human, television, and technological device. In this context, the difference between appendage arm and appendage remote control becomes negligible; indeed, the body and the artificial element are unified linguistically within Raúl's utterances. The situation simultaneously creates a moment in which the telephone and remote control become the devices that help Raúl interface and fuse with televisual reality, suggesting the creation of a kind of tele-human or media-cyborg. This combination of Raúl and his media devices reenacts Frederich Kittler's theories on media and consciousness, recalling specifically his image of airplane travelers all plugged into the earphone jacks that provide them with news and entertainment. The human consciousness melds into the technology that keeps the plane in the air, as well as into the technology that keeps the passengers informed and entertained. The result is a collective cybernetic organism that negotiates its identity among the biomechanical couplings that link airplane, news program, and passenger. For Kittler, such couplings approach invisibility, particularly in the case of media that delivers information without the need for the mediation of writing, as is the situation with televisual image and sound (Kittler's famous example is the phonograph that delivers sound without an accompanying sign). While Kittler remains objective on the implications of these ideas, such a fusion of body and media can certainly be seen as ominous. Shirin Shenassa describes a conceptualization of mass media that suggests a kind of cyborg existence where prosthesis changes from mechanical to organic, and the human becomes subject to the media rather than the media to the human.

> The third, and most radical way of viewing this connectedness is to assume that humans are not only shaped and remain in feedback with media technologies but are also, in final analysis, an integrated part of information systems. As if inverting one of McLuhan's famous axioms, humans who use media as extensions of their sensory organs now appear as an extension of media. (264)

Courtoisie presents a physical reenactment of the situation where Raúl begins with technological appendages and ends being caught within an apparently bankrupt televisual imaginary. The couplings that should join Raúl to the technological media collective apparently suffer bioelectrical "shorts."

Raúl's telephonic entrance into the televisual imaginary functions according to the experience of what television and film theorist Robert Stam calls the tele-spectator. Stam characterizes this process as such: "Larger than the figures on the screen, we quite literally oversee the world from a sheltered position—all the human shapes parading before us in television's insubstantial pageant are scaled down to lilliputian significance" (364). Raúl begins in precisely that "sheltered position," using his privileged vantage point as spectator to pass judgment on Batman and Robin. And yet, even as Raúl expresses his superiority by changing the channel, his interaction with the remote control and television set bring him to a point where he surrenders, at least partially, his position as spectator/voyeur.

By so doing, and especially when he enters the video game, he reenacts a further element of the televisual experience that Stam describes in his study on television news:

> In psychoanalytic terms, television promotes a narcissistic relationship with an imaginary other. It infantilizes in the sense that the young child perceives everything in relation to itself; everything is ordered to the measure of its ego. Television, if it is not received critically, fosters a kind of confusion of pronouns: between "I" the spectator and "He" or "She" the newscaster, as engaged in mutually flattering dialogue. (376)

Raúl's conversion into a mediated posthuman being makes real the relationship Stam describes with the other as he physically joins the television programming. That is, television's ambiguous pronouns become truly specific to him even as they simultaneously maintain the function that Stam ascribes them. Courtoisie creates, then, a situation in which Raúl's organic body becomes the corporeal reenactment of the psychological experience of television viewing with a marked blurring of the boundaries between the viewer and the viewed, the spectator's organic body and the screen image. At the same time, Stam suggests that the confusion inherent in television is the result of a failure to receive it critically or, in other words, the failure to disengage from the apparatus and inspect it from an objective distance. Raúl's loss in the game can also be seen as a loss of the ability to separate from the posthuman fusion of organic and mechanical existence.[6]

Courtoisie surrounds this central image of the metaphorical tele-cyborg with a series of episodes in which Raúl can be seen to function as a caricature of Stam's uncritical tele-spectator. In an earlier moment, Raúl watches the news:

> En la ciudad desaparecen cinco niños por día. Treinta y cinco a la semana. Más de cien por mes. Mil doscientos al año.
>
> ¿Quién se los lleva? ¿Qué hacen con ellos?
>
> Hamburguesas.
>
> La tevé pasa un aviso de MacMeat: dos ruedas de carne exacta, lechuga, unas hostias de pepino y sal fina.

96   CYBORGS IN LATIN AMERICA

> Salsa roja.
> La televisión muestra cientos de niños. La escena resulta conmovedora.
> La mezcla de ternura y caca es insoportable.
> Tráfico de órganos, prostitución infantil, dice la televisión. Algunos son adoptados.
> La pantalla muestra una cuna vacía.
> La cuna oscila. (*Tajos*, 31–32)
>
> 5 children disappear each day in the city, 35 each week, more than 100 each month, 1200 every year.
> Who takes them? What do they do with them?
> Hamburgers.
> The TV plays a commercial for MacMeat, 2 perfect meat patties, lettuces, some cucumber hosts and salt.
> Red sauce.
> The television shows hundreds of children. The scene is quite touching.
> The mix of tenderness and crap is unsupportable.
> Organ trafficking, child prostitution, says the television. Some are adopted.
> The screen shows an empty cradle.
> The cradle rocks.

Raúl's abrupt "hamburguesas," positioned very effectively at the end of page 31 in the "Lenguas de Trapo" edition, produces a darkly comic shock to the reader. The following explanation of the hamburgers sold by MacMeat provides the context, but the idea of the lost children as ground beef remains as the first interpretation of Raúl's exclamation. What is particularly remarkable is the way in which Raúl thinks within the imaginary suggested by the television. Raúl seems to respond appropriately to the emotionally manipulative scene of an empty cradle rocking sadly in the nursery. It is, however, in the moment of conjunction of lost child and hamburger that one perceives both Raúl's mental problems and the very complete suturing effect that has sewn Raúl into the televisual imaginary.[7] Indeed, he reads the commercial as one would a cut in a film where the director juxtaposes two images to create syntagmatic meaning. In Raúl's mind, the hamburger's temporal proximity to the report on missing children suggests a bleeding of meaning from the commercial to the report and vice versa. Raúl's inability to parse what Sandy Flitterman-Lewis has called "little narrative units" of television suggests the kind of complete fusion between viewer and viewed that we see in his technological "appearances" on the two television programs. It also serves as the culmination of the narrative strategies introduced by Courtoisie in the supermarket scene where the action of the novel followed a similar cinematic technique; indeed, Raúl appears to be trapped within the cinematic logic that organized the images of the first chapter. The paradox of the cut that joins helps to explain the similarly paradoxical view of posthuman identity that Courtoisie suggests, where the cut and the seam between the organic and the mechanical coexist in uncomfortable, incomplete fusion.

At the same time Raúl's inability to separate commercial from news broadcast suggests a situation in which the neoliberal policies that make "MacMeat" a global presence also serve as an unavoidable component of the posthuman's hybrid identity. The fact that Raúl is unable to distinguish commercial from news program, and that we will not be able to distinguish Raúl's imaginary from television's, associates the desire for commodity with the sign of the posthuman. This association suggests that international capitalism and the market forces that spur technological innovation are always already an inherent element of the cyborg's hybrid identity. In that sense the commercials also strengthen the idea of the televisual medium as inherently commoditized, an idea that further colors Raúl's experiences inside the television programs. Not only is his imaginary fused with the television, it is fused with a desire for commodity that unavoidably accompanies that television. The self-defeating paradox of Raúl's televisual imaginary opens a series of titular *tajos* along the seams that join viewer and viewed, organic and mechanical, in Courtoisie's vision of posthuman identity.

The confusion of organic body and television takes on further posthuman overtones when considered in the light of Deleuze's theoretical work. While Raúl's dependence on remote controls, televisions, and knives evoke images of the schizophrenic's "detachable organs" and the mechanical imagery employed by Deleuze and Guattari in their exploration of capitalism in *Anti-Oedipus*, Deleuze's work in film theory provides a theoretical opening for understanding articulations of televisual cyborgs. In his short history of the cinema he speaks of the creation of a "new Human beast," whose identity sprang from the union of technology and organic body implicit in filmmaking (1986: 43). Deleuze accompanies that image of the cinematic body with his postulation that perspective in film is alternately technological and organic. That is, in many shots the camera will act at times as the view of a character, at times the view of the audience, and at times the view of a disembodied presence that achieves perspectives impossible for any human. Deleuze's characterization of the cinematic shot is instructive in this context, "Given that it [the shot] is a consciousness which carries out these divisions and reunions, we can say of the shot that it acts like a consciousness. But the sole cinematographic consciousness is not us, the spectator, nor the hero; it is the camera—sometimes human, sometimes inhuman or superhuman" (20). When we take these ideas in light of the present discussion, we can appreciate the hybridizing possibilities of the cinema, especially in the formation of a kind of cybernetic consciousness that includes organic and mechanical participants in the production and consumption of the visual image. In the case of television news and Raúl's very specific reactions to it, we see the implications of a televisual situation in which the camera stands in for the different participants in Stam's mutually flattering dialogue. At times, it functions as the viewer to whom the newscaster speaks in the studio; at other times, as the eyes of the person viewing from their home. Just as the television viewer negotiates the human images that shift from organic reality to television screen, so too must the viewer unconsciously accept simultaneous realities in which he or she is both the human partner in an imaginary dialogue with the newscaster as well as a seeing body with prosthetic eyes.[8] Raúl's hyperbolic experience as television participant and viewer highlights this situation in which the televisual cyborg is not only a combination of physical and image-based body apparent in the news anchor or the talk show host, but also the organic body of the viewer fused with the television camera that has replaced its eyes.

Courtoisie emphasizes the physical necessity of the up-to-this-point figurative eye-replacement surgery in the coda of the novel. At the end of *Tajos* we find a section that flashes back to Raúl's childhood. At first blush, the section appears to provide the story behind the cuts in Raúl's mutilated psyche. Raúl was, unsurprisingly, a cruel child whose fascination with sharp items (such as scissors) and dislike for others culminate in an episode in which Raúl stabs an antagonistic classmate (Domínguez) in the buttocks. Up to that point, Courtoisie appears to be presenting a clichéd biography of a murderer, appropriate if we take into account the importance of televisual narratives so far. The cliché flips, though, on the stabbing, as it provokes a counterattack by the classmate who stabs Raúl in the eye. The narration then jumps to Raúl watching television (with his one good eye and a series of meditations on his elevation to "rey de los ciegos," a reference to the saying "In the kingdom of the blind, the one-eyed man is king" (91). This narrative jump frames the act of watching television that we have already commented upon with the physical trauma of the loss of an eye. The tele-cyborg figures not merely as a side-effect from too much television but as the result of technological prosthesis filling a biological need.

The news Raúl watches while thinking presents a special report, the televised execution of the country's former military dictator, none other than Domínguez, his vengeful schoolmate. Courtoisie creates two narrative filters that help Raúl process what he sees. The first consists of a series of flashes from the first page of Gabriel García Márquez's *Cien años de soledad*:

> Muchos años después, frente al pelotón de fusilamiento, el coronel Aureliano Domínguez habría de recordar aquella tarde remota en que me pinchó el ojo.
>
> Sin García Márquez.
>
> Muchos años después, Aureliano Domínguez comandó las tropas del Ejército que cercaron la residencia presidencial y terminaron por derrocar al presidente Salgado. (88)

Many years later, facing the firing squad, Colonel Aureliano Domínguez would remember that remote afternoon when he put out my eye.
Without García Márquez.
Many years later, Aureliano Domínguez commanded the Army's troops that surrounded the presidential residence and removed President Salgado from power.

We then learn that Salgado had survived the first attack with minor injuries only to be killed when Domínguez shoots him in the eye (89). The intertextual reference to *Cien años de soledad* sets up an identity flux where Raúl's childhood enemy flickers between the dictator he had become and Aureliano Buendía while Raúl fuses with President Salgado by virtue of the injury and inflictor of that injury that they share. This literary shifting becomes a coping strategy that Raúl uses to organize the execution he sees, a literal poetic justice made real as Raúl can thus witness a personal vengeance acted out on a national, televisual stage.

The second filter is the television itself, here functioning as the eyes, minds, and memories of the nation in its representation of the end of a dictatorial era. Courtoisie adds a curious loop with the mode of the execution:

> Transmitieron la ejecución del dictador en vivo y en directo.
> Por televisión y radio.
> El capitán dio la orden:...
> Domínguez cayó, miedoso, lloraba, muchos años después frente al pelotón de fusilamiento rogaba, imploraba....
> El capitán del pelotón se acercó al condenado. Sacó el revolver. Amartilló. Apuntó. Disparó.
> Le reventó el ojo derecho.
> —Así, amigos, hemos presenciado la ejecución del cruento dictador—dijo el conductor del Informativo en la televisión mientras la cámara enfocaba en primer plano el cuerpo caído del tirano—. De inmediato volvemos con la realidad internacional. Ahora vamos a unos avisos comerciales. (90–91)

> They transmitted the execution of the dictator live and direct.
> By television and radio.

The captain gave the order.
Domínguez fell, scared, crying, many years later in front of the firing squad, begging, pleading.
The captain approached the condemned. He took out his pistol. He cocked it. He aimed. He fired.
The right eye exploded.
—My friends, we have witnessed the execution of the cruel dictator—the newscaster said while the camera focused on a close up of the fallen body of the tyrant. We will return soon with international news. Now, we go to commercials.

Domínguez's form of death makes literal the biblical commandment in a web of ruptured eyes that shifts from Raúl to Salgado to the executed dictator and restores Raúl both figuratively and literally. The apparent justice, both legal and poetic, implied in the execution restores the personal and national imbalances caused by Domínguez's crimes. In that sense the connection between Raúl and Salgado discussed earlier is also a connection between Raúl and his nation, both of whom had their eyes put out by the dictatorship—literally as in the case of the biological eyes of Salgado and Raúl, but also, conceivably, figuratively in the censorship that prevented the nation from "seeing" the abuses of the dictatorship as they happened. This figurative blindness is, then, overcome by the televised nature of the event; the television sets and cameras literally becoming the prosthetic eyes of the nation (an image the U.S. television network CBS has been cultivating for decades), allowing Raúl and his compatriots a glimpse of the act that restores their ability to see. The "eye for an eye" that visits biological justice on Domínguez also applies to the mechanical eye that television appears to offer the human body that can no longer depend on organic sight. The complicated televisual and telephonic networks that create Raúl earlier in the novel culminate on a Raúl with a camera in his eye socket. At the same time, and despite the apparently positive role that television plays in the postdictatorship period, the commercial, neoliberal context associated with technology never disappears. The television announcer immediately takes the nation to the international stage with the promise of the "realidad internacional" and then reminds everyone that the presentation of the execution was made possible by "unos avisos comerciales."

Courtoisie redeploys this scene in *Caras extrañas*, his 2002 exploration of the wide-reaching effects of the political violence of the Southern Cone of the late 1960s. The novel presents this meditation in a looping narrative in which acts of indiscriminate violence perpetrated by both the Right and the Left reverberate throughout space and time, facilitated by physical and temporal reach of television reports as well as an *escrache* campaign carried out by telephone in an early twenty-first-century present.[9] In the first few pages Courtoisie describes the leftist attempt to lay siege to the fictitious town of Salvo in the vein of Argentina's *Cordobazo*, a siege that unleashes the cycle of violent reprisals that cuts through the entire novel. Just as in *Tajos* the media arrives on the scene at the end of the initial violent siege and repackages it for the television audience, turning failures into victories as it adds "sal y pimienta" to the reality it reports (2001: 17). Courtoisie then spends the rest of *Caras extrañas* tracing both the chain of violence and its televisual representation as it extends through the population and over time, commenting in particular on the way that the televisual representation replaces the organic memories of the violence as people remember not the event but the televisual report of the event.[10] In both novels, we see a preparation of the reality of governmental violence for media consumption in a process that separates and unites an event with the technological representation of that same event.

The manipulation of television as an integral component of the political struggle appears throughout the novel. In a scene that borrows equally from political horror and slapstick, a Catholic bishop is killed during the siege. The conversion of bishop into saint plays out on video through the country with important technological implications:

> El Obispo fue inhumado con honores de ministro y el gobierno, mediante una astuta campaña propagandística, lo transformó en un mártir...
>
> El obispo, aunque muerto y enterrado, hacía milagros:—Hizo hablar a un mudo—dijo la televisión.

Una prostituta se arrepintió. Se casó con un marinero calvo. Ya no volvió a las calles ni a la mala vida.

Un paralítico no pudo andar pero consiguió canjear una bicicleta de carreras que le habían donado por una silla de ruedas con freno hidráulico y luces.

Un operado de cataratas volvió a leer los diarios.

Un músico sordo se dedicó a pintar, se hizo muy famoso y ganó dinero.

Indudablemente el obispo hacía milagros. Lo repetía todo el día la televisión:—El obispo santo, asesinado por los sediciosos. (47)

The bishop was buried with ministry and governmental honors, due to an astute propaganda campaign; he was transformed into a martyr.

The bishop, though dead and buried, did miracles. He made a mute speak, the television said.

A prostitute repented. She married a bald sailor. She never returned to the street or the bad life.

A paralyzed man that couldn't walk but was able to trade a racing bike that had been donated to him for a wheel chair with lights and hydraulic breaks. A cataract surgery patient was able to read the newspapers again.

A deaf musician dedicated himself to painting; he became famous and earned money. Clearly the bishop caused miracles. It was repeated everyday on television. The holy bishop, assassinated by seditionists.

Thematically, television's role within the national consciousness is obvious; the media functions as the prosthetic mouth of the state while simultaneously functioning as the prosthetic imaginary of a nation of television viewers. Courtoisie develops an accompanying semiotics of replacement in the list of miracles that subtly supports the vision of television as a Janus-faced prosthetic. The list of miracles, in addition to not seeming that miraculous, accentuates bodies that are either physically or culturally deemed incomplete. The physically traumatized are presented as symbolically made whole through inorganic means: the paralyzed man obtains his wheelchair, a blind man's cataracts are surgically repaired, a deaf musician cannot hear, but has his hearing replaced with money. Even the prostitute, whose body is deemed incomplete because of the way in which she uses it (in a kind of prosthetic love), is completed by her marriage and saved from her "mala vida" [bad life]. The list creates a series of physical and social needs that are filled by elements extraneous to the body much in the way that television functions as it completes both the government and the populace. The syntax of the page underlines the whole process, repeating phrases and images as it imitates the cyclical structure of television news, the narrative reporting the television as it reports the supposed miracles performed by the dead bishop.

With television as the national imaginary, the rebels quickly attempt to complement their physical attack with a virtual offensive.

> Para contrarrestar, la guerrilla secuestró al travesti motivo de la confusión y lo interrogó con dureza: —Me gustan los hombres—declaró el travesti—, me muero por ellos.
> Los terroristas filmaron un video.
> Mostraban, de lejos, dos fotos, la del obispo y la del travesti con pollera larga.
> —He aquí las pruebas—afirmaban—. Por eso nos confundimos.
> El travesti fue liberado. Habló con las altas autoridades del clero, se ofreció generosamente para cumplir funciones de obispo en sustitución del sacerdote asesinado.
> Le dijeron:
> —No—al travesti.
> El travesti lloró un poco. Lo mostró la televisión. (47)
>
> To respond, the guerilla kidnapped the transvestite cause of the confusion and interrogated him harshly. I like men, the transvestite declared, I die for them.
> The terrorists filmed a video.
> They showed, from far away, two photos. One of the bishop and one of the transvestite with a long skirt.
> Here is the proof. That's why we were confused.
> The transvestite was set free. He spoke with the authorities of the clergy, he generously offered to fulfill the responsibilities of the bishop to replace the murdered priest. They told the transvestite no. He cried a little, the television showed it.

With the counterpoint of competing videos (as well as the amusing offers to supplement and replace), Courtoisie firmly establishes televisual reality as the reality. On both sides of the political debate, the story becomes the memory; the televised images and reports function as artificial memories of the events of the conflict for those whose only experience of those events came through watching them on television. As a character mentions later in the narrative:

> ¿Cómo explicar ahora lo que era la guerra?
>
> Yo tenía diez años: era fabuloso. Como la serie *Combate*, con el sargento Sanders, que daban por la televisión.
>
> Fabulosa, horrible.
>
> Yo tenía diez años cuando esa guerra, cuando escuché por primera vez en mi vida ciertas palabras y cuando murieron hombres y mujeres buenos y malos, claros y turbios.
>
> A los diez años la guerra es un programa de televisión. (79)
>
> How do we explain now what the war was?
>
> I was ten years old: it was fabulous. It was like the series Combate, with Sergeant Sanders that they played on television.
>
> Fabulous, horrible.
>
> I was ten years old during the war, when I heard for the first time in my life certain words and when good and bad men and women died, clear and troubled.
>
> When you're ten years old, war is a television program.

Courtoisie creates a generation who, as the children of those who used television as prosthetic eyes, ears, and mouths, use television as prosthetic memory, the televisual apparatus serving as a reality filter that installs itself in the child's mind. The remarks of the man, now grown, suggest television as a psychological coping mechanism as well. We have seen how Courtoisie treats television news as a staged production that artificially manipulates reality as it reports it. Here, we see the way in which fictional programs provide a way for the younger generation to understand the trauma that their nation underwent.

This theme in particular, where the result of a televised conflict is a nation that uses fictional programs to explain awful realities, becomes one of the main thrusts of the novel. Later on, Courtoisie presents the following melodramatic scene with a commentary at the end:

—Mi padre se murió hace tiempo.
—Entonces es un misterio.
—Sí, es un misterio.—dijo Jorge y le desprendió la blusa a Marcela, le soltó el pelo castaño y los pechos.
—Es un misterio—suspiró Marcela, buena.
Otra vez la telenovela. Primer plano:
Se besan. (108)

—My father died some time ago.
—So it's a mystery.
—Yes, a mystery.—Jorge said as he unbuttoned Marcela's blouse and released her hair and her breasts.
—It's a mystery—sighed Marcela, pleased.
Again the telenovela. Close-up.
They kiss.

Courtoisie then follows this scene with the conversion of the entire novel into telenovela: "Eran las seis. Encendió el aparato de televisión que tenía escondido en la habitación, detrás de una cortina. Ese día emitían uno de los capítulos cruciales de la telenovela *Caras extrañas*, por Canal 3" (156) [It was 6 p.m. They turned on the television that they had hidden in the room behind a curtain. That day they were showing one of the crucial episodes of the telenovela *Caras extrañas*, on channel 3]. Here the televisual coping mechanism that the earlier character described becomes the constant comparison between postdictatorial life, narrative, and telenovela where life is narrated multiple times as televised stories and fictions organize the chaos of the "really" real, a subject constantly undermined by the ubiquitous incursions into video fiction. At the same time, the prosthetic memory that television provides helps insure the perpetuation of stories that testify to the abuses of dictatorship. Here, Courtoisie suggests a role for television that extends beyond that kind of semi-Luddite view of television as the cause of societies' ills that appears to play out in the psychosis of Raúl in *Tajos*. With the television serving as political battlefield for what would become the memory of future generations, it seems appropriate that the subsequent attacks on the corruption that spawned those battles would also take a technological form. As one of the military begins to suffer a kind of *escrache* campaign, he receives a series of telephone calls.

> El contestador automático almacena sílabas, palabras, guarda insultos, conserva para devolver intacto, para repetirlo sin falta, sin errores de gramática, sin furcios, el jugo de los sonidos.
>
> Conserva las frases intactas. La apariencia y la carne de los sonidos para vomitarlos después, puntualmente, sin un solo temblor, cuando se pulse la tecla
>
> «Play»
>
> de la máquina, cuando el dedo al oprimir la tecla se meta en la garganta mecánica del aparato y le produzca arcadas, cuando el dedo de la mano toque «play» y el reflejo automático haga subir de las entrañas planas de resistencias, diodos y circuitos integrados, de las tripas tecnológicas de la civilización el antiguo bolo alimenticio de las palabras, y con ellas el ovillo prehistórico, primitivo, gutural del insulto:
>
> —¡Hijo de la putísima madre que te recontra mil parió! |Asesino de mierda, maricón, te vamos a matar, te vamos a cortar los huevos en pedacitos, en pedacitos, en pedacitos....! (83)

The answering machine stores syllables, words, it keeps insults, conserves them to return them intact, to repeat it without fault, without errors of grammar, without the juice of the sounds.

It keeps the phrases intact. The appearance and the flesh of the sounds to vomit them later, punctually, without a single tremor, when one presses the button.

> Play

Of the machine, when the finger presses the button, it is placed in the mechanical throat of the machine and it produces arcades, when the finger of the hand touches play and the automatic reflection makes the words emerge from the flat innards of the resistances, diodes and integrated circuits, from the technological guts of civilization, those ancient alimentary ball of words and with them the prehistoric, primitive, guttural insult: Son of the whorish mother that gave you birth. Murderous swine, faggot, we will kill you we will cut your balls in pieces, in pieces, in pieces.

Courtoisie creates a poetic system where organicity and technology elide constantly and where boundaries between the natural and the artificial disappear in waves of alternating mechanical and living imagery. The answering machine stores sounds made flesh in a technological body whose ability to "vomit" those sounds later from its "mechanical throat" stems from the interface of flesh (the finger) and machine (the "play" key). The overabundance of technological references mixed with primordial imagery creates a merry mess of flesh and metal parts that culminate in the aggressive insult that threatens the torturer with violence that he had visited upon his victims. If the original war was a televisual battle of videotaped images the reprisals must also be technological and here we see that revenge comes when the answering machine that acts as the prosthetic ear of its owner functions simultaneously as the mechanical voice of the accuser, neatly reversing the double prosthetic function of the television noted earlier. For Courtoisie the archival function of technology both visually and aurally is one where the technology cannot exist separately from the living organism that they archive, that technological and organic memories, and especially language, bleed into each other forming living circuits and mechanical flesh.

In the case of *Caras extrañas*, that replacement extends to memory where the television recording takes precedence over any biological experience of political trauma. Near the end of that novel, a man who was a young boy of ten at the time of the siege of Salvo reflects on his memory of the violence:

> Yo, y muchos otros, aprendimos mucho con la televisión.
> Al principio era en blanco y negro. Después en colores. Creo que la televisión, en términos relativos, es una fuente de vida. Y en términos absolutos una palabra más. [...]
> Creo que fue en 1969, justo cuando la toma guerrillera de la ciudad de Salvo, que el Apolo XI llegó a la Luna.

Creo que fue en ese año. Lo pasaron por televisión, en directo. Yo estaba en casa de un amigo y el padre de mi amigo, completamente estúpido e hipnotizado, no paraba de repetir:

—Qué maravilla. (*Caras*, 181–82)

I, and many others, learned much from the television. At the beginning it was in black and white. Then in color. I believe that television, in relative terms, is a source of life. In absolute terms it is just another word.

I believe that it was in 1969, exactly when the guerrillas took the city of Salvo that the Apollo XI arrived on the moon. I believe it was in that year. They had it on television, direct.

I was at my friend's house and my friend's father, completely stupefied and hypnotized, couldn't stop saying, "How marvelous."

If Raúl's inability to parse television stems from his failing biological mind, in *Caras extrañas* the man ties memory, his childhood, and history to the god-like, life-giving television. Raúl's struggles with commercialism and consumerism are reconfigured as the inhabitants of a traumatized, postdictatorship society depend on technological memories to order their understanding of the very society they inhabit. In that sense, television functions as a suture that joins a national consciousness of political trauma as represented in the later novel with the commercials that haunt Raúl's imaginary in *Tajos*. Indeed, Courtoisie anticipates *Caras extrañas* in the finale of *Tajos* where Raúl's final, and only, social act occurs as he and his unnamed nation watch the televised execution of their former dictator (a childhood enemy who had stabbed Raúl in the eye when they were classmates), the television creating in that moment a national memory (*Tajos*, 90–91).[11] In both novels, this televisual "fuente de vida" gives birth to organic bodies whose biological imaginaries have been replaced by technological representations of memory and desire while also suturing the society that shares those single televised moments.

Courtoisie articulates, then, on both individual and national levels the psychology of a posthuman television viewer, one whose absorption within the televisual imaginary is related to the cybernetic feedback loops that are produced in the webs of information that bind us to telephones and remote controls. By so doing, Courtoisie invites a consideration of cyborg identity that draws its aesthetic from the cuts or "tajos" in cinema where montages of images create meaning by the fusion of mutilated film stock. He then extends this idea into television, where commercials are the stitches that bind the cuts and introduce explicit consumerism into the semantic seam. By applying these ideas to the literal and metaphorical cybernetic couplings that create posthuman identity, Courtoisie presents his version of the cyborg that suffers from the imperfect sutures that can never fully heal the cut between organic tissue and prosthetic technology. In that sense, the novella eschews the more optimistic appraisal we see of the possibilities of the cyborg for a Jamesonian postmodern nostalgia that regrets the biomechanical hybridities that capitalism creates as it produces televisual cyborg consumers. Witold Rybczynski remarked the following when considering the development of posthuman and cyborg identity: "The artificial limbs, to continue Freud's metaphor, itch. Sometimes the scar will not heal; inflammation and infection set in. Occasionally the body rejects the implanted organ, and, if it is not quickly removed, serious damage can result" (5). *Tajos* provides a study of the posthuman at the seams of what should be seamless. The cybernetic sutures that graft the organic and the mechanical, the viewer and the televisual, begin to split, apparently ripped open by the processes that joined them in the first place. In the case of the physical trauma of the postdictatorship that Courtoisie explores in *Caras extrañas* we see television as a necessary but distanced supplement to the biological, its technology providing the only access to national history. With that foundation in mind, the commercial logic of *Tajos* becomes nearly inevitable. The shared trauma of dictatorship has become part and parcel of a televisual identity that facilitates the global consumerism within which Raúl struggles. I return to the previously quoted newscaster's remarks on the execution of Aureliano Domínguez at the end of *Tajos*: "Así amigos, hemos presenciado la ejecución del cruento dictador—dijo el conductor del Informativo en la televisión mientras la cámara enfocaba en primer plano el cuerpo caído del tirano—. De inmediato volvemos con la realidad internacional. Ahora vamos a unos avisos comerciales" [In this way, my friends, we have witnessed the execution of the cruel dictator—said the newscaster on television while the camera focused a close-up on the fallen body of the tyrant. We will return with international news. Now we go to some commercials] (*Tajos*, 90–91). Along those lines, and especially in the case of the desire for commodity, the cyborg body consumes and is consumed by those technologies that deliver global capitalism and promise the incorporation of the viewer within the logic of capitalism. If Donna Haraway speaks of "pleasurably tight couplings" between human and machine in her celebration of cyborg identity, Courtoisie suggests a space where pleasure has yet to emerge from the posthuman's itchy stitches.

Chapter 4

Neoliberal Prosthetics in Postdictatorial Argentina and Bolivia: Carlos Gamerro and Edmundo Paz Soldán

The bulk of the novels, films, and other cultural expressions under examination appear during the 1990s, a decade now notorious for the implementation and institutionalization of neoliberal regimes through much of Latin America. The political career of Carlos Menem, Argentina's president from 1989 to 1999, provides an easy chart for Latin America's own embrace and rejection of economic policies that emphasized free trade and privatization over the remnants of state-centered programs. In the case of Argentina, while the pegging of the peso to the dollar in 1991 alleviated the hyperinflation of the late 1980s and the privatization of state industry helped money flow into a bankrupted nation, by the late 1990s these policies had gutted Argentina's production capabilities, converting the country into a nation of consumers and destabilizing the economy to the point of the crisis of 2001. Argentina was only one obvious example; many other countries embraced and then rejected neoliberal policy over the course of the 1990s and the beginning of this century. We have countries such as Bolivia or Venezuela whose neoliberal experiments are now harshly condemned by the leftist governments who came to power on the backs of those economic failures. The rapid globalization and the series of economic grafts that occurred during neoliberalism contributed to the construction of hybrid sensibilities in which the Latin American subject was subjected to the influx of messages and goods specifically coded as global. The artistic representations of these newly amalgamated subjectivities have recent important critical attention. Francine Masiello's recent book, *The Art of Transition: Latin American Culture and Neoliberal Crisis*, emphasizes and explores this hybridity from its very cover, the reproduction of Juan Davila's "The Liberator Símon Bolívar." The painting depicts a transvestite, partially nude Bolívar making an obscene gesture while astride a horse that is part statue part abstract painting. Masiello examines, to great effect, the varied implications of a painting that could be considered cultural blasphemy in certain parts of Latin America, highlighting the integral importance of hybridity in the artistic expression of the last thirty years. Given this particular artistic/political background, the posthuman's essential hybridity would seem an appropriate conduit for the exploration of neoliberalism in contemporary Latin America. While the majority of the artistic expressions under examination in this book come from this time period, in this chapter I examine the work of two writers where not only is the posthuman subject on clear display but it is also explicitly linked to the neoliberal policies that helped constitute it.

The Argentine novelist Carlos Gamerro has enjoyed some success in Buenos Aires with a steady stream of works that began with *Las Islas*, a lengthy novel published in 1997 that, among other things, uncovers a group of computer enthusiasts who have planned a virtual reinvasion of the Malvinas (Falkland) Islands. The novel follows a separate designer of computer games who is hired by a business mogul to help hush the illegal activities of the businessman's son, a job that leads the designer to a series of discoveries about the connections between the neoliberal present of the 1990s and the activities of the military dictatorship of the 1970s and 1980s. If, as I argued, Argentina and Carlos Menem provide a direct way to examine the rise and fall of neoliberal policy, Bolivia suggests an even more fruitful space for the exploration of neoliberalism and, specifically, its links with dictatorship. The democratic election of Hugo Banzer in 1997 made Bolivia the first and only Latin American country to elect a former military dictator. This somewhat questionable achievement has provided the Bolivian writer Edmundo Paz Soldán ample opportunity to examine the ways in which neoliberal Bolivia simultaneously erases and reinscribes dictatorship in a series of novels. In this chapter I examine the ways in which posthuman identity is used to understand the hybrid bodies produced as the technological imports made more available by neoliberal policy are grafted onto Latin American bodies in Gamerro's *Las Islas* and Paz Soldán's *Sueños digitales* and *El delirio de Turing*. In all three novels we see the posthuman that not only functions as the scarred cyborg of chapter 1, but as the result of the economic hybridity of neoliberalism. In this dual function we find that the posthuman couplings not only fuse foreign technology and Latin American bodies, but they also couple neoliberal policy with dictatorial practice.

Las Islas loosely follows Felipe Felix, a veteran of the Malvinas War who now earns his living as a designer of computer games and as a general-purpose hacker. As he wanders his way through the narrative, he uncovers not only the standard governmental and business conspiracies prevalent in the neoliberal postdictatorship but a virtual reinvasion of the Malvinas Islands organized by fellow veterans. The novel extends from Felix's adventures as he works for the corrupt and eccentric business mogul Tamerlán, erasing all the computer evidence of a murder his son has committed, to the virtual journals of Argentine soldiers in both real and imagined invasions of the Malvinas Islands.[1]

Felix engages in the following conversation when he enters the Tamerlán office building for the first time.

—Vengo a ver al señor Tamerlán—expliqué, finalmente.
—¿Por qué?
—Él me llamó.
—¿Para qué?
—Supongo que necesitará de mis servicios—arriesgué.
—¿Cuáles?
—Especialista en seguridad de sistemas. Detección de anomalías. Redes telemáticas. Virus.
—Una palabra.

—Hacker—contesté sin dudar.

—El detector de metales—lo vi consultar apenas un comando incorporado al brazo de su sillón—indica un objeto extraño en su cabeza. Muéstremelo.

—No puedo. Está adentro.

—Aclare.

—Un pedazo de casco. Un casco de soldado. Un recuerdo…(17)

I come to see Mr. Tamerlán, I finally explained.

Why?

He called me.

For what reason?

I suppose he needs my services, I risked.

Which are?

Specialist in systems security, detection of anomalies, Telematic networks. Viruses.

One word.

Hacker, I answered without hesitating.

"The metal detector." I saw a commando consult it from his chair, is indicating a strange object in your head. Show it to me.

I can't, it's inside.

Clarify.

It's a piece of helmet, a soldier's helmet. A souvenir.

The encounter emphasizes Felix's talents with computers, the technical explanations of his abilities preceding the one word description that identifies him as a hacker. The phrasing progresses from descriptions of his contributions to the security of systems and detection of problems to the "virus" that suggests that he encapsulates both the problem and the answer, with the answer preceding the problem rather than the more traditional structure. The syntax here is important as his self-description culminates in the virus, in his ability to infect rather than his ability to resolve the infection. The one word "virus" also sets up the one word description of his occupation, "hacker," strengthening the threatening connotations of a word whose definition has been debated *ad nauseum* in computer forums at the same time that it presents Felix as inseparable from the technology that he manipulates.

The idea of the hacker as a digital computer virus is then played out on a semiotic level as this human detector of anomalies is detected as carrying something metallic in his head. The helmet shard that he carries as a souvenir of his time in the war incorporates a second level to Gamerro's creation of this posthuman protagonist. Felix's body is not completely organic, a portion of his skull converted from bone to metal as a result of serious injury. If Felix had originally characterized himself as a computer virus, associating his identity with nonorganic technology, the metal in his head makes him literally a cyborg—a true cybernetic organism. Felix is, then, particularly suited to manipulate machines as he can be seen as partly mechanical. Just as he uses his abilities to insinuate himself into information networks, the mechanical has insinuated itself into his body. Gamerro extends this rather traditional description of cyborg identity by including the function of memory within Felix's cybernetic condition. The souvenir plate inside his head acts as a kind of computer disk that contains the traumatic memory of injury. That is, in addition to his presentation as a kind of uniquely qualified cyborg hacker we have the accompanying vision of Felix as a cyborg survivor, a human whose organicity has been compromised by trauma but who also survives thanks to the reminder of that trauma.

His mechanical component prepares him uniquely for his introduction into the Tamerlán Corporation, yet another living machine. Tamerlán describes his building in the following terms: "En el centro de este organismo hecho de espejos y cañerías y cables telefónicos y fibras ópticas y redes de computadoras late un solo corazón: el mío. Todo el edificio es una mera prolongación multiplicada de mi propio cuerpo" (31) [In the center of this organism made of mirrors and pipes and telephone cables and fiber optics and computer networks beats a single heart: mine]. In that statement, Tamerlán gives the most succinct definition of posthuman identity in the novel by identifying the building with its mechanical components as technological prostheses of his own body. He appears to anticipate Hayles's position that "the posthuman view configures human beings so that it can be seamlessly articulated with intelligent machines" (3), where we could merely include Tamerlán's name in the place of the word "posthuman" in that quotation. If Felix's technological component constantly reminds him of his injury, Tamerlán's are an extension of his body—a welcome prostheses instead of the uninvited metal scar in the hacker's head. This distinction is essential to Gamerro's construction of posthuman identity as it corresponds to Argentina's history. Tamerlán's mechanical body is an agent of surveillance, his building/body functioning as a modern-day Panopticon. For example, Tamerlán can observe any of his employees instantly as he can make transparent any wall, ceiling, or floor revealing their activities not only to his gaze but to everyone in the building. This leads to remarkably full restrooms as employees try to hide in the stalls in the hope that he will not bother to watch them while they use the facilities. It also leads his receptionist to engage in a very literal form of phone sex when he calls to speak with Felix, his constant surveillance leading to strange obsessions with objects in the building that are, after all, extensions of his body. Tamerlán's position as leading businessman and most obvious posthuman subjectivity in the novel then creates a strong connection between the neoliberal regimes that he supports and to which his operations contribute and the posthuman subjectivities that global technology help create. This association extends, then, to one that includes Tamerlán as a corrupt businessman with ties to the dictatorship and the technology of control, a technology first exercised during the dictatorship in the application of various forms of surveillance and, particularly, in the application of electroshock torture with grotesque prosthetic phalluses. The technology that facilitates torture and the technology that facilitates neoliberalism become fused in Tamerlán's own monstrous building/body.

Gamerro strengthens this technology/dictatorship/neoliberal bond with an encounter between Felix and Gloria, a woman he meets as he investigates the conspiracy he uncovers while in Tamerlán's employment. As they begin foreplay, the reader is privy to Felix's thoughts:

> Descubrí que besaba despacio, la boca toda floja, la lengua remolona y lánguida, los dientes apenas amagando sombras de

mordiscos. La quiero ver a Sandra simulando esto por computadora, pensé un instante, lograr una interfase acuática como ésta va a requerir de un salto tecnológico cualitativo que cuando se dé quién va a derrocharlo apretando con una vulgar mina; Kevin tiene razón, estamos todavía demasiado apegados a la limitación de la realidad cuando las posibilidades del sexo virtual son ilimitadas: pensemos, por ejemplo, coger con tu Harley Davidson o tu Porsche o, si te da por el arte, la Venus de Botticelli o, más perverso, la de Milo, y por qué no digamos una orgía con las señoritas de Avignon, especialmente las de la derecha—se dio en vagar mi mente por el ciberespacio ilimitado y cuando volví me encontré con una mina desconocida,...(292–93)

I discovered that she kissed slowly, with the mouth loose, the tongue languid, the teeth barely giving shadows of bites. I want to see Sandra simulating this on a computer, I thought for an instant, achieving an aquatic interface like this would require a qualitative technological leap that when it does happen, who will give up being with a common girl. Kevin is right, we are already stuck against the limitation of reality when the possibilities of virtual sex are limitless. Let's consider, for example, of screwing your Harley Davidson, or your Porsche, or, if you like art, Botticelli's Venus, or, perversely, de Milo and why not an orgy with the girls from Avignon, especially the ones on the right, my mind just started wandering through unlimited cyberspace and when I returned I found myself with an unfamiliar girl.

Instead of the expected use of virtual sex as a substitute for the physical, Felix finds that real physical contact is a pale shadow of the possibilities of virtual eroticism. In this instance, contact with the flesh-and-blood Gloria makes Felix think of sex with a motorcycle, another kind of cybernetic fusion that suggests the posthuman blurring of boundaries that have appeared so prevalently in the novel. While one might attribute these thoughts to Felix's work as a hacker and his obsession with computers, we quickly find that there is something special about this woman and, in particular, her skin. As Felix returns to the real world erotic encounter, he notices:

> Esta piel, esta piel tan linda, repetía una voz adentro mío mientras refregaba en ella la nariz, los ojos, la boca como en una

> toalla secada al sol al salir del mar. Había pequeñas zonas de energía alternando con la suavidad de la piel, puntos tan intensos que las yemas de los dedos sentían casi como relieves, y perseguí el dibujo que formaban por todos los rincones de su cuerpo,...(292)

> This skin, this very pretty skin, a voice inside me repeated as I dried my nose, eyes and mouth on her as if she were a sun-dried towel and I had just come out of the sea. There were small zones of energy that alternated with the softness of her skin, points so intense that my fingertips felt them like reliefs and I followed the drawing that they formed over all the corners of her body.

Her skin is presented as a series of electrical conduits that work almost like a battery. At this point the cyborg hacker comes in contact with the woman who can fuse virtual and physical eroticism in a body that endows both his organic and his technological components with energy.

The reason for these "zones" becomes clear when he turns on the light despite her protestations.

> Le habría hecho caso, pero llegó tarde, porque mi mano ya estaba sobre el interruptor. Alcanzó a cubrirse, pero no como suele hacerlo una mujer desnuda:...sus manos habían volado a tapar zonas perfectamente inocentes del pecho y el vientre. Enseguida supe por qué. No había en diez personas manos suficientes para tapar las marcas que le cubrían todo el cuerpo, adensándose como enjambres de insectos en las áreas que intentaba ocultar...

> Eran estas pequeñas cicatrices brillosas lo que mis dedos habían detectado antes, en la oscuridad confundiéndolas con una ilusión táctil fruto de mi embeleso; el mapa que yo había trazado uniendo estos puntos con mis dedos recién ahora empezaba a tomar forma. (300)

> I would have stopped, but it was too late because my hand was already on the light switch. She was able to cover herself, but not like a naked woman usually does. Her hands flew to cover perfectly innocent areas on her chest and stomach. I quickly realized why. In 10 people, there weren't enough hands to hide the marks that covered her whole body, clustering like hives of insects in the areas that she was trying to hide.

It was these small shining scars that my fingers had detected before, confusing the tactile fruit of my charm in the dark, this map that I had traced uniting those points that were now taking form.

Just as the metal in Felix's head identifies him as a kind of wounded cyborg, Gloria's scars create a body that is more than its organic components. While the scars are not literally mechanical prostheses, they fulfill the same semiotic function as Felix's metal plate as they act as emblems of trauma—reminders of the injury that has altered the nature of the body. Indeed, the scars form a map, a series of written markers on her body just as the metal plate was referred to as a souvenir of the war. What cements this interpretation of Gloria's body as a kind of cyborg survivor is the already observed description of these scars as zones of energy, as if they emitted the electricity that the skin had absorbed from the *picanas* that produced the scars in the first place.

As she describes the torture that converted her skin from flesh to electrical map, we see a development of this type of body imagery where organic identity converts into technological prosthesis. In the case of Gloria torture severs the link between mind and organic body, much as Elaine Scarry has described in her work on pain and the body. Gloria's posthuman nature comes not as a mechanical prosthesis replaces flesh as in the case of Felix but as the relationship between consciousness and flesh is fundamentally altered, converting her abused and violated body into merely one more interchangeable prosthesis among many. Gamerro develops this idea by having her recount experiences that include the grotesque rapes and tortures that Nunca Más uncovered in its report, noting that relief would only come when she blacked out—disconnecting from her body. Gamerro then takes it a step further when Gloria remarks that her body was used as the literal conduit for a horrible practical joke that her torturers would play on each other; that is, they would apply the *picana* to her while one of them was raping her so that her body would absorb and transmit the electrical current to the man engaged in her violation. The act literally makes her flesh an extension of the *picana*, thereby converting flesh into machine and completing the creation of a literal cyborg body. We see that kind of thinking repeated when she talks about her twin daughters, both of whom suffer from Downs Syndrome. As she reflects on their innocence she repeatedly refers to her body as a kind of filter, an apparatus that served to remove the evil of the moment of their procreation. Once again the flesh of the victim serves as mechanical device rather than as an aspect of self and the cyborg body becomes the physical representation of the torture that engendered it. In that sense, Gamerro's posthumans are the embodiment of Scarry's theories on what she calls the "objectless" state of the being in pain where the imagination (the post-pain being) consists of "wholly its objects" (162). At the same time, their conversion into a kind of cybernetic text rescues the very real trauma that they have suffered from any kind of textual or semiotic obfuscation. That is, these cyborg bodies (and especially Gloria's skin) function as unmediated physical texts where prostheses and cybernetic scars tell the abstract story of dictatorial abuses while simultaneously exhibiting the personal horror suffered by a single human victim of those abuses.

Felix, our posthuman hacker, functions within this symbolic system as not only a traumatized cyborg-survivor, but also as the figure that can read the map of torture and that can decipher the prosthetic scars left by the technological implements used in that torture. Gamerro proposes, then, a Latin American cyborg whose ability with technology qualifies him uniquely to "hack" a traumatic past, to crack the mechanical codes that guard governmental secrets. His ambiguous presence as a by-product of governmental abuse and threat to its technological existence taps into the overarching cyborg mythology while contextualizing specifically for an Argentina marked by brutal political realities much more real than situations in which cyborgs usually appear. If classic science fiction presents the cyborg as a symbol of the scientist's hubris run amok, Gamerro proposes the figure as the unwitting result of the application of the machinery of state terror or neoliberal policy to the organic body of the victim—an image we also find in Piglia's *La ciudad ausente* or even in Puig's *Pubis angelical*. By separating this image from its traditional science fiction context, Gamerro provides a way to understand the relationship between the technologies of control first exercised by the military dictatorship and the new technologies made available by the neoliberal policies of the 1990s.

The Bolivian novelist Edmundo Paz Soldán's recent narrative has focused on the representation of his country bleeding at the seams of a bewildering series of cultural sutures. His novels extend from difficult conjoinings of third-world social realities with first-world technology and neoliberalist policy to a political landscape too strange to be fiction where bloody dictators become democratically elected presidents. In *Sueños digitales* and *El delirio de Turing*, especially, Paz Soldán engages contemporary theories on posthuman identity in his construction of a Bolivia struggling in the face of a virtual reality where bodies are their images, machines gain equal footing with flesh as extensions of the human, and identity is inseparable from the numbers, bytes, and codes used to represent it.[2] These two novels form a narrative arc in which Paz Soldán begins by suggesting that the strange political hybridization caused by Hugo Banzer's unsettling presidential resurrection can be imagined in terms of the similarly unsettling fusions of flesh and technology inherent in posthuman identity. He then expands that construction to examine the way dictatorial power and oppression duplicate themselves within virtual realities that are unable to deliver on their promise of an escape from the "really" real. Throughout this arc, Paz Soldán delivers a nuanced meditation on the implications of posthuman thinking within a distinctively Latin American context. I outline briefly *Sueños digitales*'s contribution to this construction and then turn the majority of my attention to the more recent *El delirio de Turing*, the Bolivian national book award winner for 2003.

In his 1999 novel, *Sueños digitales*, the Bolivian novelist Edmundo Paz Soldán has explored the implications of this kind of reality, one in which technology has destabilized the representational power of photography and, by extension, the very definition of what it means to be human. The novel recounts the experiences of one Sebastián, a young Bolivian computer professional who earns his living working for a magazine, digitally retouching photographs and creating "seres digitales," hybrid images that combine one person's body with another's head (the novel begins with the line, "Todo había comenzado con la cabeza del Che y el cuerpo de Raquel Welch" (11) [Everything started with the head of Che and the body of Raquel Welch]). The success of these "seres digitales," the magazine makes it a contest in which its readers are to guess to whom the body belongs, attracts the attention of the country's president Montenegro, a former military dictator now democratically elected president based on Bolivia's now former president Hugo Banzer. Sebastián is hired to alter photographs from Montenegro's past as a dictator, erasing people and evidence that implicated the president in past crimes. As Sebastián becomes uneasy with his work he begins to notice the president's forces conspiring against him, erasing his image from personal photographs and then moving to erase his body physically—something that Sebastián avoids only by committing suicide. This narrative arc is complemented by a dissolution of Sebastián's marriage and a coworker's descent into insanity fueled by computer games and the Internet.

Paz Soldán imbues the novel with a technological atmosphere from the very beginning. From the immediate presentation of digitally hybridized photos to a language loaded with references to computers and digital image technology, the novelist creates a world in which technology is at first simply ubiquitous and, then, turns menacingly inescapable. The first description of Sebastián provides one example of the omnipresence of technology:

> Sebastián se encontraba en la sala de diseño gráfico de Tiempos Posmodernos, dándole los últimos toques a Fahrenheit 451, la revista semanal cuyo primer número, en papel couché y a todo color—predominaban el rosado, el amarillo chillón, el turquesa y el naranja—, saldría el domingo. Flaco, ojeroso, con un Marlboro en los labios y encandilado frente a la pantalla de la G3, Sebastián arrastraba el mouse entre resoplidos y tecleaba combinaciones de letras y números, órdenes para que, a través de la interpretación de Adobe Photoshop, la foto de Fox Mulder en la pantalla ganara en colores contrastantes para la portada, una sombra oscura como una aureola sobre la cabeza, el pelo negro convertido en amarillo vangoghiano, magenta que te quiero magenta en la tarea de las compensaciones. (12)

Sebastián found himself in the graphic design room of Tiempos Posmodernos, putting the final touches on Fahrenheit 451, the weekly magazine whose first issue, in full color—pink, yellow, turquoise, and orange—, would come out on Sunday. Thin, with a Marlboro in his lips and lit in front of the G3's screen, Sebastián dragged the mouse between puffs of smoke, and keyed in combinations of letters and numbers, orders so that, through the interpretation of Adobe Photoshop, the photo of Fox Mulder on the screen acquired contrasting colors to the cover, a dark shadow like an aurora around his head, the black hair converted into vangoghnian yellow and magenta I want you magenta in the compensatory work.

Throughout the novel, Paz Soldán employs references to Macintosh computers, software, the Internet, and virtual gadgets that impart a technological tone to the novel that permeates the reality in which the characters move. The precise references to the computers and software titles, G3's, and Adobe Photoshop, the artificial colors of the magazines, overwhelm the passage, making the character nearly inseparable from the technology that complements his physical description. The references combine to create a world that would seem to be one of science fiction if it were not for the fact that a very early part of this book was written on a G3 computer whose glare illuminated my own face as I manipulated text with keyboard and mouse.

It is within this digital setting that Paz Soldán begins his depiction of the assault on the human body—most obviously on the image of the body, through the alteration of the photographs—but also, and of equal importance, on the very constitution of the human body as exhibited in the characters that populate the novel. That is, the novel is not only about the altered photographs but also about the technologically altered bodies of those who manipulate photographic bodies. Again near the beginning of *Sueños digitales*, we find a passing description of a photograph that serves as an important image of both these themes:

> Desde la pared enfrente suyo, Naomi Campbell y Nadja Auermann observaban a Sebastián observando a la Welch. El

rostro de Campbell, escaneado de una portada de American Photo y luego ampliado por Pixel hasta tomar la forma de un poster, era el de un androide recubierto de metal, la piel de plata reluciente y los labios de un rojo supersaturado (calva, las uñas verdes). Era una Naomi futurista. (16)

> From the wall in front of him, Naomi Campbell and Nadja Auermann looked at Sebastián looking at Welch. Campbell's face, scanned from a cover of American Photo and then blown up by Pixel until taking the form of a poster, was one of an android covered in metal, the silver skin shining and the lips of an oversaturated red (bald, green fingernails). She was a futuristic Naomi.

On one level, this passage humanizes the image of the body; that is, the pictures of Campbell and Auermann are able to observe Sebastián as he observes the image of Raquel Welch. The photographs exhibit the same abilities as the people they represent, deepening the link between the image and the body and suggesting that the manipulations of those images exercise a corresponding effect on the bodies themselves. The depiction of Campbell specifically as an android, a robot human with metal skin, cements this idea, where not only does the photograph gain human abilities but the human body itself becomes mechanized. This relation of photograph, human, and machine becomes the guiding image for the events of the novel, where the definition of the human is wrapped up in technology.

Indeed, this literal depiction of a futuristic cyborg anticipates the metaphorical cyborgs that appear in the novel. Sebastián's friend and colleague Pixel serves as one obvious example. Pixel's nickname (his real name is not mentioned) comes from his interest in computer and image technology, as well as his contribution to an ad campaign for a digital camera—te ves mejor en pixels [you look better in pixels]. This naming of the human body as an element of the computerized image creates a kind of linguistic cyborg, where the language used to define human identity is mediated by the technology that surrounds it. Paz Soldán extends this image of Pixel as he narrates the life of a drug- and Internet-addicted person who is finally driven mad by a virtual reality game in which he is known as Laracroft, the name of the popular computer game heroine and a further example of the naming of the human body as an expression of a technological world. Pixel loses his humanity within this purely digital world; the feedback loop that had flowed between him and his technology has become a feedback noose.

Paz Soldán complements this almost stereotypical image of the lonely hacker cum digital being with that of the main character Sebastián, an apparently happily married, better-adjusted twenty or thirty something young man. The presentation of Sebastián as a metaphorical cyborg is at once more subtle and more insidious, creating what some have called an electronic fable in the novel—warning of the dangers of technologically based definitions of the human. If we return to the passage I referred to earlier, we find one such image of the process by which Sebastián is cyberneticized. As Sebastián smokes in front of his G3, moving his mouse and typing on his keyboard, Paz Soldán describes him as "encandilado frente a la pantalla de la G3" (12) [lit up in front of the G3's screen]. The lighting of Sebastián's body creates an exchange in which not only does the human use the computer to manipulate photographic images but also the computer in some way illuminates the human, lighting the human figure in much the same way Sebastián tries to light Fox Mulder digitally. This bidirectional effect insinuates another cybernetic feedback loop and suggests a situation in which the mere operation of technology alters the person who uses it. We see another such situation in the passage where the photos of the supermodels watch Sebastián watching Raquel Welch. Hayles speaks of the "flickering signifiers" of text written with computers, the levels of code that move between the electrical polarities on hard disks to the photons that translate to text on a screen while passing through compiler codes and the word-processing program (1999: 31). Here the computer's flickering lights reach out and include the human subject within the play of electrons and photons that convey computational instructions. Not only does Sebastián find himself on equal terms with the altered supermodel photographs but the specially lighted image of him at his computer becomes yet another digital photograph, one that displays this human/computer hybrid as its principal subject.

The novel follows up on this initial image with several situations in which Sebastián begins to operate as an element of this computer/human hybridization. Throughout the novel Sebastián imagines the people he encounters with different heads and/or different bodies. Take, for example, the description of a conversation with his boss Isabel at the Ciudadela, President Montenegro's secret base of operations: "Isabel tenía una camisa de seda roja y mucho maquillaje en las mejillas. Sebastián se dijo que su rostro tenía algo de la Scully de Los Expedientes X, y trató de imaginarla con el cuerpo de Fox Mulder" (95) [Isabel had on a red silk shirt and a lot of makeup on her cheeks. Sebastián decided that her face had something of Scully from the X-Files and tried to imagine her with Fox Mulder's body]. As Sebastián mentally manipulates Isabel's body his consciousness acquires the qualities of Adobe Photoshop, his mind functioning as the computer software he uses in the creation of his digital beings. It is in these situations that we see the extension of the earlier image in which the light from the computer illuminated Sebastián's body; in this case, his working relationship with the computer has affected the operation of his imagination, a computational model now ordering the functioning of his thoughts.

This presentation of Sebastián as a metaphorical cyborg is made clear in an earlier episode in which he prepares for his work at the Ciudadela.

> Isabel miró alrededor suyo, como cerciorándose de que no la espiaban. Sacó unas fotos de su cartera y las puso sobre la mesa. Eran las fotos de una parrillada. Sebastián vio rostros satisfechos de políticos conocidos, las cervezas en la mano y las mesas llenas de platos de asados con papas y soltero y llajwa. Se le abrió el apetito, pediría un sándwich de jamón y queso. ¿Lo estaría esperando en su computadora un email de Nikki? Jugueteó con la rosa de plástico en el florero al centro de la mesa. ¿Soñaban los androides con rosas artificiales? (42)

> Isabel looked around, as if making sure that no one was spying on her. She took some photos out of her purse and put them on the table. They were photos of a barbecue. Sebastián saw the satisfied faces of well-known politicians, beers in hand and the

tables full of barbecue. He got hungry, he would ask for a ham and cheese sandwich. Is there an email on my computer from Nikki waiting for him? He played with the plastic rose in the vase in the middle of the table. Do androids dream of artificial roses?

The images presented here are at once innocent and suggestive. Sebastián merely examines the photographs that he will alter (making one of the generals disappear), sees the food, gets hungry, thinks of his wife, and plays with a plastic flower. At the same time, we see the way in which technology has infiltrated all levels of Sebastián's thought. After examining the photographs that metonymically represent his work with computers, his thoughts turn to his wife; thoughts mediated by the email technology that facilitates their communication, the computer becoming the location of the relationship with his wife. Indeed, just as Sebastián has begun to think as a computer, he is unable to conceive of interpersonal relationships separate from the technology that permeates his existence. The crowning moment of this mediation is found in Sebastián's idle thoughts about the plastic rose, "Do androids dream of artificial roses?" The question is a play on Phillip Dick's important cybernetic novel *Do Androids Dream of Electric Sheep*, later adapted for film as Ridley Scott's *Blade Runner*. The reference invokes the multiple literal androids found in that novel as well as the cyberpunk novels it inspired such as William Gibson's *Neuromancer*. It simultaneously forges a connection between that genre and the present novel, as the android dreams seem to find an echo in Paz Soldán's digital dreams. The resulting connection suggests the reading of the Bolivian novel not only as a meditation on the nature of the photographic image in the digital age, but also as a consideration of the nature of the human body in a cybernetic, posthuman age in which the human body is not imagined apart from the technology that surrounds and permeates it.

Even as Paz Soldán evokes and engages the work of North American writers and critics, he incorporates narrative elements that situate the novel within a uniquely Latin American context. Despite the heavy use of references to North American culture such as the X-Files, Paz Soldán continually resituates the action within a Bolivian context with geographical and cultural references. Furthermore, the portrayal of the Bolivian protagonist threatened by the dictator, now president, and his secret police establishes ties with the Latin American tradition of the *novela del dictador* [novel of the dictator]. The atmosphere of fear at the end of the novel especially, where Sebastián watches friends and then images of himself disappear, also evokes important aspects of that genre. Paz Soldán extends, then, his meditations on the nature of the body and the image in the posthuman age to the nature of the body and the image in a postdictatorial age in which the threats of oppression lurk beneath a neoliberal façade. Just as a metaphorically mechanical Sebastián erases people from photographs and alters history along with its images, oppressive political machinery continues to attempt to alter history and threatens the continued disappearance of its citizens. The combination of computers and political terror in the novel suggests the image of Latin American neoliberal society as a massive G3 where the government acts like an Adobe Photoshop that digitally alters and erases the past and present reality of its inhabitants, attempting to ignore the horror of the past by erasing it, both literally and figuratively.

It is here that we find a Latin American plotting of the posthuman, in Edmundo Paz Soldán's literary exploration of the digital manipulations of photographs and the political manipulations of history and people in contemporary Latin America, where memory has become so short that people can elect the dictators who had earlier repressed them. Returning to Hayles's "flickering signifier," the biological bodies of the disappeared and of the criminals who disappeared them are digitalized and altered so that the link between signifier and signified flickers away—the signifier no longer signifying an historical reality or a physical body. This destabilization of the photograph, one of the most potent symbols of the resistance to dictatorship (I am thinking here of the photographs that the relatives of the disappeared have used in several countries to denounce various military dictatorships), is particularly unsettling. At the same time the stable connection that does remain is this posthuman digitalized body, a product of both the dictatorship—as we have seen in the first chapter of the book as well as in Gamerro's novel—and the neoliberal policies and programs that Paz Soldán outlines with such detail in *Sueños digitales*. Rosario Ramos González has called the novel *fábula electrónica*. Indeed it is; as the digital and political reconfiguration of the human body, its image, and its context result in the horror that serves as the moral of this digital tale.

El delirio de Turing extends and refines the views on posthuman identity that he first articulated in *Sueños digitales*; extending especially the idea that the present political realities encode terrible histories in posthuman bodies. The novel occupies the same literary universe as his previous novels; the city of Río Fugitivo in a Bolivia controlled by Montenegro the dictator-cum-president whose present administration is not so different from his former. The city suffers from all the neoliberal contradictions that appear in Bolivian and Latin American culture and society where cyber-cafes and extreme poverty exist side by side and a technological future never completely covers the tortured past of economic and political disaster. The novel begins with a mid-level government employee who receives an encrypted email message. As his job is cryptography, he decodes the message only to discover the accusation: "ASESINOTIENESLASMANOSMANCHADASDESANGRE" (23) [MURDERERYOURHANDSARESTAINEDWITHBLOOD]. This is disconcerting, of course, for while the man worked in both iterations of Montenegro government, he always felt disconnected from the affairs of government, willfully ignoring the effects of the work he did decoding intercepted communiqués. His name is Saenz, but goes by the nickname Turing as his dedication and talent in cryptography inspired his coworkers to consider him Bolivia's Alan Turing, the pioneering computer scientist who was among the first to conceptualize the human as a computer and was famous for his thought experiment in which a human and a machine were indistinguishable. (He also occupies a prominent position in the introduction to Hayles's book.) The novel then follows several interweaving story lines that range from the leader of a group of anticapitalist, antigovernment hackers code-named Kandinsky to the American-born head of the Cámara Negra [Black Chamber], Montenegro's version of the NSA that fights them, to the psychotic ramblings of a German ex-CIA member of Montenegro's detail to the prosecutor whose sister was killed as a consequence of one of the Turing's decoded messages. Parts of the novel occur in cyberspace, in Internet chatrooms, and text-message conversations as well as in a virtual reality called the Playground, a commercialized Internet site where people can create characters that live and interact in a digital city.

Within this narrative world, Paz Soldán constructs a series of characters and images that link posthuman identity with dictatorial oppression, both in the exercise of power as in the traumatic impacts of that exercise. From the beginning of the novel the Cámara Negra appears as the main representative of political power within the novel, an organization that occupies a unique place in the Montenegro government as its existence spans both the dictatorial and democratic iterations of the not-quite-fictional dictator's government. The Cámara Negra is described as Bolivia's answer to the NSA, an organization dedicated to the interception and decoding of communiqués and messages used by any organization deemed oppositional. In the novel it appears at the intersection of the various story lines, functioning as a narrative focal point that causes the motion of the various events narrated. The Turing referred to in the novel, Miguel Saenz, is the mid-level employee who worked decoding messages during the dictatorship and continues to work in cryptography without any sense of responsibility for the results of his actions. It is he who receives the cryptic emails accusing him of assassination and whose daughter and lover occupy an important place in the events of the novel. Furthermore, it is this organization that hunts the hackers that have been attacking governmental and commercial businesses, and the narrative also relates the stories of the various bosses and employees.

The Cámara Negra's hybrid position as synecdoche of both dictatorship and democracy suggests a rubric through which to understand Paz Soldán's meditation on posthuman identity. People and organizations become uncomfortable fusions of opposites, where being and identity are founded at the seams of cultural and physical definition and where images, doubles, and machines constantly supplant the original referents. The head of the Cámara, for example, is an American ex-NSA agent born in the United States of Bolivian parents. He is hired by the Bolivian government to head up the computer security section and immediately is granted Bolivian citizenship, producing in that way a situation where Bolivian identity is grafted onto an American who speaks a heavily accented Spanish bereft of the subjunctive and longs for his home in Washington DC. Saenz himself becomes the double of Turing with his nickname, his own body turning metaphorically into a duplication of the computer scientist. The organization itself is infiltrated by one of the hackers, whose play of identities borders on the absurd as he is simultaneously a loyal employee of the Cámara Negra, one of the lieutenants of Kandinsky, the legendary hacker who leads the group attacking the government and, in the end, Kandinsky (he takes the name Kandinsky from the original hacker to throw off the authorities). When one combines this play of identities with the fact that the purpose of this organization is the computerized decoding of messages, codes that serves as cryptic doubles of the meaning they carry, we see a situation where the posthuman conceptualization of identity reigns as bodies are transformed from stable individualized bearers of meaning to mere loci of doubles, codes, and hyphens that create and supplant identity. The fact that this dynamic occurs within an arm of a politically oppressive government only cements the connection between oppression and the posthuman.

Paz Soldán, like Gamerro, develops the triangular relationship between the posthuman, past dictatorship, and present neoliberal policies by focusing on the figure of the hacker, a body whose own slippery virtual identities provide a site in which these three forces come into contact. However, while Gamerro's hacker is used symbolically, Felix's skills are more of a pretext to the different encounters with technology and with posthuman bodies, Paz Soldán employs a thorough knowledge of hacker culture in a nuanced consideration of the links between global markets, technology, codes, and the posthuman in contemporary Bolivia.[3]

Cultural constructions of the hacker figure invest it with a unique ability to signify being and representation of being, simultaneously. Douglas Thomas, in his study of hacker culture, has explored extensively the ways in which hackers move between states of embodiment and disembodiment as they interface with computer technology in their quest to free information from the security that keeps it secret. On one level, they become their handles, the names they invent for their online personas that come to represent their achievements in software programming and in gaining access to secret systems. As society has become more aware of the presence of the hacker and of their influence on an increasingly computerized world, these figures have also morphed into the, at times impossible, menaces that tend to appear when a society is at the cusp of massive cultural shifts. That is, the hacker becomes a kind of wizard or guru who has access to knowledge that mere mortals are unable to attain. In that sense, the hacker ceases to be the body of the person and becomes the vague menace that can represent several forces and ideas, simultaneously. Due to his or her perceived ability to steal those codes that make up our financial identities, bank account numbers and passwords, credit card numbers, governmental identification numbers, and so on, the hacker comes to signify that metaphorical process at work in society where codes are identity, where bodies are constituted by the numbers and language that computers use to refer to them. The hacker, then, is that being that exults in this process, using names such as Phiber Optic and Acid Phreak and spelling that trades 3s for Es and 1s for ls all in an effort to foreground their place in an evolving representational reality (Thomas 56–61). Paz Soldán uses this dynamic as a conduit for his exploration of this metaphorical reality where poststructuralist theories on the interconnections of language and reality culminate in a world where people are their pin numbers, hackers' bodies melt into their virtual avatars, and dictatorships recodify themselves as democratic governments dedicated to neoliberal policy.

El delirio de Turing uses computers and hacker culture as a pervasive backdrop to the events that occur. We find two story lines devoted to self-described hackers, the notorious leader of the Resistencia Kandinsky and, Miguel Saenz's daughter Flavia, webmaster of a page titled "TodoHacker." As we navigate the chapters devoted to these two characters we encounter various other hackers, all modeled on descriptions we find of hacker culture in Thomas's work. We encounter, for example, Phiber Outcast, a self-identified script kitty who gives Kandinsky his start and attempts to persuade him to continue with the illegal hacking that has made them both rich. The name is a fairly clear reference to one of the more famous hackers of the 1990s (the aforementioned Phiber Optik), a move that shows both the author's familiarity with hacker lore as it serves to describe a character who is always derivative (A script kitty is a hacker who is unable to write his or her own code and, therefore, depends on the work of more skilled hackers in order to carry out intrusions of secure systems). Characters constantly access the Internet, chat on IRCs, and play in the Playground, a virtual reality world inspired by Neal Stephenson's Metaverse in his well-known novel *Snow Crash*, a novel Paz Soldán references with an epigraph. While *Turing* revolves around the impact of Albert and Saenz's work in the Cámara Negra under both iterations of the Montenegro regime, the computerized world of the hacker is omnipresent and literally infects the reality occupied by all of the interlacing stories and characters.

Paz Soldán presents Miguel Saenz as a kind of unwitting proto-hacker. While he certainly shares none of the revolutionary tendencies ascribed to hackers, he does exhibit several characteristics in common. We have already mentioned Saenz's alias "Turing," a nickname his boss Albert gives him assumedly based on his uncanny ability to decrypt the messages he receives as a part of his work. This moniker becomes Saenz's handle, a name that replaces his identity as Miguel Saenz, husband, father, and embodied individual with an identity that emphasizes his ability to decode, that conflates the man with his cryptographical ability—in a sense converting him into one of the codes that he cracks. The novel casts him in this vein from the beginning, presenting him first in the context of his work, decoding messages and, in particular, the email that accuses him of murder. Saenz, or Turing, is what he does, much as a hacker's online identity is based on his exploits rather than on any kind of embodied presence. The bilingual pun on his name (Saenz = Signs) only adds to the play of signifiers at the locus of the character.

Both the proto- and actual hackers inhabit a country navigating a new global culture and economy where people are identified by their ability (or lack of ability) to consume goods and, in particular, to consume technology. Aside from Montenegro's corrupt government, neoliberal policies are also represented in the Playground—a multinational virtual computer world that charges its participants monthly fees to participate. Its arrival in Bolivia was heralded by advertisements and excitement and its reality is marked by more advertisements and surveillance software that makes sure that its citizens comply with the rules of commerce. The novel presents this virtual reality world in the following terms:

> Hacía poco más de un año, tres adolescentes que acababan de graduarse del colegio San Ignacio se habían prestado dinero de sus papás para adquirir la franquicia del Playground para Bolivia. Creado por una corporación finlandesa, el Playground era al mismo tiempo un juego virtual y una comunidad en línea. Allí, cualquier individuo, por medio de una suma mensual básica— veinte dólares que podían convertirse en mucho más de acuerdo al tiempo de uso—creaba su avatar o utilizaba uno de los que el Playground ponía a la venta, e intentaba sobrevivir en un territorio apocalíptico gobernado con mano dura por una corporación. El año en que transcurría el juego era 2019. El Playground era exitoso en varios países; Bolivia no había sido la excepción. (72–73)

> A little more than a year ago, three recent graduates from San Ignacio High School had borrowed money from their parents in order to acquire the rights to the Playground franchise for Bolivia. Created by a Finnish corporation, Playground was both a virtual game and an online community. There, for a modest monthly fee—twenty dollars, which could grow to much more, depending on the time you spent—anyone could create an avatar or use one of those that Playground put up for sale. The game takes place in the year 2019. Participants try to live in an apocalyptic land governed by the strong arm of a corporation. Playground's success in other countries was replicated in Bolivia. (58)

The Playground functions as a hyper-commercial, global entity, with virtual streets characterized by their advertisements for global brands such as Nike. The commercialism and consumerism extends far beyond the advertisements. Not only do people pay for the privilege of "living" in the virtual city but the virtual characters they inhabit become themselves traded commodities, with people developing digital beings that are then sold to people who do not want to have to dedicate the time to starting the experience from scratch. The ubiquitous virtual prostitutes are, then, commodities on commodities as the avatars that sell themselves for cyber-sex have already been packaged and sold to their flesh-based operators. The Playground becomes an avatar of reality that attempts to supplant the "real realidad" that it recreates. Indeed, one of the most important rules of the Playground is that no one can make reference to its artificial nature. If anyone does so, the Playground police appear and expulse the avatar of the person making the illegal statement. With the inclusion of this police force, Paz Soldán suggests that the Playground recreates the kind of oppressive, disciplinary society that was explicitly used in the dictatorial iteration of Montenegro's government and implicitly in the democratic version. The way in which both global capitalism and governmental discipline are reconstituted within the virtual playground allows the computerized reality to function as a metaphorical link between contemporary neoliberal regimes and the 1970s Operation Condor dictatorships. The computer code that creates the images and sounds of the Playground simultaneously point at the global trade and consumerism of neoliberal policy and at the restrictions on expression so widespread under the anticommunist dictatorships.

While all the characters are aware of the Playground, with everyone from Saenz complaining about his daughter's bills to those government officials involved in Cámara Negra's surveillance of possibly subversive activities, the hacker characters are those that we see interact within this virtual space. Their exploits in the Playground both establish the themes already seen even as they introduce other elements of the meditation on technology and identity that we see throughout the novel. The use of virtual characters as extensions of self introduces the concept of posthuman identity in the representation of the hacker. As Flavia and Kandinsky send these avatars of themselves into cyberspace, their identity shifts from one that is fundamentally corporeal and organic to one that exists at the interaction between flesh and technology. Here the avatars become prosthetic bodies, arms, legs, and sexual organs made up of bytes that respond to the instructions that emanate from the organic bodies that direct them. This very obvious construction of posthuman identity is reinforced by a series of references throughout the novel that emphasize these characters' dependence on technological prostheses. Flavia is never without her cellular phone, a device she uses to view Lana Nova, the digital newscaster, as well as to access the Playground. She engages in cyber-sex via the Playground in a meeting that prefigures the physical erotic encounter with another hacker in an Internet café booth. Her room and her descriptions are always mediated by the technology that surrounds her. The same is true of Kandinsky and, as we read the chapters that make up his biography, we see a person whose reality is always configured according to his relationship with computers, his name (handle) a reference to a hacker whose work he appreciates. His very reputation depends on his use of various avatars, from the Playground "Recuperación" movement that is the digital avatar for his antiglobalist Resistencia to the various personas he inhabits— Kandinsky not the least of them. The fact that we never learn his real name, even when we see him in contact with his biological family, further emphasizes the presentation of Kandinsky as an identity that appears not within the body of the adolescent hacker but in his relationships with computers and with his various cyber-personalities.

In fact Kandinsky especially desires a "true" cyborg body to flesh out, as it were, his already very posthuman existence. At one point we find Kandinsky in a cyber-cafe, watching the clerk when he notices:

> Esos días Kandinsky suele visitar Portal a la Realidad, un café Internet en el barrio de Bohemia. Lo atiende una joven con el brazo derecho de metal. Kandinsky la observa, desde lejos, alzar vasos de cristal con delicadeza, pasar las páginas de su agenda, teclear en la computadora. El brazo está controlado por el cerebro, aprende a moverse de manera intuitiva, reconoce las formas y las texturas de los objetos y se adapta a ellas. La joven tiene una cara redonda y sosa y un cuerpo plano, pero Kandinsky es seducido por ella, o acaso por la relación que tiene con su brazo.

Así quisiera relacionarse con su computadora, intuitivamente: programar códigos sin necesidad de usar el teclado. (190)

During that time Kandinsky went to Portal to Reality, an Internet café in the Bohemia district. He was waited on by a young woman with a metallic right arm. From afar, Kandinsky watched her delicately hold a glass, flip through the pages of her agenda, type on the keyboard. The arm was controlled by her brain, learned to move intuitively, recognized the shape and texture of objects and adapted to them. The young woman had a round, dull face and flat chest, but Kandinsky was drawn to her, or perhaps to the relationship she had with her arm. It was the kind of relationship that he would have liked to have with his computer—intuitive: to program without needing a keyboard. (157)

The waitress literally embodies that to which Kandinsky can only aspire, a cybernetic body in which the feedback loop between metal and flesh produces "intuitive" actions. The direct connection that Kandinsky makes between the girl's arm and his computer further underscores his cyborg aspirations and the posthuman possibilities that his relationship with his computer presents. That Kandinsky sexualizes this attraction is also of note. The narrative makes it clear that Kandinsky's desire is based specifically on the girl's cybernetic nature, that the relationship that she has with her arm is not only one that he desires with his computer but one that he desires on an erotic level. Here, though, we do not see a repetition of the dynamic that we observed in Gamerro's novel. Felix was already a literal cyborg and was attracted to Gloria without knowing her metaphorical position. Kandinsky merely desires the connection and anything related to it.

This presentation of the hacker figure as posthuman forges yet another connection with the old guard of Turing and Albert, an ex-Nazi and his superior at the Cámara Negra. Throughout the chapters dedicated to the ramblings of the senile Albert, we see him described more as a cyborg than as a human being. Note his initial presentation.

Mi nombre es Albert. Mi nombre no es Albert.
Nací.... Hace. Muy. Poco.

Nunca nací.... No tengo memoria de un principio. Soy algo que ocurre. Que siempre está ocurriendo.... Que siempre ocurrirá. Soy. Un. Hombre. Consumido. Y. Terroso.... Ojos. Grises.... Barba. Gris.... Rasgos. Singularmente. Vagos.... Me. Manejo. Con. Fluidez. E. Ignorancia. En. Varias. Lenguas.... Francés. Inglés. Alemán. Español. Portugués de Macao. Estoy conectado a varios cables que me permiten vivir. Por la ventana de la habitación miro el fluir del día en la avenida.... No recuerdo de qué pueblo se trata.... Pero la imagen está.... Hay un niño. Que corre y corre. No soy yo. No puedo ser yo.... Yo no tengo infancia. Nunca la tuve.... Soy una hormiga eléctrica. (31)

My name is Albert. My name is not Albert.

I was born.... Not. Very. Long. Ago.

I was never born.... I have no memory of a beginning. I am something that happens. That is always happening.... That will always happen.

I. Am. An. Emaciated. Grimy. Man.... Gray. Eyes.... Gray. Beard.... Singularly. Vague. Features.... I. Express. Myself. With. Untutored. And. Uncorrected. Fluency. In. Several. Languages.... French. English. German. Spanish. Portuguese from Macao.

I am connected to several wires that allow me to live. Through the window I watch the day pass by on the avenue.... I don't remember which village it is.... But the image is there.... There's a boy. Who runs and runs.

It's not me, I can't be me.... I have no childhood. I never have.... I am an electric ant. (19)

As Paz Soldán describes the machinery surrounding Albert, we see created a kind of medicalized cyborg whose existence functions as a product of the failing organic body and the medical apparatuses that have fused with it. Albert's rejection of an infancy, of an existence outside of organic procreation, also configures him as posthuman; the lack of an origin myth, of a birth within a nuclear family to human parents, is one of the principal characteristics of posthuman identity, at least as critics such as Donna Haraway or Ira Livingston have described it.

Albert's presentation as flesh dependent upon tubes and machines raises a disturbing theme. Kandinsky and, to a lesser extent, Flavia are seen to fight against the neoliberal policies that have become avatars for the Montenegro dictatorship in the metaphorical flux of the novel. The cybernetic imagery that connects these iconoclastic hackers with the establishment undercuts the ability of Kandinsky to function as a kind of folk hero (in fact, Flavia spends most of the novel trying to prove that Kandinsky is as corrupt as the corporations and government against which he works). In the case of the moribund Albert, his cyborg nature is akin to a kind of virus that has infected his organic body. That is to say, his continued contact with the oppressive state via its obsession with decrypting coded messages has resulted in the kind of cybernetic monster that is dependent upon medical machinery.[4]

This vilification of technology and of the technological component of the posthuman, while not in keeping with the most recent theorizations of the cyborg, does fit within hacker representation and, specifically, self-representation. Thomas notes:

> The hacker, unlike technology itself, which is almost exclusively coded as evil, is an undecidable character. Both hero and antihero, the hacker is both cause and remedy of social crises. As the narratives point out, there is always something dangerous about hacking, but there is also the possibility of salvation. While hacking is about technology, it is also always about the subversion of technology. (52)

Jon Adams concurs in his discussion of hacker literature, noting that one is as likely to see an anti-cyborg theme as one is to encounter the kind of subversive cyborgs that we see in the novels of writers such as Philip K. Dick and William Gibson (296). In this sense, Paz Soldán's choice of *Snow Crash* as the source of one of his epigraphs is once again pertinent as Hayles uses it as a counterexample to her generally positive vision of posthuman identity in science fiction literature. She observes, "So it is necessarily bad that humans and computers merge in this way? For Stephenson, apparently, the answer is 'yes.' For all his playfulness and satiric jabs at white mainstream America, Stephenson clearly sees the arrival of the posthuman as a disaster" (1999: 276). The fact that much of the novel's posthuman identities appear in the markedly neoliberal space of the Playground further suggests a vision of cyborg identity where the market forces that drive technological innovation and adoption are never overcome by the hybrid possibilities that the cyborg's body promises to some. Indeed, the carpal tunnel syndrome that Kandinsky suffers functions as another indicator of the posthuman condition as a virus, one that damages the organic body rather than completing a new kind of identity.

The culmination of this condemnation of the posthuman hacker comes in Albert's reasoning behind Saenz's nickname Turing. He states:

> Se me viene a la mente una imagen borrosa. La de Miguel Sáenz en su primer día de trabajo en la Cámara Negra. La espalda inclinada sobre el escritorio.
>
> Me dio la impresión de un ser tan dedicado a su labor. Tan poco afecto a las distracciones.... Que parecía una computadora universal de Turing.... Todo lógica.... Todo input.... Y todo output.... Ahí se me ocurrió bautizarlo como Turing.
>
> Él siempre creyó que el apodo se debía a su talento para el criptoanálisis.
>
> La razón era otra. (284)
>
> A blurry image comes to mind. That of Miguel Sáenz on his first day of work at the Black Chamber. Hunched over his desk. He appeared to be so dedicated to his work. So unaffected by distractions.... That he looked like a Universal Turing Machine.... All logic. All input.... All output.... That's when I decided to call him Turing.
>
> He always thought that the nickname was because of his talent for cryptanalysis.
>
> The real reason was different. (255)

The description of Turing, not as a genius of cryptography but as a Universal Turing Machine, becomes the ultimate condemnation of posthuman identity. Paz Soldán sets mechanistic thinking in opposition to mercy, equating it with a kind of bureaucratic mindset that allows people to participate in murder without feeling any guilt or responsibility. While the organic bodies of Albert and Kandinsky are ravaged by technology, Saenz's conscience is presented as mechanical and, therefore, culpable. The different avatars of the technological reality, the extensions of the flesh found in the codes that both hide and reveal humanity, all those things that allowed Saenz and others to distance themselves from the organic bodies of the victims of the dictatorial regime, become symptoms of the deeper disease that the novel condemns—that tendency to forget the bodies of those affected by state terror. The hackers' representational undecidability links the technologies of dictatorship and of commerce and visits that linkage on the bodies of those that are caught within and contribute to those systems.

If in *Sueños digitales* the attack on human bodies came through their photographic digitization, here the attack on organic subjectivity comes as bodies are reduced to codes and ciphers. The lives of the revolutionaries that were murdered because of Saenz's works were made palatable to Saenz precisely because their flesh could be converted into the codes that could hide their identities and plans. The murders that occur as part of Kandinsky's resistance were made possible because of the computer codes and virtual avatars that obscured their organic bodies. Once again, though, we see violence and the posthuman body as essential symbolic connections between the neoliberal technology of the 1990s and 2000s and the practices of the dictatorships of the 1970s. The danger of forgetting or obscuring the past is overcome if one has the ability to read the codes inscribed in the posthuman bodies that remain.

Both Paz Soldán and Gamerro create posthuman, Latin American, hackers that extend and challenge the U.S. visions of both posthuman identity and the representation of hacker culture. We do not see the standard cyborgs of science fiction, menacing creations of a culture with too much faith in technology, nor do we see an acting out of Haraway's cyborg myth. What we do see are the inevitable results of an abusive culture that appears either as dictatorship or as neoliberal regime, but always in conjunction with technology. These posthumans are survivors, scarred by their experiences and left as texts of flesh and metal that can subvert the authoritative structures that engendered them because they remain and can use their bodies as testimony in acts of "ciberhacktivismo," for, even in the case of Paz Soldán's more pessimistic view, we still have ravaged bodies whose technological infections cannot be silenced. Hayles concludes her book with the following passage: "Although some current versions of the posthuman point toward the anti-human and the apocalyptic, we can craft others that will be conducive to the long-range survival of humans and of the other life-forms, biological and artificial, with whom we share the planet and ourselves" (1999: 291). The posthuman bodies we see in these novels sidestep the dichotomy that Hayles suggests, they are neither apocalyptic nor are they wholly positive. They are certainly not antihuman; indeed, they suggest a vision of humanity where the combination of the mechanical and the organic assures the survival of both the individual and the subversive story that the individual has to tell. By including hackers in the mix, Paz Soldán and Gamerro extend this posthuman mythology by including a cyborg body that is not only a text but also a reader who can hack the codes imprinted on the flesh of the victims of political and economic trauma.

Chapter 5

Video Heads and Rewound Bodies: Cyborg Memories in Rodrigo Fresán and Alberto Fuguet

Throughout this book posthuman and cyborg realities have always been "about" something else, from surviving dictatorship to not surviving in neoliberalism. In this final chapter I examine a series of articulations of the posthuman that are merely what they are, cyborged subjectivities constructing "like" places to inhabit without much reflection on what caused their appearance. The posthumans that appear in the novels of Rodrigo Fresán and Alberto Fuguet appear as remarkable and unremarkable bodies existing within glocal matrices in highly individualized attempts to construct meaning. In so doing and being, these bodies appear in sharp contrast to the politicized posthumans that occupy Fresán and Fuguet's literary compatriot Paz Soldán's narrative. The figures that flit through *Mantra* (2001) and *Por favor, rebobinar* (1998) appear as the realities of the age, they are posthuman because there is not another way to be and are interested in the construction of memories and mythologies that explain an existence not obviously marked by political trauma.

By making this argument I situate these novels within the sometimes ferocious criticism leveled at Fuguet's McOndo movement, criticisms that left Fuguet unwilling to republish the anthology of short stories that gave the group its name and that included work by Fresán and Paz Soldán among various twenty- and thirty-something male writers from Latin America and Spain. The writers embraced, or appeared to embrace, the then new global realities of 1990s neoliberal Latin America, rebelling against stereotypes of Latin America as rural and magical as well as against traditions of committed political narrative. Such a characterization led to much of the criticism of the movement, with other critics and writers offended by the call to move on from the narratives and themes that examine and review the trauma of the dictatorships and postdictatorships found in many Latin American countries.[1] Most of the authors who have been associated with McOndo (principally because they published a story in the anthology) have, however, included the themes of global culture, new technology, and a highly developed individualism that have been rejected in some circles. Because of the interest in precisely these themes we also see various articulations of posthuman identity, as previous analysis in this book has hopefully made clear. Paz Soldán's focus on new technologies and the posthuman acts as one particularly potent argument against those that would dismiss the McOndo writers as apolitical or as guilty of assent by silence.

As I suggested earlier, the cases of Rodrigo Fresán and Alberto Fuguet provide another perspective to Latin American posthuman identity. In both *Mantra* and *Por favor, rebobinar*, we see articulations of posthuman identity that begin with the cyborg reality of technological bodies and then situate them not within a history of dictatorship or a present of political and economic abuses but as a reality that requires new mythologies and different ways of remembering individual experience. What these novels show in the context of the present study is the extent to which posthuman realities have become integrated within Latin American narrative and cultural expression, beyond narrative genre and beyond social and political ideologies, and how the cyborg body has gained traction as an important vehicle for the exploration of a variety of sometimes competing ideas and themes.

Mantra is part of the Mondadori series Año 0 where various novelists were asked to write novels about, and I quote from the series description, "algunas de las ciudades más importantes del mundo" [some of the most important cities in the world].

Fresán chooses Mexico City, following the example of his friend and mentor Roberto Bolaño's award-winning novel *Los detectives salvajes* [The Savage Detectives]. Fresán's novel presents a series of interwoven narratives, narrated in first person by various characters. In the first, Martín Mantra's childhood friend, who came to Mexico City as a young Argentine during the 1970s, reflects on his experiences with Mantra as he comes to terms with a brain tumor that looks, to him, like a "sea monkey," a reference to the comic book ads the two read when they were young. In the second, a new narrator, this time French, is a cadaver who is reminiscing as his body is expatriated from Mexico to France. In the last, a robot from the future searches among the ruins of Mexico City for evidence of Mantrax, now an historical figure and near deity. Throughout all the narratives we see a series of attempts to understand culture, both Mexican and global, as the conglomeration of popular discourses and especially television and film. Edmundo Paz Soldán has characterized the novel in this way: "*Mantra... se anima a explorar qué es lo que ocurre a la psiquis del individuo, y al género novelístico, cuando estos son sometidos a una descarga múltiple y continua de información a través de medios como el cine, las revistas y, por supuesto, la televisión*" (108) [*Mantra* explores what it is that happens to the psyche of the individual and the genre of the novel when they are subjected to a multiple and continuous download of information through media such as film, magazines, and, of course, television]. I would argue that as a function of this exploration of mass-media culture we find a literary reconfiguration of the cyborg figure that displaces it from its tortured position in the Argentine literary tradition and resituates it as the basis for the construction of a new cultural imaginary. What we see is an attempt to imagine a new mythology, a new set of stories, that explains the posthuman fusion of organic flesh and technological apparatus that constitutes subjectivity in the novel.

At this point in our study, it seems appropriate to stir in theories of being and media that we find in Marshall McLuhan's work. As we do so we follow on theorizations of the posthuman that we explored in Courtoisie's narrative, but this time with more of a focus on those subjectivities that function ably within the media-based imaginaries rather than those that fail to integrate (as was so evident in the case of *Tajos*). To arrive at this quotidian fusion of mass media and the posthuman, we begin with Haraway's revolutionary mode of cyborg identity, we continue through the evolutionary process that Hayles describes, and end in a state of posthumanity so ubiquitous as to seek a theoretical grounding in a theorist who used media and identity theory not so much to describe what will happen or what is about to happen but rather to describe what has already happened. McLuhan brings (or actually brought, well before the work of Hayles and Haraway) the idea that this type of identity appears especially when humans and the technological delivery systems of the mass media share "informational patterns" and televisions and cameras function as fundamental prostheses for identity. These "new organs," according to McLuhan's Laws of Media, constitute real extensions of a human identity configured in the fusion between human body and technological media apparatus (96–97).

The narrator with the sea-monkey tumor suggests, near the beginning of the novel, a new way to conceive of memory and biography. He muses:

> En el futuro todos seremos directores de cine, todos filmaremos películas de nuestras vidas. Pienso en una mañana cinematográficamente autobiograforme....
>
> El olvido será olvidado y ya no sabremos lo que es la memoria ni sus deformaciones que todo lo complican. Ya no recordaremos nuestro pasado como si fuera una película, porque nuestro pasado *será* una película de la que seremos primero protagonistas para poder ser espectadores después. (67)
>
> In the future we will all be film directors, we will all make films of our lives. I am thinking of a tomorrow cinematographically autobiograformed.... Forgetting will be forgotten and we will no longer know what memory is nor its deformations that complicate everything. We will no longer remember our past as if it were a film, because our past will be a film in which we will first be protagonists in order to then become spectators.

The dynamic here is intriguing, not only for the idea of lives as literal films but for the way that the idea is presented as a solution for organic failure. The act of forgetting is presented as a malfunction of memory; a concept inherently flawed in and of itself as it constitutes an act that deforms the past instead of documenting it. As a solution to those failures, film serves as a prosthetic brain that stores faithfully recorded images and sounds of the past. But not only do we see a reconfiguration of the human body as both organic and mechanical, possessing human life and the mechanical ability to record and store audio-visual data, we also see a multiplication of identity that further erodes the idea of a single human subject. The human is simultaneously a writer, actor, and director in this new situation, and is then converted into spectator when accessing the celluloid memories that the filmic life has produced.

The novel follows this line of thinking to its logical conclusions in the figure of Martín Mantra, the namesake of the novel though never a narrator. In a subsequent section, the boy makes an appearance as the dead narrator remembers meeting him for the first time:

> Se abre una puerta y entonces entra un niño raro, con una cabeza enorme que se mueve al caminar, como si apenas estuviera pegada al cuerpo. Al acercarse me doy cuenta que no es exactamente su cabeza sino un gigantesco casco con luces y lentes de filmadora con luces parpadeantes lo que le hace parecer deforme y extra-terrestre. Hace mucho ruido. Adentro de todo eso sonríe su cabecita. El niño me enfoca y sonríe. "Siempre quise conocer a alguien enmascaradamente luchadoriforme," me dice. (202)

> A door opens and a strange boy enters, with an enormous head that moves as he walks, as if it were barely attached to his body. As he approaches me, I realize that it isn't exactly his head, it's a giant helmet with lights and film lenses with blinking lights that make him seem deformed and alien. It makes a lot of noise. Inside all of this, his little head smiles. The boy focuses on me and smiles. "I always wanted to meet someone maskedly wrestlerformed" he says.

Mantra is the future that our sea-monkey narrator foresaw, a person who constantly films what he lives and who does so thanks to the technological apparatus that he constantly wears. Note how this narrator's reactions to the boy confirm the posthuman nature of the relationship between child and media-prosthesis. The helmet is first interpreted as an odd, but organic, head. It is only upon closer inspection that differences between the helmet and the boy are made clear. Nevertheless, Mantra's behavior is described as based on technology. His helmet makes him, all of him, differently formed, even alien, and when he looks at the narrator he does not merely look; he focuses: his attention and his shot-selection process are one and the same.

The dead narrator was a masked *luchador* [wrestler], and Mantra's fascination with that particular aspect helps us appreciate the service to which these posthuman images are put in the novel. While the man that reads the boy as alien does not share the same bio-technological configuration, Mantra does perceive an identity that extends beyond the organic. The boy's description of the narrator as "enmascaradamente luchadoriforme" names the man both as his profession and as his mask, elements that are prosthetic to the person's identity. Furthermore, the way in which Mantra takes two nouns, "máscara" and "luchador" and adverbizes or adjectivizes them suggests a subjectivity based on process rather than location. The combination of this kind of identity in flux between costume, technological prosthesis, and human body adds to the posthuman imaginary that is presented throughout the novel as it simultaneously relates it to Mexican popular culture and particularly to the successful Santos and Blue Demon films.

It is at this point that we appreciate the other thrust of the novel when it comes to the presentation of new kinds of human beings: that is, the attempt to rewrite mythology so as to include a genesis story of the posthumans and televisual cyborgs that populate a modern Mexico perceived by foreign eyes. The section of the novel devoted to the dead French wrestler begins with "Así, creo yo, es como empiezan las mejores religiones" and continues with a series of musings about the importance of science fiction for the creation of a national identity, with emphasis on the importance of Rod Serling's *The Twilight Zone*. These musings are especially revealing as they intersect with Mexican history. At one point, we see a recital of the conquest of Mexico that culminates in a series of descriptions of maps and of their study. As the stream of consciousness connections build, we find the following series of historical figures engaged in cartographic contemplation:

> Retratos de personas mirando mapas: Julio César, Hernán Cortés, Napoleón, Adolf Hitler, Darth Vader.... Hay algo de conquistador en todo aquel que mira un mapa (al mirar un mapa miramos desde las alturas de un dios) y hay algo de conquistador también en la primera vez que miramos mapa de la isla del Tesoro (trazado por Robert Louis Stevenson a partir del contorno de un estanque en una plaza frente a su casa en Edimburgo) o de la Tierra Media (porque J.R.R. Tolkien necesitaba todo un mundo donde poner el idioma que venía inventando desde los ocho años). (245)
>
> Portraits of people looking at maps: Julius Caesar, Hernando Cortés, Napoleon, Adolph Hitler, Darth Vader.... There is something of conqueror in anyone that looks at a map (when we look at a map, we look from the perspective of a god) and there is something of a conqueror in us the first time we look at a map of Treasure Island (drawn by Robert Louis Stevenson by the side of a pond in a park in front of his house in Edinburgh) or of Middle Earth (because J.R.R. Tolkien needed an entire world in which he could put the language that he had been inventing since he was eight years old.

By situating these ruminations at the end of a long recounting of Mexican history and by including Hernán Cortés and "conquistador" in the passage, we see a juxtaposition of the staples of Mexican history with important figures of Western history and, of course, Darth Vader. The fact that we, as readers, ape Caesar and Cortés when we look at maps of Treasure Island and Middle Earth underscores the way in which the popular culture that feeds our childhoods contributes to the formation of this kind of hybridized identity, one made cybernetic not only by the heavily cyborged figures that populate *Mantra* but also by the fact that our list of historical figures culminates in Darth Vader, popular culture's best known cyborg. By sensing the presence of the infamous conquerors in the list in the construction of Vader and combining that with the fact that Darth Vader's dependence on a mask makes him, unwittingly, especially appropriate for adoption into a Mexican mythological imaginary, we see how Fresán suggests a new popular mythology that generates the cybernetic figures that run through the novel.

The novel's end, a robot's search for his origin, brings all of these threads into another hybrid whole. This section begins as follows:

> He aquí el relato que solían relatar los viejos:
> «En un cierto tiempo que ya nadie puede contar, del que ya nadie puede acordarse...un día llegó caminando un hombre que se decía mitad momia y mitad metal a "Mexico City is known to Mexicans simple as México—pronounced 'MEH-kee-ko.' If they want to distinguish from Mexico the country they call it either 'la ciudad de México' or el DF—'el de EFF-e' "».
> Era un hombre extraño. (513)
> Behold the tale that the elders used to tell.
> "In a time that none can now count, that none can remember...one day a man came walking that was said to be half mummy and half metal to 'Mexico City is known to Mexicans simple as México—pronounced 'MEH-kee-ko.'' If they want to distinguish from Mexico the country they call it either 'la ciudad de México' or el DF—'el de EFF-e.' "
> He was a strange man.

At this point the novel has become myth (the passage in English is mentioned repeatedly throughout the novel), and we see how the cyborg image has combined with passages from the narrative to create the mythology of Mantrax, the god that the robot seeks. In so doing, the novel invites a comparison between the grafting and editing that occurs as history and story are fused in myth, as organic flesh and technological prosthesis are fused in cyborg, and as disparate scenes are cut together in film. Indeed, the narrative structure that moves us from a young, dying man, to a corpse, to a robot, outlines the evolution of the posthuman. *Mantra* as a novel sees in the cyborg a body peculiarly prepared to mediate and explore that process, one whose essential hybridity and fused nature helps understand identity and myth in the media age.

By so doing, we see a reimagination of the cyborg figure in Argentine narrative (this is another graft of sorts, it feels odd, and necessarily so, to read this as an Argentine novel though it is by the writer whose earlier work includes *Historia argentina*). Because of this reimagination, I think we need to be careful of reading this as merely a novel about what happens when you watch too much TV. For example, Edmundo Paz Soldán has observed that,

> Rodrigo Fresán explora en *Mantra* la intensa relación que existe entre el hombre y los artefactos tecnológicos en la sociedad contemporánea. Gracias a su relación con la máquina (en este caso, la televisión), el ser humano pierde agencia, se convierte en parte de los procesos de intercambio de una sociedad capitalista y globalizada. (2003: 106)

> In *Mantra*, Rodrigo Fresán explores the intense relationship that exists between man and technological artifacts in contemporary society. Thanks to their relationship with machines (in this case television), human beings lose agency and are converted into a part of the processes of exchange of a globalized, capitalist society.

While I completely agree that the novel examines this intense relationship, articulating new identities that arise from that communication of information between body and mass-media machine, I would argue, however, that the novel goes much further than simply describing the dehumanizing effect of that relationship. Instead, Fresán takes the intimate interactions between human and television to posit a new kind of globalized body, one that is neither dehumanized nor rehumanized, but posthumanized. In so doing, he reconfigures the Argentine cyborg from unholy monster or scarred survivor to citizen of a new global culture in need of a new, cybernetic, mythology.

Fresán presents another vision of this globalized, cyberneticized culture in his short story "Señales captadas en el corazón de una fiesta" [Signals Captured in the Heart of a Party]—this time on a scale less grand than that of new mythologies and future civilizations. The story, published in Fresán's collection *La velocidad de las cosas* (1998) [The Speed of Things], earlier served as Fresán's contribution to the *McOndo* anthology. In it, we find a series of reflections on what it means to be a "party animal," with considerations of popular music (David Byrne, The Pet Shop Boys) as well as drug culture and dealing with AIDS. The narrator functions as a collector of voices and thoughts that occur at parties, reporting snippets of conversations and situations that are overheard as one moves through the dialogues that constitute the series of parties that is one never-ending party.

The story begins with a first-person narrator musing on the titular signals:

> Aquí están, estas son, las señales captadas en el corazón de una fiesta. Las metálicas y frías señales. El derrotado himno de batalla, la triunfante marcha fúnebre, los sombreros en la mano.
>
> Me gusta oír las señales. La cabeza ligeramente torcida sobre un cuello que apenas la sostiene. Sísifo separa unas de otras con cuidado, las ordena por color y por peso, y en seguida empuja y sigue empujando montaña arriba. (65)
>
> Here they are, these are the signals captured at the heart of a party. The cold and metallic signals. The defeated battle hymn, the triumphant funeral march with hats in hand.
>
> I like to hear the signals. The head lightly twisted on a neck that can barely keep it up. Sisyphus separates them carefully, puts them in order by color and weight and then pushes and keeps pushing them up the mountain.

The accumulation of organic and metallic body parts here is impressive. The heart of the party gives way to the receptor of signals, in this case a head too big for its body that appears to presage Martín Mantra's headgear. Fresán intercuts the list of body parts with signals, suggesting a mechanical nature to this biologically described party—signals that are particularly technological given their cold metallic nature. As the signal collector, a grotesque body, is able to listen to these mechanical signals, we see quite clearly the kind of relational dynamics that constitute the posthuman identity for which Hayles argues. While the party and its participants are biological, with bodies and organs, the messages that circulate among these bodies are mechanical—making not only the narrator's body but also the party itself a truly cybernetic organism. As the story continues the narrator makes frequent reference to the signals, sometimes as "latidos digitales" [digital heartbeats] of the aforementioned heart of the party; at other times as more traditional radio signals that are broadcast and then lost in the ether. In all cases, we see the development of a discourse of the technological as a way to describe the supposedly organic system of parties.

These parties appear as the cause of the metaphorical transformation of human to cybernetic partygoer. The narrator explains his particular power as radio receiver, "Me refiero a aquellas señales que sólo puede captar alguien para quien las fiestas han dejado de ser interesantes. Ese al que las fiestas ya nunca le resultarán dignas de interés salvo para compararlas con las *otras* fiestas" [I refer to those signals that can only be picked up by someone for whom parties have ceased to be interesting. He for whom parties will never be interesting except as they are compared with the *other* parties] (65). This boredom with the party culture is what attunes the narrator's receptors and qualifies him to receive the titular party signals. This process extends beyond the auditory nature of radio signals and converts the narrator into a radio/camera/television watcher as the story progresses:

> Miro las fiestas como si fueran cuadros. Las miro y las fijo en el negativo invertido de mi retina cansada. Basta que cierre los ojos para sentir que las fiestas comienzan a desaparecer del mismo modo en que yo, con la siempre elegante lentitud de lo inexorable, he ido desapareciendo para el resto de los concurrentes, que ahora prefieren mirar para otro lado antes que concentrarse en el hombre invisible...
>
> Si, es posible que me hayan visto hace poco en los bordes de alguna fiesta, apartando enseguida la mirada—otro cuadro—, negando mi existencia como se niega una noticia desagradable al cambiar de canal. Zapping. (66)

> I look at parties as if they were paintings. I look at them and fix them in the inverted negative of my tired retina. It suffices to close my eyes to feel that the parties begin to disappear the same way that I, with the always elegant slowness of the inexorable,

have been disappearing for the rest of the partygoers, who now prefer to look away than to concentrate on the invisible man. Yes, it is possible that they have seen me on the edge of some party, looking away very quickly—another painting—, denying my existence like one denies bad news by changing the channel. Zapping.

The narrator does not merely receive the conversations and sounds of the party as signals; he also captures the images, his tired retina is described in its camera-like functions as he looks and fixes each scene, recording it as he did the overheard sounds. This process erases him as a man, making him invisible but also converting him into television. That is, his ability to receive signals makes him more akin to the quotidian device that also receives and fixes image and sound. For that reason, the logical response to the narrator at parties is "zapping"; that is, the other partygoers change him as they would a channel.

This combination of party as cybernetic organism and partygoer as human television suggests the development of a posthuman society that Fresán would use *Mantra* to mythologize. Furthermore, the story employs this cybernetic discourse as merely a semiotic system for describing the human condition. That it, to this point in the story, the technological imagery is not explicit or literal as we saw in *Mantra*; it merely functions as the most appropriate way to express the condition that the narrator seeks to describe.

However, the story takes a supernatural turn at the end, when we discover that the narrator is actually a ghost, the spirit of a man who has died of AIDS and continues to frequent the parties that he had attended when alive. While the spirit suggests a more fantastic arrangement than the implied science fiction of the technological metaphors, Fresán quickly resituates his ghost story within a cyborg matrix. As the narrator adopts the dead Willi's voice, he encounters first a deformed girl—una de ellas parece macrocefálica, una cabeza inmensa sobre un cuerpito delgado (89) [one of them seems macrocephalic, an immense head on a thin tiny body]—in reality a girl wearing a Teenage Mutant Ninja Turtle costume. The combination of animal and human, and especially the oversized head, both anticipates the wrestler's reaction to Mantra as it simultaneously emphasizes Haraway's inclusion of human/animal couplings as an element of cyborg identity. Willi then remembers his death, a collapse that happens as his parents play a game based on Morse code that mirrors Willi's conversion from flesh to transmission, his spirit sending signals through the Ouija board that serves as a fixture in the parties he attended. This image culminates in Willi's final messages: "Me muero. Me despido. Cambio y fuera. Fin de transmisión" (90) [I'm dying, I say goodbye. Over and out. End of transmission].

The story ends with more reflections from the dead Willi, who appears to exist because of the series of films that were made of him and his family before he passed away. Fresán again (or rather, first) works through the themes of memory as film and of the reality of the past as that which is recorded on celluloid. Willi's afterlife is proscribed by his continued existence as a visual and audio signal, as the digital and analog reproduction of his once organic life. Among other themes the story presents a reflection on the role of technology in the preservation of life and the necessary conversion of organic life into television signal, a conversion that he would then mythologize in *Mantra*.

From the rather grand gestures we find in *Mantra* and the supernatural "Señales" that anticipated Fresán's novel, we move to smaller, more personalized movements in Alberto Fuguet's popular novel *Por favor, rebobinar*, a novel whose title was so grounded in the video culture of the 1990s that it has already become obsolete (as we no longer rewind DVDs or computer files). The novel, a series of meditations, reviews, interviews, and stories based on the lives of a group of twenty-something middle-class Chileans, is replete with the mass media made evident in the "Be kind, rewind" instructions of the title. Film, television, radio, newspapers, and magazines all provide the material that constitutes the lives of this young Chilean middle class at the beginning of the post-Pinochet era. This focus on mass media in the novel helped define the McOndo moment, as I noted earlier, and has also given a focus to the majority of the criticism that has been written about Fuguet's narrative. What this criticism has missed is the relationship between mass media and technological identity that becomes clear only in the consideration of the posthuman characters that appear in the novel. These posthumans are not, however, the camera-headed filmmakers and origin-seeking robots of *Mantra*; the closest these characters get to the science fiction denizens of Fresán's world is by watching the same movies that Mantra and his cohort watched. Nevertheless, we find a series of moments where Fuguet's characters can only express their experiences in posthuman terms; the mass media world that they inhabit has reconfigured them as consciousnesses dependent upon prosthetic imagery for the articulation of self.

The majority of criticism dedicated to *Por favor, rebobinar* has looked specifically at the Lucas, the aspiring film critic who lives through the films that he watches—principally videotapes that he rents. Over the course of his narration, he indicates that he best understands his life as a film and that his memories and his interaction with the world make most sense when taken as elements of a script. This positioning of subjectivity within a cinematic matrix helps set up a series of articulations of a posthuman-like identity, where a pronounced identification with film bleeds into a body configured by the technological tools used to make that film.

> Así, creo, funciona un poco mi mente: más que creer que los ojos de Dios siempre me están mirando, siento que lo que tengo dentro del cerebro, conectado a los ojos, es una cámara que registra cada uno de mis actos. Creo que cuando uno se muere, se va a un gran microcine que está en el cielo y, junto a un comité ad hoc, uno se sienta a ver lo que ya vio.
> Eso se llama el infierno.
> Algunos, supongo, creen que es el cielo. (19)
>
> That, I believe, is a little like how my mind works: rather than believe that the eyes of God are always watching me, I feel like what I have inside my brain, connected to my eyes, is a camera that records each of my acts. I believe that when someone dies, they go to the great theater in the sky and, with an ad hoc committee, one sits and sees what they already saw. That is hell. Some, I suppose, believe that it's heaven.

VIDEO HEADS AND REWOUND BODIES

A couple of pages later, he remarks:

> Soy un maestro del zapping, de la cultura de la apropiación. Digamos que afano, pirateo, robo sin querer. Es como si tuviera un digital sampler en mi mente que funcionara a partir de puras imágenes. No soy un tipo creativo. No invento, absorbo. Trago. (22)
>
> I am a master of zapping, of the culture of appropriation. Let's say that I steal, I pirate, I rob without meaning to. It's as though I had a digital sampler in my mind that functions with pure images. I'm not a creative type, I don't invent, I absorb, I swallow.

Ana María Amar Sánchez's take on these passages is that they form the manifest of the novel, that with Lucas's absorption of popular culture we see a narrative cannibalization of the novel as just one more artifact of the same pop-culture system of representation (210). What I would propose as an extension of the critical consideration of the novel and of Lucas specifically is the way in which Lucas's attempts to articulate his own subjectivity result in an elaboration of a posthuman body where memory is able to occur as well as the sociocultural implications of such a body.

In the first passage, we observe a dynamic between technology and flesh, surveillance and behavior. In Lucas's mass media world, the camera functions on several levels. At first, we see a connection between a god that controls all humans' actions, a kind of superego/Panopticon that disciplines the organic body by means of constant surveillance. Lucas then modernizes the religious overtones of his musings, transforming "los ojos de Dios" into a camera, a technological device that fulfills the same function as the divine—therefore configuring a mass media world where celluloid is the creator/judge. Notwithstanding the metaphysical implications of such a transformation, what interests me most in this passage is the insertion of the camera into Lucas's head. Lucas combines the final judgment story with a cybernetic image, one in which his brain becomes cyborg as his cerebral memory centers are configured as a camera that records. In that moment, Lucas's organic body ceases to exist separately from the film technology with which he has interacted for so long. In this sense, Lucas's lifestyle has contaminated his sense of self profoundly. If we follow (and bend) the implications of the film and television theory associated with suture and flow to their cybernetic ends we find that the spectators are programmed by their experience with mass media to conceive of themselves as cameras, constantly seeing and recording the world through the eyes of that machine. In the case of Lucas, his long relationship with his television has trained him to experience the world as a camera would. On this level, it is not important that Lucas is not a literal cyborg like those we see in more traditional science fiction (though we should recognize that Lucas cites films from science fiction frequently). What is important is that Lucas no longer conceives of himself as separate from his prosthetic memory machine. What we see is a shift in thinking that follows the last portion of Katherine Hayles's description of posthuman thinking that I cited earlier: "In the posthuman, there are no essential differences or absolute demarcations between bodily existence and computer simulation, cybernetic mechanism and biological organism, robot teleology and human goals" (3). Lucas, as he constructs an identity based on cybernetic prosthesis and, in particular, presents his ability to interact with reality as based on that same prosthesis, also presents himself as a part of the evolving "posthuman view."

Regarding the second passage (about zapping), Lucas's technological absorption develops his posthuman identity in various directions. He repeats the idea of a cybernetic brain, one that is extended to various characters over the course of the novel. (Indeed, the title itself, in addition to being the phrase that one finds on a rental VCR cassette, also refers to using this prosthetic memory organ to keep from forgetting.) Beyond that image, Lucas foregrounds the role of "zapping" within the consumerist logic that the character advances over the course of his section of the novel. This time, the mechanical brain is associated with the reception of the televisual image rather than its production as was the case with the camera eyes of the first passage. Now the video head is a receptive machine, a digital sampler that records a variety of images that are seen thanks to the use of another machine—a remote control that exercises a cybernetic effect not only on his body but also on culture in general, especially if we take into account Sarlo's analysis of zapping. What unites the two descriptions, beyond the prosthetic brain, is the function that the organ performs. As both camera and digital sampler, the robot that lives inside Lucas remembers experiences by recording them and saving them to tape. The technological and artificial nature of these memories appears to be the result of their conversion into the organic celluloid matrix that is Lucas's brain.

If Lucas were the only metaphorical cyborg in the novel, we could use his particular conceptualization of posthuman identity as yet another support for the thesis that Christian Gundermann has presented about the very conservative posture he sees taken in the novel, especially when compared to the Argentine writer Manuel Puig. Lucas is presented as just one more "couch potato," infected by the technology for which he feels an unhealthy attraction and identification. If we remember the cyborg trope in the traditional science fiction I mentioned, the standard version of the cyborg is the accidental and traumatic result of uncontrolled technophilia. Rather than exercise the subversive possibilities that Haraway has argued as inherent to the cyborg this traditional science fiction figure is a cautionary tale, a victim of the scientific hubris of Doctor Frankenstein—a warning to those who would disregard the limits on creation imposed by the divine. Even the AI robots and machines of the Terminator films, of the Matrix, or even the recent remake of Battlestar Galactica are threats to humanity because human pride in technology produced robots that were too good at what they did. The cyborg that Fuguet describes, however, does not fit within this model so easily and not merely because it is not a literal creation of metal and flesh. Lucas is a metaphorical cyborg that does not function as designed. He is a broken robot, so to speak. Note what the character expresses as he speaks of his own ability to remember, an ability supposedly facilitated by the prosthetic organ that we have discussed.

> Lo único que tengo relativamente claro es que si no siento, si ya no me involucro en cosas que me importan, si ya no pueden

> usarme como depositario de nada, no es del todo a propósito.
> Pero tampoco es una pose. O algo planeado. No es como si
> hubiera apretado un botón, todo se borró, y listo: adiós a mis
> sensaciones. Simplemente pasaron a mi lado, se fueron. A veces,
> incluso, trato de que vuelvan. Intento rebobinar, pero me es
> imposible. (29)
>
> The only thing that I have relatively clear is that if I don't feel,
> if I no longer involve myself in things that I care about, if they
> can no longer use me as a deposit of anything, it's not completely on purpose. It's not a pose either, or something planned.
> It's not as though someone had pressed a button and everything
> was erased, goodbye to all my feelings. It's just that everything
> passed by me, it's gone. Sometimes, in fact, I try to make them
> come back. I try to rewind, but for me it's impossible.

His inability to feel is connected, not with the insensitivity stereotypically associated with those that watch too much television and are isolated by that technology but with something very different. The button, that implement so important for a literal cyborg, does not receive the blame that Lucas assigns as he tries to understand his situation. The problem is that his electronic archive simply does not work. He is unable to rewind, unable to access the information that his prosthetic organ, be it camera or digital sampler, should have archived electronically. The problem from which Lucas suffers is not that he is a cyborg in a world of humans; it is that he is not cyborg enough, he is not able to use his electronic memory to access the past in the way that others supposedly can.

This vision of cyborg identity is developed in the title of Baltasar Daza's novel, Daza being the pop novelist who appears at various points in *Por favor, rebobinar*. The title of his novel is, unoriginally, *Disco Duro* [Hard Disk], and Daza describes his novel in the following terms:

> Es una idea, un juego. Es moderno, remite a los computadores
> y a los discos, o a los compacts, debería decir. Y lo duro, lo
> *heavy*, tiene que ver con la agresión y las drogas. Pero, más que
> nada, tiene que ver con nuestra memoria colectiva, con nuestro
> inconsciente, con aquello que tenemos insertado en el cerebro y
> no podemos borrar. (264)

It's an idea, a game. It is modern and it evokes Computers and disks, compact discs, I should say. And the hard, the heavy, has to do with aggression and drugs. But, more than anything, it has to do with our collective memory, with our unconscious, with that which we have inserted in our brains and that we can't erase.

What Daza postulates is a cybernetic condition that extends throughout human identity, a situation in which the only way to conceive of a collective memory is through technology. Lucas is, then, one more cyborg among a generation of posthuman beings, his prosthetic organ simply does not function like the rest of his generation. In this sense, the parasitical relationship that Lucas has with film impedes his function as a posthuman rather than facilitating it. In so doing, Fuguet articulates an innovative vision of identity quite far afield of the typical neo-luddite reaction of the conservative stance.

Andoni Llovet's long chapter develops Daza's vision second-hand (the model and aspiring writer reports on Daza's novel in its embryonic form over the course of his own autobiography). Throughout the chapter Llovet revisits the title of Daza's masterpiece, relaying Daza's own views on "Disco Duro" even as he adapts and expands it to fuel his own thought on the subconscious and on the artistic process. Llovet first mentions the novel as a long-promised text that has yet to appear, one that Daza mentions to his friends from writing classes but will not let them read:

> Ése va a ser el epígrafe *Disco Duro*, la gran novela de Baltasar Daza. *Caída libre* es uno de los temas de Pascal Barros. Es el tema favorito de Baltasar. Daza lleva años trabajando en *Disco Duro*, pero nunca le ha mostrado nada a nadie. Sí ha contado cosas. Va a ser, se supone, su trabajo más autobiográfico y toma como punto de partida su familia.
>
> —Quiero hacer una saga, pero sin caer en la fórmula del realismo mágico. Puro realismo virtual, pura literatura McOndo. Algo así como *La casa de los espíritus* sin los espíritus. (145)

That will be the epigraph of *Hard Disk*, Baltasar Daza's great novel. *Free Fall* was one of Pascal Barros's songs. Baltasar's favorite song. Daza has spent years working on *Hard Disk* but he's never shown any of it to anyone. He has told some of it. It's going be, one assumes, his most autobiographical work and it takes his family as a starting point.

—I want to do a saga, but without recurring to the formula of magical realism. Pure virtual realism, pure McOndo literature. Something like *The House of the Spirits* without the spirits.

The novel serves as an example of Fuguet's McOndo group, with emphasis on the rejection of magical realism as well as the sacred writers of the Chilean canon. The phrase that most attracts our attention, especially considering the title's later posthuman implications, is "realismo virtual," referring to Daza's attempt to distance his work from Allende's as well as the international market's view of what Latin American literature should be. With the phrase virtual realism, we see a new vision of literature constructed that associates it with virtual reality worlds. In that sense not only does the literary act anticipate the virtual computer worlds that we would later see so well explored in Edmundo Paz Soldán's work, but Fuguet suggests that there is no distinction—that the literary virtual and the technological virtual are ultimately the same. In that sense the novel's title not only suggests a way for thinking about posthuman memory but also a way to conceive of the entire artistic process.

In this same passage, Llovet reports further on Daza's view of the virtual nature of the artistic process,

> Este apoyo, más el contrato con una editorial y la ayuda de una agente, me daría el suficiente ánimo y seguridad para sacar de mi disco duro cerebral un montón de materia prima disponible con la cual lanzarme a escribir todas esas novelas que nadie, por cobarde o mediocre, ha tenido la ocurrencia de escribir. (146)

> This support, plus the contract with the press and the help of an agent, will give me the needed will and security to access from my own cerebral hard disk a ton of available original material with which I can begin writing all the novels that no one, because they're cowards or mediocre, has been able to write.

Here Daza links not only the artistic product with virtual realities, but also the process of literary production with cyborg embodiment. The business aspect of literature, invoked by the agent and the contract, become the market keys to the technological organ of creativity that resides within Daza's cerebrum. This fusion of art, business, and the metaphor of the posthuman body creates a posthuman reality in which the cybernetic is a state to which artists aspire, a state from which Lucas finds himself isolated because his organs do not function properly.

Llovet continues in this mode later in his narrative as he continues to muse on the creative process,

> ¿De dónde salió esto? Ni siquiera me acordaba de que tenía todo esto adentro, guardado, escondido.
> ¿Escondido?
> Rebobinado.
> *Así que esto es lo que llaman inconsciente, ¿ah?*
> Me acuerdo que una vez leí en un *New York Review of Books* que tenía Balta un largo artículo sobre creatividad, rockeros y drogadicción. Algo así. Estaba basado en Jung, el psiquiatra favorito de Sting, que lo puso de moda con *Synchronicity*. Esta información inútil la aportó Gonzalo McClure. El asunto es que el artículo analizaba y exploraba el por qué un tipo—un artista, más bien—crea. Compone, escribe letras, qué sé yo. La conclusión final era que la creatividad salía del inconsciente. Nada nuevo ahí. Lo interesante, lo que a mí más me llamó la atención y aterró, fue la definición que el tal Jung le daba al inconciente. Según él, es todo lo que sabemos pero que no estamos pensando. (1999: 172)

> Where did this come from? I don't even remember that I had all this inside, kept safe and hidden.
> Hidden?
> Rewound.
> So that's what they call the unconscious, right?
> I remember that one time I read an article in a *New York Review of Books* that Balta had about creativity, rock musicians, and addiction. Something like that. It was based on Jung, Sting's favorite psychiatrist, that he made fashionable with Synchronicity. This useless information was given by Gonzalo McClure. The idea was that the article analyzed and explored why a guy—an artist rather, creates. He composes, writes lyrics, whatever. The

final conclusion was that creativity came from the unconscious. Nothing new there. What was interesting, what caught my attention and scared me was the definition Jung gave of the unconscious. According to him, it is everything that we know but that we are not thinking.

Llovet's discussion of Jung and the role of the unconscious is rather basic; he is, after all, merely processing what he read in the newspaper. What is telling is the fact that his access to the artistic subconscious is controlled by the word "Rebobinado." Fuguet underscores this with the very layout of the writing. The telegraphic style of the beginning of the passage reproduces the breaks in movements that the act of rewinding presupposes. Hence, not only does Llovet invoke "Rebobinar" but the text's structure also invokes the action. Fuguet then accompanies this structural evocation with a memory; Llovet's memory functioning now that he has been rewound.

The culmination of Llovet's musings on Jung, Sting, and the subconscious makes the posthuman elements of the process even more clear:

> O sea, es todo aquello de lo que alguna vez tuvimos conciencia, pero ya se nos olvidó. Algo así como el disco duro de los computadores. El disco duro que todos llevamos dentro, seamos compatibles o no. La luz se te puede cortar, te pueden robar el Mac, un virus te atacó, da lo mismo, tu disco duro sigue adentro, contigo, vayas donde vayas, hagas lo que hagas. (172)

> That is, it is everything of which we were once conscious, but that we have since forgotten. Something like the hard disk of computers. The hard disk that we all have inside, whether we're compatible or not. The electricity can go out, they can steal your Mac, you can get a virus, it doesn't matter, your hard disk continues inside, wherever you go, whatever you do.

Llovet, then, as a being that must be rewound, can only find the vocabulary to describe the human condition in computers. And yet the metaphor of the hard drive does not suggest a situation in which the organic is completely replaced by the technological. Humans are not better off as robots. Llovet's human hard drive improves on the purely mechanical original in that it cannot be stolen, it cannot be erased by a power outage, and it is impervious to computer viruses. What we see proposed here is the posthuman as the condition that solves both organic shortcomings and technological drawbacks. Fuguet strengthens this interpretation with a series of metaphors that develops posthuman identities as various characters. In a specific chain of cybernetic images, we see the description of the city as a technological body. "En el city hay de todo, como una radio interna propia y un sistema de videos las 24 horas, que funciona por room service y que sólo se especializa en cintas raras, de culto (seleccionadas por el joven crítico Lucas García)" (232) [In the city there is a bit of everything, like one's own internal radio and a 24-hour video system, that works by room service and specializes only in rare, cult tapes (selected by the young critic Lucas García)]. Urban identity is transformed here in a network of interrelated machines. Moreover, the archival and surveillance functions of this machine city create a direct connection with Lucas's cyborg body. This particular combination of technology and surveillance situates Fuguet's cyborg city alongside that proposed by Jesús Martín Barbero:

> [es un] mareamiento de circuitos y trayectos que de-velan en las cibernéticas metrópolis actuales de ciudades invisibles: místicas, esotéricas, vivenciales. Y desde las cartografías catastrales construidas *desde arriba*, y a las que "nada escapa" como el panóptico aquel que estudiara Foucault, sólo que ahora su centro es móvil—la cámara colocada en el helicóptero—. (2003: 13)
>
> [It is a] dizzying collection of circuits and trajectories that is uncovered in the real cybernetic metropolises of invisible cities, mystics, esoteric and filled with life. And it is from the maps constructed from above and that nothing escapes like the Panopticon that Foucault studied, though now the center is mobile, the camera is in the helicopter.

The perspective that Fuguet contributes to this articulation of the city is the way in which the body of the posthuman being becomes the map of the cybernetic metropolis, the fusion of flesh and prosthesis as an exact replica of what is found in the cities that Martín Barbero describes. In fact, Fuguet expresses the connection between body and city explicitly when he writes: "Las calles de la ciudad son tus arterias, en los parques se esconde tu pasado y entre los sitios baldíos se reparte tu corazón" (229–30) [The streets of the city or your arteries, your past hides in the parks and your heart in the places]. In this statement, we see the way in which the organic elements of the body function as a map of the streets. This combines with the earlier passage in which places in the city employ a surveillance technology that evokes specifically the mechanical brain that Lucas describes and to which he alludes constantly with his references to a "rewinding" memory.

The novel ends with the chapter, "Gonzalo McClure: Adulto contemporáneo." McClure, half of a couple that is expecting their first child, reflects on the past that he shared with several of the characters who have told their stories over the course of the novel as he simultaneously distances himself from them with the formation of a "traditional" relationship (i.e., heterosexual, monogamous, with children). Gundermann highlights, obviously, this as clear evidence of the conservative vision that Fuguet develops over the course of the novel. As I mentioned previously, Gundermann has a basis for his argument, especially if we view Lucas as an infected couch potato. In fact, McClure mentions one character, the famous musician/actor Pascal Barros, in a situation that suggests that he has successfully abandoned a cybernetic aesthetic: "Pascal no toca en vivo hace tiempo. Ahora está abocado a grabar su nuevo disco: Perdidos, interferidos, desenchufados. Es, claro, un disco acústico, unplugged. Tiene más de veinte temas listos" (383) [Pascal hasn't played live for a while now. He's recording a new record: Lost, interfered, with and unplugged. It is, of course, an acoustic disk, unplugged. He has more than twenty songs ready]. After so many "plugged-in" bodies the fact that Barros is now playing acoustic music suggests a certain de-evolution, at least in posthuman terms. That noted, Lucas is not actually a couch potato infected by technology, he is the result of broken prostheses and, within that logic, Fuguet creates a continuity between the ubiquitous posthumanity in the early part of the novel and a continued cybernetic discourse in this rather nostalgic denouement. McClure notes that his prosthetic memory organ continues to function: "Sólo el pasado, con sus hechos y sus recuerdos, podrá esclarecer lo que hoy nos parece tan enredado y oscuro. Quizás. Pero entiendo a los que se niegan a rebobinar hacia cualquier lado" (380) [Only the past, with its facts and memories, can clear up what today seems so twisted and dark. Maybe. But I can understand those that refuse to rewind toward any side]. The fact that the act of remembering continues to be expressed in terms of rewinding suggests that this particular aspect of the posthuman condition endures, in spite of the evolution of the postadolescents that populate the narrative.

Indeed, the arrival of a child at the end of the novel can be seen within this ongoing exaltation of posthuman identity. McClure is careful to discuss at length his work and his wife's; he in radio, she as a former model, now photographer. In both professions, we see a particular relationship between technology and the body. McClure and the other characters who work in radio comment several times on the displacing effect of the decorporealized voices that are an essential part of any radio personality. Their relationship with the mass media has let them, to borrow a phrase from cyberpunk, move away from the meat of the body and toward mass conversation with their listeners. When we combine that with the posthuman discourse of the novel, we see McClure as yet another articulation of the changing relationship between bodies and technology that occur in the realm of the mass media. Importantly, Pía, McClure's wife, also works in the production of image, in the conversion of body into photograph, much as we saw in the novels of Paz Soldán and Prado. Moreover, Pía has moved from one side of the camera to the other as she changes professions, creating a situation in which she always appears defined by the camera, but ending in a place where the camera functions as her prosthetic eye rather than one in which she offers her body up to the consuming gaze of the lens. That these two would procreate, then, suggests the arrival of an audiovisual child that combines the professions of both parents. The conservative ending that Gundermann dismisses is also the arrival of a new kind of posthuman, one that combines both mass media technology with a heteronormative nuclear family.[2]

In Fuguet's subsequent fiction, we see a more detailed exploration of the intersections of technology and the formation of "traditional" families. The story "Hijos" [Children], from his 2005 collection, *Cortos* [Shorts], displays just such an example where Fuguet examines the dynamics of parenthood implicit in the relationship a married couple has with their computers. The story follows the lives of a couple in their late twenties, content with their childless life. Over the course of the narrative, they meet an elderly couple, also childless, and become friends with them, sharing films and giving them a Macintosh laptop. The elderly couple receives the gift with some trepidation, and then enjoys what it has to offer—the elderly man being a film scholar who is amazed with all that the Internet Movie Database (www.imdb.com) has to offer. The story ends unremarkably, the elderly couple's cat passes away and life continues. Fuguet structures the story in chapters with sections, the chapter numbers appearing in the screen of a laptop that appears at the top of the page, the sections divided by Apple Computer's trademark .

The posthuman nature of the story again functions on an implicit level (aside from the ubiquitous references to Macintosh), underpinning much of the younger couple's relationship even as it begins to suggest ways to understand the relationship between film and interpersonal relationships. Near the beginning of the story, the narrator describes his relationship with his wife Carla.

> Somos una pareja joven, sin hijos. Lo de joven es relativo. Ninguno de los dos ha cumplido los treinta, es cierto, pero llevamos siete años juntos y no hemos sentido comezón algún. Diría que somos más *ambient* que *transient*...
> Nos gusta surfear la red tomados de la mano. Tenemos un computador al lado del otro. Recientemente pasamos a banda ancha. Contamos con varios Apple. Los coleccionamos. Es donde más gastamos, pero nos parece más una inversión que un despilfarro. Nos gusta renovarlos cada tres años.... A veces le envío emails cariñosos y le escribo el tipo de cosas que no me atrevo a decirle en persona. A ella le gusta tomar fotos digitales a cosas en las que nadie se fija: vitrinas, letreros, carteleras de cine. Cuando no podemos estar juntos, chateamos vía Messenger. (117)

> We're a young couple with no children. But being "young" is relative. It's true neither of us has turned thirty yet, but we've

VIDEO HEADS AND REWOUND BODIES

been together for seven years and haven't felt any real itching desire to start a family. I'd say we're more ambient than transient.... We like to hold hands while surfing the net, which is why we've got our computers set up next to each other. We recently went to broadband, and use several Apple products. We collect them. It's where much of our budget goes, but we look at it as more of an investment than a waste. We like upgrading every three years.... Sometimes I'll send her affectionate emails in which I describe things that I'd never dare to reveal in person. She likes to snap digital photos of things that people usually overlook: display cabinets, billboards, cinema marquees. When we can't be together, we chat over Instant Messenger. (125)

Clearly what makes the couple remarkable is the extent to which the Macintosh computers mediate their relationship. Email and chats provide a virtual intimacy at times more direct than that which they enjoy when physically together. The image of the two holding hands as they surf the Internet is particularly powerful as it not only displays Katherine Hayles's image of the posthuman computer user but it combines that with the interpersonal dynamics of a married couple. Fuguet produces a kind of triad in which the human couple commune with each other even as they fuse with the Internet through their laptops. For that reason, it should not surprise us that they renew their computers every three years. Fuguet's image of human/human/computer fusion naturally would produce metaphorical children; in this case, the updated PowerBooks.

As the younger couple befriends an elderly film professor and his wife, Fuguet begins to use elements of film theory as an engine for the exploration of interpersonal dynamics in an age of computers and cinema. In one scene that occurs near the beginning of the friendship, we see the beginning of this theorization,

> Un par de semanas atrás, el doctor nos mostró una vejada copia en 16 mm de *El acorazado Potemkin*. Si bien el curso no incluía cine ruso, Paternostro Villalba usó la obra de Eisenstein para ilustrarnos dos ideas que, para él, son claves: el montaje como instrumento revolucionario y el cine como manifiesto. La famosa escena de las escaleras de Odessa me recordó la secuencia

> en la estación de tren de Chicago de *Los Intocables* con Kevin Costner. Se lo hice saber. Paternostro no sabía de qué hablaba. Tampoco conocía, ni de referencia, el trabajo de Brian De Palma. (121–22)
>
> Two weeks ago, the professor showed us an old 16mm copy of *Battleship Potemkin*. Though the syllabus didn't include any Russian films, Paternostro Villalba used Eisentstein's work to illustrate two ideas he felt were crucial: the use of cinema as a revolutionary instrument, and cinema as manifesto. The famous scene on the steps leading to the Odessa harbor immediately reminded me of the Chicago train station sequence in *The Untouchables* with Kevin Costner. I pointed out the connection, but Paternostro didn't know what I was talking about. He didn't know—nor had he heard of—Brian De Palma's work. (130)

Eisenstein's appearance in the story advances the theme of an implicit posthumanity in a way similar to the concept of posthuman cleavage that I introduced in chapter 3 of this book. That is, Eisenstein here functions as a metonymy of his theories on cinema and montage, specifically on the unique importance of editing in a cinematic aesthetic. Eisenstein's insistence on the power of the cut in the creation of meaning becomes a metaphor for Fuguet's thinking on the ways in which humans join together in interpersonal relationships.

The narrator's response to the class is instructive, as is Paternostro's use of Eisenstein as an example in a class not explicitly about Russian film. Paternostro introduces Eisenstein as a foreign element, as an edited-in sequence that alters the meaning of the course by highlighting the revolutionary potential of montage. The narrator then repeats this move, using the Eisenstein sequence in conjunction with his own cinematic background, the more contemporary De Palma film, *The Untouchables*. The narrator has performed an Eisensteinian operation in which an editing-in of the subsequent film enriches the Eisenstein original, an idiosyncratic move certainly as the De Palma film was clearly referencing Eisenstein. This series of cinematic moves in a collection of short stories titled *Cortos* in Spanish emphasizes not only the cinematic aesthetic that Fuguet develops in the short stories, but also opens up the possibility of thinking of the shorts as a montage, as a series of cleavages that produce meaning at the seam of the cut.

The subsequent development of the story shows how this logic then controls both the structure and the thematics that continue. The shared interest in cinema brings the younger and older couples together; the younger couple gives the Paternostros an old laptop and the lives of all four begin to change. The editing together of the generations produces alterations in meaning even as it suggests a way to understand the relationship of technology with the lives of the characters. That is, just as these lives are joined through cinematic cuts, the relationships between bodies are joined at sutures forged by computers. Here we return to the image of the younger couple surfing the web and holding hands, but also to the Apple trademarks that divide and join the sections of the story. Fuguet's achievement in the story is, then, not so much in the story of two couples whose lives are changed by one another, but in the way in which he uses cinematic aesthetics and an implicit posthuman context to narrate what is ultimately a Hollywood feel-good story.

Fuguet's narrative provides a vision of posthuman life much more radical than one would expect and in a much more subtle way than one sees in posthuman literature, certainly more subtle than Fresán. Without any science fiction figures, no robots, androids, or kids with Mantra-vision, Fuguet constructs a world in which technology permeates and penetrates every character, reconfiguring its auto-discursive strategies in such a way that they cannot articulate their own identities without depending on technological imagery. It may be that these figures do not achieve the subversive ends that Haraway dreams for her cyborgs, but they do present a markedly different cultural reality in which posthuman identity has become a fact of the everyday world.

The McOndo writers have been criticized, extensively, for their perceived lack of political engagement. My analysis here certainly does not do anything to defend them from that criticism. Indeed, what we see in the posthumans that wander through Fresán and Fuguet's novels do not perform the same kind of political and social critiques that we see in other Latin

American novels. We do not see Piglia's traumatized cyborg whose prostheses tell the story of state torture, we do not see the cybernetic products of neoliberalism run amok that Paz Soldán and Courtoisie describe in their recent novels, nor do we see explorations of gender and sexuality that appear in novels by Borinsky, Boullosa, and Prado and that engage more directly North American and European cultural theory. What we see is the construction of narrative realities where posthuman identity is a given, a quotidian condition of a shared experience. The link to memory that we see in both novels becomes not the attempt to remember a traumatic past or to recoup a pretechnological world; what we see is the need to construct a new history, a new mythology in which the posthuman finds its forebears in the machines that helped make them.

Conclusion

Slavoj Žižek recently weighed in on the proliferation of theories of the posthuman when he summarized as follows:

> Furthermore, a whole school of cyberspace theorists advocate the notion that cyberspace phenomena render palpable in our everyday experience the deconstructionist "decentered subject": one should endorse the "dissemination" of the unique Self into a multiplicity of competing agents, into a "collective mind," a plurality of self-images without a global coordinating center, which is operative in cyberspace, and disconnect it from pathological trauma—playing in virtual spaces enables me to discover new aspects of "me," a wealth of shifting identities, of masks without a "real" person behind, and thus to experience the ideological mechanism of the production of Self, the immanent violence and arbitrariness of this production/construction. (25)

What strikes me as we work our way through these various Latin American articulations of the posthuman is that the "real person behind" never goes away completely. The masks, the bodies, the play of signifiers that Žižek appears to conflate with the now tired poststructuralist conceptualizations of identity do not occur in the way that one would assume. What we find in these texts is a profoundly human posthuman, though not in the knee-jerk rejection of technology that we find in Sabato and other mid-twentieth-century writers. What we do see are the strategies that art employs as it attempts to think through realities and identities, both collective and individual, in a world that is increasingly mediated by the technologies of culture.

The scarred cyborgs, the confused posthumans, the ungendered and regendered motherless bodies, the products of neoliberalism, and even the normal folk just trying to remember their individual lives are all cybernetic organisms of one sort or another. What the literature and other expressions of culture that we have considered in this book suggest is the power of these figures to enunciate contemporary realities, be they those traumatized realities of the postdictatorship, be they the everyday lives of individuals surrounded by effects of neoliberal policy.

It is in this combination of the quotidian and science fiction that we see emerge a more Latin American articulation of the posthuman. The cyborg image is that which, in these cases, helps think through the contradictory realities of local histories and global consumerism in a way that is at once an expression of global popular culture and an autochthonous gesture unique to the various countries in which it appears. Oddly enough, it also becomes a gesture that renews and revises previous stories about Latin American culture and literature. Elsewhere, I have written of the surprising and fundamental elements of the neobaroque in Piglia's *La ciudad ausente* (Brown 2009). While literal cyborgs play an important part in this baroque-ness— Angela Ndalianis has argued persuasively that the hybridity that cyborgs bring make them merely the most recent expression of cyborg sensibility—, I find that Piglia's use of obscure underground music and film references in the novel create the kinds of "zonas de condensación" that Carpentier found so central to his thinking about the baroque. As we consider the way that cyborg imagery and identity has been folded into expressions of Latin American culture, from Holmberg's automatons to Diego Rivera's murals to the very recent narrative considered in this book, we see a possible baroque sensibility at work, one that then extends from the biomechanical to a broader incorporation of global underground and popular culture that is so apparent in Piglia initially and then in Paz Soldán, Fuguet, and Fresán. What strikes as ironic is the fact that this science fiction imagery and its introduction in apparently realist fiction like that of Paz Soldán and Fuguet would appear to follow a similar line of argumentation to that used by Carpentier as he argued for a "marvelous real" in Latin America. Carpentier's position was that Latin American reality was sufficiently unique so as to require a marvelous description, the basis for the popularity of magical realism throughout a last third of the twentieth century. With such a strong appearance of posthumans, both literal and figurative, in roles that are at once global and specifically local, we see magic replaced by science fiction in a similar dynamic.

The rise of an even younger generation of writers, including the southern cone novelist Mike Wilson Reginato, whose 2008 *El púgil* explores a cybernetic Buenos Aires with figures that range from a talking refrigerator to a clone of Orson Welles to a cybernetically reanimated corpse, suggests that the cyborg will continue its presence in newly globalized yet stubbornly localized Latin American cultural expression. Indeed, Wilson works with a group of Chilean writers including Álvaro Bisama, Francisco Ortega, and Jorge Baradit, who have embraced a mix of realism and science fiction to a success that promises many more years of plumbing the posthuman implications of technology and identity. We also see a series of epistolary novels that are based on electronic mail rather than the traditional handwritten letter, from Daniel Link's *La ansiedad* to Gustavo Sainz's La *novela virtual* to Luis López Nieves's *El corazón de Voltaire*. In each of these cases, we see explorations of an older genre from a technological perspective that adds to the changing sense of identity and the Internet in Latin America. The richness and variety of the treatments of technological identity and the cyborg body suggest an important aspect of Latin American cultural production that certainly deserves further study. I hope to have pointed out some directions in this book, but there remain many texts and ideas left to explore, including, especially, the cases of Brazil and the Caribbean and how these areas grapple or do not grapple with the themes I have covered here. While posthuman sutures will continue to itch and the cyberpunk rejection of the materiality of the body is never quite embraced, the southern cyborg appears to have taken its place in the pantheon of Latin American artistic concerns.

Notes

Introduction

1. See my "Humanismo cyborg" for a lengthier discussion of this vein of technophobia in Argentine literature.

1 Posthuman *Porteños*: Cyborg Survivors in Argentine Narrative and Film

1. The book is a reader of feminist and cyborg theory that collects fourteen articles, three of which focus on the film, with several more using *Blade Runner* as example. Linda Janes summarizes Mary Ann Doane's interpretation this way: "these films [Alien and Blade Runner] rework connections between the maternal, history and representation in ways that suggest contradictory response of both nostalgia for, and profound horror of, the maternal function and toward technologies of reproduction" (96).
2. Various studies have analyzed the semiotic value of Maria and *Metropolis*. See, e.g., Peter Ruppert's work.
3. Translation is my own. Throughout the book, all translations are my own unless parenthetical references indicate otherwise.
4. This interpretation of the ending challenges those of critics such as Currie Thompson who maintains that "Aristarain's film is remarkable...because its final sequence, in which the protagonist cuts out his tongue, is a thinly veiled critique of people who had allowed themselves to be silenced by the dictatorship" (35). The temptation to interpret Bengoa's final act this way is certainly present, but previous images of a silent fight made possible by prostheses suggests an act more rebellious than one of capitulation.
5. See Idelber Avelar's, Gareth Williams's, and Francine Masiello's recent books.

6. Jagoe tempers this position somewhat, recognizing the female's subjugation to the male in several instances in the novel.
7. See Avelar, Williams, and Balderston. Also see Bratosevich's chapter "¿Hacia una estética cibernética?" (1997: 215–60).
8. This and all following translations of passages from *La ciudad ausente* come from Waisman's 2000 translation.
9. See Laura Demaría's excellent analysis of the use of these patients and other characters as emblematic of the oppression and torture of the dictatorship (1999155–86).
10. Marie-Laure Ryan uses the term "wreader" in an ironic mode to describe the different kind of reader that appears when a traditional reader is confronted with hypertext (9).
11. Ryan's analysis of Baudrillard's work on virtual realities, in *Narrative as Virtual Reality* 27–35 in which she mentions specifically the latter critic's description of the Disneyland museum, has guided my thinking here.
12. Ryan's discussion of the development of hypertext theory is enlightening here; she also first highlighted the quotation from Landow (8).
13. The various Frankenstein movies that show the role of lightning in the creation of the monster suggest yet another connection between Piglia's cyborgs and Shelley's creature.
14. See his interview with Marco Antonio Campos in *Cuentos con dos rostros*, 101.
15. Without referring specifically to the Senator's cyborg nature, Levinson argues for a related interpretation of
    the Senator's body...[as]...a product of both mourning and melancholy. On the one hand, the unspeakable portions of Argentina's past cling to the Senator's body like a disease, like melancholia: "una extensión de mi cuerpo, algo que está fuera de aquí." They remain as an incessant presence that overwhelms his body, leaving him fixed in the same spot, crippled, virtually immobile: a living corpse. On the other hand, speech about history allows the Senator to continue: to recall, to account for and thus to move past the past, to mourn and to live. (111)

2 Missing Gender: The Posthuman Feminine in Alicia Borinsky, Carmen Boullosa, and Eugenia Prado

1. See also Gabriela Romero-Ghiretti's article on subjectivity and the cyborg body in *Cine continuado*.

2. I develop the idea of posthuman cleavage further in chapter 3.
3. See "Humanismo cyborg" for an extended discussion of Boullosa's novel in the context of earlier technophobia.
4. The group called the event an "installation novel" to emphasize the hybridized genre of the work. It included music, a theatrical stage with an actress, and texts that were at times acted and at times read. There was also an exhibition that complemented the dramatic portion of the installation.
5. Martin Hopenhayn comments upon this textual hybridity specifically in his review of the novel.
6. The hyperbaton of the English translation is much more pronounced in the original Spanish.

3 Ripped Stitches: Mass Media and Televisual Imaginaries in Rafael Courtoisie's Narrative

1. Haraway's iconoclastic cyborg has become the champion of various critiques of capitalism. Note Negri and Hardt's discussion of the figure in their recent *Empire*:

    The will to be against really needs a body that is completely incapable of submitting to command. It needs a body that is incapable of adapting to family life, to factory discipline, to the regulations of a traditional sex life, and so forth....

    Donna Haraway's cyborg fable, which resides at the ambiguous boundary between human, animal and machine, introduces us today, much more effectively than deconstruction, to these new terrains of possibility. (216, 218)
2. See, in particular, her section on "zapping" pp. 57–73.
3. Remarkably, the telephone functions as a technological weapon in *Caras extrañas*, where one military leader is pursued by a series of phone messages accusing him of torture and murder.
4. This representation of the remote control as a tool designed to assist the acquisition of goods counters Nestor García Canclini's discussion of zapping. García Canclini emphasizes business's efforts to stop zapping as it allows the viewer to avoid commercials and, hence, the invitation to consume (1997: 52–53).
5. In that sense, Courtoisie participates much more within the theoretical framework that Rob Latham has proposed in his recent *Consuming Youth*. For Latham the cyborg is essentially a figure of post-Fordist consumption, an image related to the vampire and one whose biomechanical nature allows it to participate more fully in capitalistic consumerism.

6. This idea is also developed in Alejandro Agresti's 1996 film *Buenos Aires Vice Versa*, especially in the case of the woman who seats her television at her dinner table so that she can serve *milanesas* to the newscaster who appears on her television at dinnertime. For further analysis see articles by Sorbille and Thompkins.
7. I use "suturing" here in allusion to cinematic suture theory while being aware that the dynamic I describe here, and that of television/viewer in general, operates in a much different way in film than it does in television. Still, the concept of the inclusion of the spectator within a Lacanian imaginary is useful for describing the kinds of bio-media fusions that I see occurring.
8. Frederic Jameson's characterization of television viewing is quite similar. See especially 73–74 and his description of the camera as a gun that imprisons both filmed subject as well as spectator.
9. *Escrache* refers to the act of using street signs and graffiti to identify the homes of people accused of participating in Argentina's Dirty War. See Masiello (2001) for a discussion of its political and cultural aspects.
10. Jesús Montoya Juárez examines Courtoisie's use of a televisual aesthetic in *Caras extrañas* remarking in particular the way in which Courtoisie blends narrative, cinematic, and televisual genres in the novel.
11. This vision of the role of television in the role of national trauma has been the focus of an important area of Holocaust Studies. See, in particular, Dominick LaCapra (1994) and (2001).

4 Neoliberal Prosthetics in Postdictatorial Argentina and Bolivia: Carlos Gamerro and Edmundo Paz Soldán

1. The majority of the scant criticism that currently exists on *Las Islas* focuses on its depiction of the aftermath of the Malvinas War. See Molina as one such example.
2. The majority of criticism of Paz Soldán's work is devoted to *Sueños digitales*. See especially Amar Sánchez, Ramos González, and Montoya Juárez.

3. The figure of the hacker has been appearing more often in Latin American film and literature. In addition to *Las Islas* and *El delirio de Turing*, we see the figure in the Mexican film *Nicotina* and in the novel *Milonga de Hackers* by the Argentine writer Dante Garavaglia.
4. The passage is also an allusion to the literary nature of Albert's identity. He quotes Borges's story "El inmortal" almost verbatim when he discusses his knowledge of language. The repetition of "Soy una hormiga eléctrica" is a direct reference to Philip Dick's story "The Electric Ant," a story in which a robot, designed to think he was human, awakes from an accident to discover his mechanical nature. I develop these references in the article "Edmundo Paz Soldán and His Precursors."

5 Video Heads and Rewound Bodies: Cyborg Memories in Rodrigo Fresán and Alberto Fuguet

1. I refer, in particular, to Diana Palaversich's criticism of Fuguet as uninterested in anything that is not himself and as more inclined to criticize the Left than Right-leaning neoliberal policies of 1990s Chile (37–38). Ana María Amar Sánchez is more generous with her evaluation of the politics of McOndo; see her essay "Literature in the Margins" as well as her book.
2. See also Cárcamo Huechante's book for an examination of the various conservative economic forces at play in Fuguet's work.

Bibliography

Adams, Jon K. "Hacker Ideology (aka Hacking Freedom) in Recent Science Fiction Novels." In *Bildschirmfiktionen: Interferenzen zwischen Literatur und neuen Medien.* Ed. Julika Griem. Tübingen: Narr, 1998, 295–303.
Amar Sánchez, Ana María. "Literature in the Margins: a new canon for the XXI century?" *Ciberletras* 15 (2006).
———. *Juegos de seducción y traición. Literatura y cultura de masas.* Rosario: Beatriz Viterbo, 2000.
Avelar, Idelber. *The Untimely Present: Postdictatorial Latin American Fiction and the Task of Mourning.* Durham, NC: Duke University Press, 1999.
Badmington, Neil. "Approaching Posthumanism." In *Posthumanism.* Ed. Neil Badmington. New York: Palgrave, 2000, 1–10.
Balderston, Daniel. "Lecturas repetidas." In *Ricardo Piglia: Una poética sin límites.* Ed. Adriana Rodríguez Pérsico. Pittsburgh, PA: IILI, 2004, 293–98.
Baudrillard, Jean. *Art and Artefact.* Ed. Nicholas Zurgrugg. London: Sage, 1997.
Benjamin, Walter. *Illuminations.* Ed. Hannah Arendt. Trans. Harry Zohn. New York: Schocken, 1968.
Blade Runner. Dir. Ridley Scott. Warner Bros., 1982.
Borinsky, Alicia. *All Night Movie.* Trans. Cola Franzen and Alicia Borinsky. Evanston, IL: Northwestern University Press, 2002.
———. *Cine continuado.* Buenos Aires: Corregidor, 1997.
———. *Mina cruel.* Buenos Aires: Corregidor, 1989.
Boullosa, Carmen. *Cielos de la tierra.* Mexico City: Alfaguara, 1997.
———. *Duerme.* Mexico City: Alfaguara, 1995.
Bratosevich, Nicolás. *Ricardo Piglia y la cultura de la contravención.* Buenos Aires: Atuel, 1997.

Brown, J. Andrew. "Cyborgs, Post-Punk and the Neobaroque: Ricardo Piglia's *La ciudad ausente*." *Comparative Literature* 61.3 (2009): 316–26.

———. "Humanismo cyborg: El poshumano letrado en América latina." *Revista de crítica literaria latinoamericana* 34.68 (2008): 19–32.

———. "Identidad poshumana en *Lóbulo* de Eugenia Prado." *Revista Iberoamericana* 73.221 (2007): 801–12.

———. "Edmundo Paz Soldán and His Precursors: Borges, Dick and the SF Canon." *Science Fiction Studies* 34 (2007): 473–83.

———. "Sobrevivientes y cyborgs: Cine argentino al final de la dictadura." In *Cine, Historia y Sociedad: Cine argentino y brasileño desde los años 80*. Ed. Gastón Lillo and Walter Moser. Ottawa: Legas, 2007, 115–29.

———. "Hacking the Past: Edmundo Paz Soldán's *El delirio de Turing* and Carlos Gamerro's *Las Islas*." *Arizona Journal of Hispanic Cultural Studies* 10 (2006): 87–107.

———. "Ripped Stitches: Consumerism, Technology, and Posthuman Identity in Rafael Courtoisie's *Tajos*." *Journal of Latin American Cultural Studies* 15.2 (2006): 127–42.

———. "Life Signs: Ricardo Piglia's Cyborgs." In *Science, Literature, and Film in the Hispanic World*. Ed. Jerry Hoeg and Kevin Larsen. New York: Palgrave, 2006, 87–107.

———. "Reading *Rayuela* in the Rayuel-O-Matic." *Revista Canadiense de Estudios Hispánicos* 29 (2005): 379–96.

———. *Test Tube Envy: Science and Power in Argentine Narrative*. Lewisburg, PA: Bucknell University Press, 2005.

Buenos Aires Vice Versa. Dir. Alejandro Agresti. Agresti Films, 1996.

Bundtzen, Lynda K. "Monstrous Mothers: Medusa, Grendel, and Now Alien." In *The Gendered Cyborg*. Ed. Gill Kirkup. London: Routledge, 2000, 101–09.

Cárcamo Huechante, Luis. *Tramas del mercado: imaginación económica, cultura pública y literatura en el Chile de fines del siglo veinte*. Santiago: Cuarto Propio, 2007.

Carpentier, Alejo. "The Baroque and the Marvellous Real." In *Magical Realism: Theory, History, Community*. Ed. Wendy Faris and Lois Parkinson Zamora. Durham, NC: Duke University Press, 1995, 89–108.

Colás, Santiago. *Latin American Postmodernity*. Durham, NC: Duke University Press, 1994.

Cortázar, Julio. *Rayuela*. Ed. Julio Ortega and Saúl Yurkievich. Paris: ALLCA XX, 1991.

Courtoisie, Rafael. *Caras extrañas*. Madrid: Lengua de Trapo, 2001.

———. *Tajos*. Madrid: Lengua de Trapo, 2000.

Decante Araya, Stéphanie. "Del valor material al valor simbólico: Tensiones y negociaciones con el horizonte de expectativas en el Chile de los 90. El 'caso Fuguet.'" *Arizona Journal of Hispanic Studies* 9 (2005): 181–91.

Deleuze, Gilles. *Cinema I: The Movement Image*. Minneapolis, MN: University of Minnesota Press, 1986.

Deleuze, Gilles and Félix Guattari. *Anti-Oedipus: Capitalism and Schizophrenia*. Minneapolis, MN: University of Minnesota Press, 1983.

Demaría, Laura. *Argentina-s: Ricardo Piglia dialoga con la generación del 37 en la discontinuidad*. Buenos Aires: Corregidor, 1999.

Dick, Philip K. *Selected Short Stories of Philip K. Dick*. Ed. Jonathan Lethem. New York: Pantheon, 2002.

———. *Do Androids Dream of Electric Sheep?* New York: Del Rey, 1968, 1996.

Doane, Mary Ann. "Technophilia: Technology, Representation and the Feminine." In *The Gendered Cyborg: A Reader*. Ed. Gill Kirkup. London: Routledge, 2000, 110–21.

Durán, Javier. "Utopia, Heterotopia, and Memory in Carmen Boullosa's *Cielos de la Tierra*." *Studies in the Literary Imagination* 33.1 (2000): 51–64.

Flitterman-Lewis, Sandy. "Psychoanalysis, Film, and Television." In *Channels of Discourse, Reassembled*. Ed. Robert Allen. Chapel Hill, NC: University of North Carolina Press, 1992, 203–46.

Foster, Thomas. *The Souls of Cyberfolk: Posthumanism as Vernacular Theory*. Minneapolis, MN: University of Minnesota Press, 2005.

Foucault, Michel. *Discipline and Punish*. Trans. Alan Sheridan. 2nd ed. New York: Vintage, 1995.

Fresán, Rodrigo. *Mantra*. Barcelona: Mondadori, 2001.

———. *La velocidad de las cosas*. Buenos Aires: Tusquets Editores, 1998.

Fuguet, Alberto. *Cortos*. New York: HarperCollins, 2005.

———. *Shorts*. Trans. Ezra E. Fitz. New York: HarperCollins, 2005.

———. *Por favor, rebobinar*. Santiago: Alfaguara, 1999.

Fuguet, Alberto and Sergio Gómez. *McOndo*. Barcelona: Grijalbo Mondadori, 1996.

Gabilondo, Joseba. "Postcolonial Cyborgs: Subjectivity in the Age of Cybernetic Reproduction." In *The Cyborg Handbook*. Ed. Chris Gray. New York: Routledge, 1995, 423–32.

Gamerro, Carlos. *Las Islas.* Buenos Aires: Simurg, 1998.
Garavaglia, Dante. *Milonga de hackers.* Buenos Aires: La Colmena, 2001.
García Canclini, Néstor. *Cultura y comunicación.* La Plata: University of La Plata Press, 1997.
———. *Culturas híbridas: Estrategias para entrar y salir de la modernidad.* Mexico City: Paidos, 1990.
Gibson, William. *Neuromancer.* New York: Ace, 1985.
Gray, Chris Hables. *Cyborg Citizen.* New York: Routledge, 2002.
Gundermann, Christian. "Todos gozamos como locos: Los medios de comunicación masivas como módulo de filiación entre Manuel Puig y Alberto Fuguet." *Chasqui: Revista de Literatura Latinoamericana* 30.1 (May 2001): 29–42.
Gutiérrez Mouat, Ricardo. "Literatura y globalización: Tres novelas post-macondistas." *Inti: Revista de Literatura Hispánica* 55–56 (Spring–Autumn 2002): 3–28.
Halberstam, Judith and Ira Livingston. "Introduction: Posthuman Bodies" In *Posthuman Bodies.* Ed. Judith Halberstam and Ira Livingston. Bloomington, IN: Indiana University Press, 1995, 1–22.
Haraway, Donna. *Modest Witness@Second Millenium. FemaleMan Meets OncoMouse: Feminism and Technoscience.* New York: Routledge, 1997.
———. *Simians, Cyborgs, and Women: The Reinvention of Nature.* New York: Routledge, 1991.
Hardt, Michael and Antonio Negri. *Empire.* Cambridge: Harvard University Press, 2000.
Hayles, N. Katherine. *My Mother Was a Computer: Digital Subjects and Literary Texts.* Chicago, IL: University of Chicago Press, 2005.
———. *Writing Machines.* Cambridge: MIT University Press, 2003.
———. *How We Became Posthuman: Virtual Bodies in Cybernetics, Literature, and Informatics.* Chicago, IL: University of Chicago Press, 1999.
Herbrechter, Stefan and Ivan Callus, eds. *Cy-Borges: Memories of the Posthuman in the Work of Jorge Luis Borges.* Lewisburg, PA: Bucknell University Press, 2009.
Hoeg, Jerry. *Science, Technology, and Latin American Narrative in the Twentieth Century and Beyond.* Bethlehem, PA: Lehigh University Press, 2000.
Holmberg, Eduardo. *Horacio Kalibang o los autómatas.* Buenos Aires, 1879.

Hopenhayn, Martin. "No Way Out: Comentario a Lóbulo de Eugenia Prado." *Critica.cl.* 24 February 2005, http://www.critica.cl/html/m_hopenhayn_01.htm.

Jagoe, Eva-Lynn Alicia. "The Disembodied Machine: Matter, Feminity and Nation in Piglia's *La ciudad ausente.*" *Latin American Literary Review* 23.45 (1995): 5–17.

Jameson, Fredric. *Postmodernism, or, the Cultural Logic of Late Capitalism.* Durham, NC: Duke University Press, 1991.

Janes, Linda. "Introduction to Part Two." In *The Gendered Cyborg: A Reader.* Ed. Gill.

Kirkup, Linda Janes, Kath Woodward, and Fiona Hovenden. London: Routledge, 2000, 91–100.

Kirkup, Gill, Linda Janes, Kath Woodward, and Fiona Hovenden. *The Gendered Cyborg: A Reader.* London: Routledge, 2000.

Kittler, Friedrich. *Gramophone, Film, Typewriter.* Stanford, CA: Stanford University Press, 1999.

LaCapra, Dominick. *Writing History, Writing Trauma.* Baltimore, MD: Johns Hopkins University Press, 2001.

———. *Representing the Holocaust: History, Theory, Trauma.* Ithaca, NY: Cornell University Press, 1994.

Landow, George. *Hypertext 2.0: The Convergence of Contemporary Critical Theory and Technology.* Baltimore, MD: Johns Hopkins University Press, 1997.

Latham, Rob. *Consuming Youth: Vampires, Cyborgs, and the Culture of Consumption.* Chicago, IL: University of Chicago Press, 2002.

Levinson, Brett. "Trans(re)lations: Dictatorship, Disaster and the 'Literary Politics' of Piglia's *Respiración artificial.*" *Latin American Literary Review* 25.49 (1997): 91–120.

Liu, Alan. *The Laws of Cool.* Chicago, IL: University of Chicago Press, 2004.

Martín-Barbero, Jesús. *Oficio de cartógrafo.* Mexico City: UNAM, 2003.

———. *Al sur de la modernidad: Comunicación, globalización y multiculturalidad.* Pittsburgh, PA: IILI, 2001.

Masiello, Francine. *The Art of Transition.* Durham, NC: Duke University Press, 2001.

———. "Este pobre fin de siglo: Intellectuals and Cultural Minorities during Argentina's Ten Years of Democracy." In *Latin American Postmodernisms.* Ed. Richard Young. Amsterdam: Rodopi, 1997, 239–55.

The Matrix. Dir. Andy Wachowski and Larry Wachowski. Warner Bros., 1999.

McLuhan, Marshall and Eric McLuhan. *The Laws of Media: The New Science*. Toronto: University of Toronto Press, 1992.

Metropolis. Dir. Fritz Lang. Universum Film, 1927.

Molina, María Elena. "Guerra de Malvinas: la literatura argentina y el desafío de la autocrítica." *Espéculo* 13.39 (July 2008), http://www.ucm.es/info/especulo/.

Montoya Juárez, Jesús. "Ni apocalípticos ni integrados: medios audiovisuales en tres narradores del Sur de América." *Revista Iberoamericana* 73.221 (2007): 887–904.

Ndalianis, Angela. *Neo-Baroque Aesthetics and Contemporary Entertainment*. Cambridge, MA: The MIT Press, 2004.

Nicotina. Dir. Hugo Rodríguez. Arenas Entertainment, 2003.

Niebylski, Dianna. *Humoring Resistance: Laughter and the Excessive Body in Latin American Fiction*. Binghamton, NY: State University of New York Press, 2004.

———. "Spectacle and Nomadic Bodies in Alicia Borinsky's *Mina cruel* and *Cine continuado*." *Letras Femeninas* 27.2 (2001): 54–67.

O'Connell, Patrick. "Santiago's Children of the Dictatorship: Anamnesis versus Amnesia in Alberto Fuguet's *Por favor, rebobinar*." *Chasqui: Revista de Literatura Latinoamericana* 34.1 (May 2005): 32–41.

Palaversich, Diana. *De Macondo a McOndo. Senderos de la postmodernidad latinoamericana*. Mexico City: Plaza y Valdés, 2005.

Paz Soldán, Edmundo. *El delirio de Turing*. Buenos Aires: Alfaguara, 2005.

———. "*Mantra* (2001), de Rodrigo Fresán, y la novela de la multiplicidad de la información." *Chasqui: Revista de Literatura Latinoamericana* 32.1 (May 2003): 98–109.

———. "Escritura y cultura audiovisual en *Por favor, rebobinar* de Alberto Fuguet." *Latin American Literary Review* 30.59 (May 2001): 43–54.

———. *Sueños digitales*. La Paz: Alfaguara, 2000.

Piglia, Ricardo. *The Absent City*. Trans. Sergio Waisman. Durham, NC: Duke University Press, 2000.

———. *Artificial Respiration*. Trans. Daniel Balderston. Durham, NC: Duke University Press, 1994.

———. *Cuentos con dos rostros*. Mexico City: UNAM, 1992.

———. *La ciudad ausente*. Barcelona: Anagrama, 1992, 2003.

———. *Respiración artificial*. Barcelona: Anagrama, 1980, 2001.

Poblete, Juan. "La voz del amo: Representación e instituciones en los estudios latinoamericanos." *Dispositio* 22.49 (1997): 103–20.

Porush, David. *This Soft Machine: Cybernetic Fiction.* New York: Metheun, 1985.
Prado, Eugenia. *Lóbulo.* Santiago: Cuarto Propio, 1998.
———. *Cierta femenina oscuridad.* Santiago: Cuarto Propio, 1996.
Pubis angelical. Dir. Raúl De la Torre. Arte Diez, 1982.
Puig, Manuel. *Pubis angelical.* Buenos Aires: Seix Barral, 2004.
Ramos González, Rosario. "La fábula electrónica: Respuestas al terror político y las utopías informáticas en Edmundo Paz Soldán." *MLN* 118 (2003): 466–91.
Romero-Ghiretti, Gabriela. "Fleeing Subjectivities and Politics of Resistance in Alicia Borinsky's *Cine continuado*." *Letras femeninas* 35.2 (Winter 2009): 289–310.
Ruppert, Peter. "Technology and the Construction of Gender in Fritz Lang's Metropolis." *Genders* 32 (2000). http://www.genders.org/g32/g32_ruppert.html.
Ryan, Marie Laure. *Narrative as Virtual Reality: Immersion and Interactivity in Literature and Electronic Media.* Baltimore, MD: Johns Hopkins University Press, 2001.
———. *Possible Worlds, Artificial Intelligence, and Narrative Theory.* Bloomington, IN: Indiana University Press, 1991.
Rybczybski, Witold. *Taming the Tiger: The Struggle to Control Technology.* New York: Penguin, 1983.
Sabato, Ernesto. *Hombres y engranajes/Heterodoxia.* Madrid: Alianza Editorial, 2002.
Sandoval, Chela. "New Sciences: Cyborg Feminism and the Methodology of the Oppressed." In *The Cyborg Handbook.* Ed. Chris Gray. New York: Routledge, 1995, 404–22.
Sarlo, Beatriz. *Escenas de la vida posmoderna: Intelectuales, arte y videocultura en la Argentina.* Buenos Aries: Ariel, 1994.
Sassón-Henry, Perla. *Borges 2.0: From Text to Virtual Worlds.* New York: Peter Lang, 2007.
Scarry, Elaine. *The Body in Pain: The Making and Unmaking of the World.* New York: Oxford University Press, 1985.
Shenassa, Shirin. "The Lack of Materiality in Latin American Media Theory." In *Latin American Literature and Mass Media.* Ed. Edmundo Paz Soldán and Debra Castillo. New York: Garland, 2001, 249–69.
Sorbille, Martín. "Argentine Military Terrorism (1976–1983): Insatiable Desire, Disappearances, and Eruption of the Traumatic Gaze-Real in Alejandro Agresti's Film *Buenos Aires Viceversa* (1996)." *Cultural Critique* 68 (Winter 2008): 86–128.

Stam, Robert. "Television News and Its Spectator." In *Film and Theory*. Ed. Robert Stam and Toby Miller. Malden, MA: Blackwell Publishers, 2000, 361–80.

Stephenson, Neil. *Snow Crash*. New York: Bantam, 1992.

Taylor, Claire. "Cities, Codes and Cyborgs in Carmen Boullosa's *Cielos de la tierra*." *Bulletin of Spanish Studies* 80.4 (2003): 477–92.

Taylor, Claire and Thea Pitman, eds. *Latin American Cyberculture and Cyberliterature*. Liverpool: Liverpool University Press, 2007.

Thomas, Douglas. *Hacker Culture*. Minneapolis, MN: University of Minneapolis Press, 2002.

Thompkins, Cynthia. "Experimentación y concientizacón en *Buenos Aires Viceversa* de Alejandro Agresti." *Literatura e Autoritarismo* 4 (December 2001): 27–33.

Thompson, Currie. "Against All Odds: Argentine Cinema, 1976–1991." *Post Script: Essays in Film and the Humanities* 11.3 (1992): 32–45.

Tiempo de revancha. Dir. Adolfo Aristarain. Aries Cinematográfica, 1982.

Williams, Gareth. *The Other Side of the Popular: Neoliberalism and Subalternity in Latin America*. Durham, NC: Duke University Press, 2002.

Wilson Reginato, Mike. *El púgil*. Santiago: Forja, 2008.

Žižek, Slavoj. *On Belief*. London and New York: Routledge, 2001.

Index

abuse, 15, 19, 101, 106, 121–22, 146
  see also dictatorship, Dirty War, rape, torture, violence
Adam, Villiers de l'Isle, 39
Adobe Photoshop, 124, 125, 128, 130
advertising, 2, 6, 77–78, 136, 110
  see also commercial, marketing, media
aesthetic, 39, 82, 84, 182
  cinematic, 172–73
  cybernetic, 28, 168
Agresti, Alejandro, 182
AI, 161
AIDS, 154, 156
Alien, 179
alien, 149, 150
Allende, Isabel, 164
ambiguity, ambiguous, 10, 29, 32, 37, 45, 46, 48, 73, 74, 75, 95, 122
  biological, 10
  of the body, 7
  boundary 11, 181
La ansiedad (Link), 177
answering machine, 107
  as mechanical voice, 108
  as prosthetic ear, 108
anticommunist, 6, 137
Anti-Oedipus (Deleuze and Guattari), 61, 98
antitechnological, 72

apocalypse, apocalyptic, 49, 52, 53, 136, 144
Apollo XI, 109
Apple computer, 170–71, 173
  see also computer
Argentina, 1, 2, 4, 5, 6, 9–42, 75, 102, 113–15, 118, 122, 147, 153, 161, 179, 180, 182, 183
  see also dictatorship, Dirty War, neoliberal, police state
Aristarain, Adolfo, 4, 5, 10, 15–23, 179
art, 2, 5, 89, 114, 119, 164, 165–66, 175, 177
  artistic process, 163–64
  artists, 1, 7, 57, 165
  performance, 2
  see also media, photography, theater
artificial, 1, 2, 4, 11, 15, 19, 20, 22, 24, 26, 30, 31, 33, 34, 35, 36, 38, 39, 41, 48, 54, 55, 59, 63, 64, 70, 74, 84, 105, 108, 125, 129, 137, 144, 161
heart, 4, 5, 9, 13, 14, 15
human, 1
limbs, 110
Auermann, Nadja, 125, 126
autism, 25
avatar, 134, 136, 137, 138, 141, 143
  see also computer, hacker, identity
Avelar, Idelber, 42, 179, 180

Balderston, Daniel, 180
Banzer, Hugo, 114, 123, 124
Baradit, Jorge, 177
Barbie, 10
baroque, 176
Batman, 85–86, 87, 88, 94
Battleship Potemkin, 171–72
Battlestar Galactica, 161
Baudrillard, Jean, 29, 32, 180
Benedetti, Mario, 80
Bible, 53
biography, 93, 99, 138, 148, 163
bio-media, 182
birth, 22, 34, 37, 41, 51, 72, 74, 93, 108, 109, 140
   see also child, family, genesis story, origin, pregnancy, procreation, reproduction
Bisama, Alvaro, 177
bisexuality, 46–47
   see also erotic, feminine, heteronormative, heterosexual, heterotopia, queer
Blade Runner, 9–10, 13–15, 22, 129, 179
blind, blindness, 99, 101, 103
   see also eye
body, 2, 4–7, 9, 10–14, 16–23, 25, 27, 32–35, 37–38, 40, 42–48, 50, 54, 55, 58–62, 64–75, 79, 80–82, 84–85, 87, 90, 92–95, 97–99, 101, 103–04, 108–10, 111, 115, 117–18, 120–31, 133–34, 138, 140–50, 152–56, 158–61, 168–69, 173, 175–77, 180–81, 183
city as, 167
codes inscribed in posthuman, 143
constituted by numbers and computer language, 134
cybernetic/cyborg, 5, 14–15, 18–22, 34–36, 38, 41–42, 48, 66–67, 74–75, 85, 111, 122, 138–39, 142, 144, 146, 167, 177, 180

digitalized, 130
as filter, 122
food functioning as, 82
globalized, 153
and machine, 16–17, 20, 24, 29, 67, 69, 74, 118
as meat, 70
postfamilial, 13
posthuman, 5–7, 13, 34, 50–51, 54, 56, 66, 71, 75, 79, 81, 130–31, 133, 143–44, 159, 165, 167
reduced to codes, 143
techno-organic, 7
and text, 3, 25, 56
   see also flesh, scar
Bolaño, Roberto, 147
Bolívar, Simón, 114
Bolivia, 2, 6, 113–15, 123–44, 182
Borges, Jorge Luis, 4, 183
Borinsky, Alicia, 5, 10, 43–48, 75, 174, 180
Boullosa, Carmen, 5, 43, 48–59, 75–76, 174, 180, 181
boundary, 12, 56, 81–83, 87, 95, 108, 119
ambiguous, 11, 181
between human/animal/machine, 10–11, 83, 181
between natural and artificial, 108
between science fiction and social reality, 12
boundary-crossing cybernetic life forms, 10
cyborg's ability to challenge/transgress, 10, 35, 38, 56, 58, 61, 81, 83
set by history/race/gender, 56
brain, 27, 88, 139, 158, 159, 163, 168
cybernetic, 160
prosthetic, 149, 161
tumor, 147
Brazil, 177

INDEX

breath, breathing, 41–42, 55, 64, 89, 90
Buenos Aires, 5–6, 77, 114, 177, 182
Buenos Aires Vice Versa, 182
building, 16, 20, 115, 117–18
  see also corporation, skyscraper
Byrne, David, 154

cadaver, 147
  as mother of text, 74
camera, 13, 16, 58, 60, 98, 101, 111, 126, 155, 156, 158, 159, 160, 161, 162, 167, 169
  as gun, 182
  as prosthesis for identity, 148
  as replacement for eyes, 99, 101, 169
  see also cinema, film, photography, television, video
Campbell, Naomi, 47, 125–26
cancer, 37
  see also death, medical
capitalism, capitalist, 4, 10, 12, 14, 16, 59, 93, 98, 110, 111, 153, 181
  critiques, 131, 181
  dehumanizing effect of, 17
  Fordian, 14
  international, 79, 97, 111, 137
  patriarchal, 11, 12
  see also market, money
Caras extrañas (Courtoisie), 5, 6, 80, 102, 106–10, 181, 182
Caribbean, 177
carpal tunnel syndrome, 142
Carpentier, Alejo, 176–77
La casa de los espíritus (Allende), 163–64
cattle prod, 36–38
  as sexual prosthesis, 38
  see also dictatorship, pain, picana, police state, torture, violence
CBS, 101
celluloid, 149, 157, 159, 161
  see also film

censorship, 10, 21, 101
child, childhood, 27, 55, 72, 95, 96–97, 99, 100, 105, 109, 140, 147, 150, 151, 168–69, 170, 171
  audiovisual, 169
  see also birth, family, parent, procreation
Chile, 2, 5, 57–59, 157, 164, 177, 183
CIA, 132
Ciberhacktivismo, 144
Cielos de la Tierra (Boullosa), 5, 43, 48–58
Cien años de soledad (Márquez), 49, 99, 100
Cierta feminidad oscura (Prado), 59
Cine continuado (Borinsky), 5, 43–48, 58, 180
cinema, 2, 9, 10, 14, 16, 21, 60, 81, 84, 85, 97, 98, 110, 148, 158, 171–73, 182
  cinematic aesthetic, 172, 173
  cinematic suture theory, 182
  cinematographic consciousness, 98
  hybridizing possibilities of, 98
  as manifesto, 172
  as revolutionary instrument, 172
  see also film
city, 4, 16, 77, 96, 109, 131–32, 137, 147, 152, 167–68
  as technological body, 167
La ciudad ausente (Piglia), 4, 22–42, 74, 122, 176, 180
cleaving, cleavage, 45, 80–81, 172–73, 181
  see also cut, seam
code, 2, 54, 123, 127, 131, 133–35, 137, 141, 143, 157
  inscribed in posthuman bodies, 131, 143, 144
  mechanical, 122
  see also computer, hack

commercial, commercials, 96–97, 101, 109, 111, 132, 136, 181
  as stitches, 110
  see also advertising, marketing, media, television
commercialism, 109, 136
commodity, commoditize, 81, 93, 97, 137
  commodization of emotion, 93
  desire for, 93, 97, 111
communication, 17, 19, 45, 72, 88, 129, 153
  subversive, 31
  see also language, voice
community, 12, 49, 50, 52–56, 136
computer, 2, 11, 20, 20, 54, 59, 78, 88, 114–17, 119, 123–31, 133–39, 141, 143, 157, 160, 163, 164, 166, 167, 170, 171, 173
  as location of relationship, 129, 171
  scientist, 131, 133
  see also Apple computer, code, email, hack, hard drive, MacIntosh, PowerBook
conscience, 143
consciousness, 24, 31, 42, 58, 59, 66, 67, 71, 88, 93, 98, 121, 128, 158
  cinematographic, 98
  media and, 93
  national, 103, 109
  posthuman, 62
  see also psyche, unconscious
consumerism, consumerist, 80, 81, 92, 93, 109, 110, 113, 136, 137, 160, 176
  bodies, 80
  capitalistic, 181
  identity, 79, 81
  see also advertising, marketing
Consuming Youth (Latham), 181
consumption, 29, 79, 93
  cyborg as a figure of post-Fordist consumption, 181

media, 7, 102
  of the visual image, 98
control, 9, 14, 18–19, 29, 30, 46, 69, 70, 74, 75, 82, 88, 131, 138–39, 159, 161, 166, 173
  technology of, 17, 54, 118, 123
  see also surveillance
El corazón de Voltaire (López Nieves), 177
Cordobazo, 102
corporation, 16, 17, 19, 20, 117, 136, 141
  biomechanical corporate body, 17
  multinational, 14, 15
  see also building, capitalism, money
corporeal, 42, 48, 60, 62, 70, 92, 95, 137, 169
  identity, 1, 80
  reactions, 64
corruption, 17, 20, 21, 107, 115, 118, 136, 141
  see also corporation, government
Cortázar, Julio, 1
Cortés, Hernán, 151
Cortos (Fuguet), 170, 172
Costner, Kevin, 172
coup, 6
  see also military
coupling, 42, 46, 59, 60, 93, 94
cybernetic, 110
fuse foreign technology and Latin American bodies, 115
human/animal, 157
neoliberal policy with dictatorial practice, 115
"pleasurably tight," 10, 22, 36, 58, 69, 81, 111
  see also body, flesh, machine
Courtoisie, Rafael, 5–6, 77, 79–111, 147, 174, 181, 182
creator, 159
  see also genesis story, origin
crime, 5, 38, 41, 79, 101, 124
criminals, 130
Cuentos con dos rostros (Piglia), 180

INDEX

cultural, 3, 77, 103, 123, 130, 132, 133, 134, 147, 159, 173, 182
   blasphemy, 114
   expression, 2, 113, 146, 177
   identity, 2, 6
   minorities, 23
   production, 1, 2, 4, 7, 32, 177
   studies, 2
   theorists, 7
   theory, 7, 10, 32, 174
culture, 1–3, 5, 7, 22, 23, 36, 49, 53, 58, 75, 86, 114, 129, 131, 143, 147, 154, 155, 157, 159, 161, 175, 176
   abusive, 143
   cyberneticized, 153
   global, 79, 135, 146, 153, 176
   hacker, 133–35, 143
   mass, 7
   popular, 79, 150, 151, 159, 176
cut, 13, 15, 21, 80–85, 88, 96, 97, 99, 108, 110, 152, 172–73, 179
   between organic tissue and prosthetic technology, 110
   see also cleaving, seam
cybermestiza, cybermestizaje, 48, 56
cybernetic, 1, 2, 5, 10, 11, 14, 15, 18–23, 27, 31, 34–36, 38, 41–42, 54, 66–68, 70, 73–74, 78–79, 93, 98, 109–10, 117, 119, 122, 127, 129, 139, 141, 151–53, 155–56, 160–61, 163, 165, 167, 174, 176–77
   aesthetic, 28, 168
   brain, 160
   discourse, 156, 168
   fiction, 31
   film as "cyberneticizing" agent, 7
   language, 27, 31
   nature of narrative, 23
   state, 56
   theory, 31, 68
   see also bodies
cyber-personalities, 138

cyberpunk, 54, 69, 129, 169, 177
   literature, 3
cyberspace, 119, 132, 137, 175
   theorists, 175
"A Cyborg Manifesto" (Haraway), 10, 51, 75

Data, 52
death, 12, 14, 33, 34, 37, 56, 58, 69, 70, 73, 74, 80, 101, 157
   see also Dirty War, torture, trauma, war
deceit, 13, 84
decode, decrypt, 131, 132, 135, 141
   see also code, computer
deconstruction, deconstructionist, 11, 175, 181
dehumanizing, 17, 54, 153
Deleuze, Gilles, and Felix Guattari, 7, 58, 60–61, 67–68, 72, 74, 97–98
El delirio de Turing (Paz Soldán), 6, 115, 123, 131, 134, 183
democracy, 132
democratically elected, 6, 123, 124
De Palma, Brian, 172
desaparecido/a, disappeared, 27, 130
   photographs of, 130
desire, 13, 14, 40, 46, 48, 53, 55, 60, 62, 64, 66, 70, 72, 92–93, 109, 138, 139, 171
   for commodity, 93, 97, 111
   female, 72
Los detectives salvajes (Bolaño), 147
Dick, Philip K., 9, 129, 141, 183
dictatorship, dictatorial, 6–7, 9–10, 23, 39, 41, 80, 99–101, 109, 111, 115, 118, 123–24, 130–32, 137, 141, 143, 179
   corporation and, 17
   neoliberalism and, 114–15, 118, 133–34, 143, 145

dictatorship, dictatorial—*Continued*
   trauma & abuses, 14–15, 20, 22,
      24, 36, 38, 42, 43, 101, 106,
      110, 122, 123, 132, 146, 180
   see also Argentina, Dirty War,
      government, military,
      postdictatorship, surveillance,
      trauma
digital, 78, 79, 117, 123–32, 137,
   138, 155, 157, 170–71
   age, 4, 129
   sampler, 159–62
Dirty War, 9, 39, 182
   see also dictatorship, torture,
      violence
discipline, 17, 137, 159, 181
   technology of, 54
   see also Panopticon
discourse, 5, 49, 67, 147, 155, 169
   cybernetic, 156, 168
   networks, 29
   see also narrator
disease, 37, 143, 180
   see also virus
disembodiment, 58, 59, 70, 98
   hackers and, 134
   see also body, embodiment
dismember, 10, 36
Disneyland, 29, 180
*Do Androids Dream of Electric
   Sheep?* (Dick), 9, 129
doctor, 24, 26, 27, 35, 82, 161
   see also hospital, medical, surgery
Downs Syndrome, 122
dream, 12, 13, 14, 28, 46, 50, 51,
   52, 63, 129, 173
   see also nightmare
drug, 27, 126, 163
   culture, 154
Duerme (Boullosa), 56
dystopia, dystopic, 9, 53, 55
   see also utopia

ears, 17, 64, 66, 78
   answering machine as prosthetic,
      108

television as prosthetic, 105
   see also body, prosthesis
economic, economy, 3, 14, 19, 113,
   115, 131, 144, 146, 183
   global, 135
   policies, 113
   see also market, money
Eisenstein, Sergei, 171–72
"The Electric Ant" (Dick), 183
electroshock, 26–27, 37
   as representative of torture, 36
   torture, 36, 118
email, 128–29, 131, 132, 135,
   170–71
   see also computer
embodiment, 82, 122, 165
   hackers and, 134
   see also body, disembodiment
emotion, 34, 96
   commoditization of, 93
empire, 54
Empire (Negri and Hardt),
   11, 181
erotic, eroticism, 45, 48, 65,
   67–70, 74, 75, 119,
   138, 139
   virtual, 119, 120
   see also sex
Escenas de la vida postmoderna
   (Sarlo), 86
escrache, 102, 107, 182
Europe, 2, 3, 5, 15, 24, 41, 43, 49,
   55, 93, 174
L'Éve future (Adam), 39
evolution, 71, 152, 168, 169
   of the human body, 75
eye, 46, 56, 73, 78, 98, 99–101,
   109, 120, 140, 150, 155,
   158, 160
   "eye for an eye," 101
   prosthetic, 98, 169
   television functioning as, 99,
      101, 105
   television sets and cameras
      become prosthetic eye of
      nation, 100, 101

INDEX

fable
  cyborg, 11, 181
  electronic, 127
  see also myth
family, 5, 28, 33, 46, 52, 57, 59, 62, 71, 74, 75, 91, 138, 140, 157, 164, 169, 171
  destabilization of traditional structure, 50
  life, 181
  organic, 12, 50–51, 55, 59
  see also nuclear family, parents, pregnancy
father, 4, 13, 20, 36, 48, 50, 57, 59, 61–63, 74, 106, 109, 135
  crimes of mechanical father (torture), 38
  cyborg as unfaithful to, 38
  as inessential, 12, 52, 62–63
  see also birth, family, maternal, parent, pregnancy, reproduction
fear, 1, 35, 37, 39, 46, 63–64, 130
  see also pain, torture, trauma
feedback, 88, 94
  cybernetic, 67, 109, 127
  loop, 18, 67, 68, 90, 92, 109, 127, 139
  noose, 127
female, 9, 10, 11, 13, 23, 38, 39, 43, 44, 48, 58, 59, 60, 72, 75, 180
  instability and hybridity of female cyborg, 44
  rebellious/subversive figure, 14, 44, 48
  victim, 84
  see also feminine, feminist, woman, body
feminine, 5, 43–44, 46, 48, 59, 180
  identity, 44, 56
  see also gender, heteronormative, nuclear family, woman
feminist, feminism, 5, 10, 43, 73
  cyborg as element of, 10, 23, 43, 75

theory, 12, 179
third world, 48
  see also gender, woman
Fernández, Macedonio, 24, 25
fiction, 3, 11–12, 15, 23, 31, 42, 106, 123, 125, 132, 169
  cybernetic, 31
  machinery or technology of, 31
  realist, 176
  science fiction, 3, 6, 9, 12, 13, 15, 23, 50, 54, 58, 59, 64, 72, 78, 122, 141, 143, 150, 156, 158, 160, 161, 173, 176, 177
  video, 106
  as a way to understand trauma, 105
  see also language, narrative, novel, story-telling
film, 2, 4, 7, 9–10, 13–17, 20–22, 42, 64, 84–85, 96, 98, 104, 110, 113, 129, 147, 148–49, 150, 152, 157–58, 160, 161, 163, 170, 171, 172, 176, 179, 182, 183
  as "cyberneticizing" agent, 7
  memory as, 157
  noir, 14
  as prosthetic brain, 149
  theory, 7, 94, 98, 171
  see also cinema, media, radio, television, video
Finnegans Wake (Joyce), 30
first world technology, 123
  see also third world
flesh, 4, 9, 11, 13, 14, 18, 21, 22, 25, 34, 36, 38, 40–42, 44, 55, 58, 60–62, 66, 69, 70, 75, 81, 107–08, 119, 121–23, 137–39, 141, 143–44, 147, 152, 157, 159, 161, 167
  see also body
"flickering signifier" (Hayles), 127, 130
Flitterman-Lewis, Sandy, 97
food, 68, 79, 129
  functioning as body, 82

199

forget, 4, 36, 38, 63, 143, 148, 160
forgetting as a malfunction of memory, 149
  see also history, memory, past, story-telling
Foster, Thomas, 3
Foucault, Michel, 18, 167
France, 140, 147
Frankenstein (Shelley), 1, 38, 54, 161, 180
free trade, 113
  see also capitalism, market
Fresán, Rodrigo, 7, 145–47, 152–54, 156–58, 173, 176, 183
Freud, Sigmund, 110
Fuguet, Alberto, 7, 79, 145–46, 157–58, 161, 163–64, 166–73, 176, 183

Gamerro, Carlos, 6, 10, 113–15, 117–18, 121–22, 133, 139, 143–44, 182
García Canclini, Nestor, 7, 181
García Márquez, Gabriel, 57, 99–100
Garden of Eden, 12, 50, 53, 63
  see also genesis story, origin, religion
gender, 5, 10, 12–13, 23, 32, 43, 45–48, 51, 52, 56, 57, 58, 75, 174, 176, 180
  identity, 43, 59
  liberation, 59
  see also feminist, heteronormative, nuclear family
The Gendered Cyborg (Kirkup), 10
genesis story, 150
  see also birth, Garden of Eden, origin, religion
Gibson, William, 129, 141
global, 7, 97, 110, 111, 136, 137, 138, 146, 175, 176, 177
  culture, 79, 135, 146, 147, 153, 176
  economy, 133, 137

messages and goods specifically coded as, 114
  technology, 118
globalization, 113, 153, 177
god, goddess, 87, 109, 151, 152, 158, 159
  see also religion
government, 9, 17, 39, 74, 103, 104, 113, 115, 130–34, 136, 137, 141
  abuse, 102, 122
  secrets, 122
  see also dictatorship, power
Gray, Chris, 2
Guevara, Ernesto "Che", 124
gun
  camera as, 182

hack, hacker, 7, 115–19, 122, 127, 131–35, 137–38, 141, 143–44, 183
  culture, 133–34, 143
  as hero and antihero, 141
  iconoclastic, 141
  literature & lore, 135, 141
  as menace, 134
  posthuman/cyborg, 120, 122, 139, 142
  and revolutionary tendencies, 135
  see also code, computer, decode, handle, software
Halberstam, Judith, 13, 50
hallucinations, 72
  see also insanity, madness, paranoia
handle, 134–35, 138
  see also hack
Hannah, Darryl, 10
Haraway, Donna, 2, 4, 5, 7, 10–13, 23, 25–27, 31, 32, 34, 36, 38, 41, 45, 46, 48, 50–54, 58–60, 62–63, 69, 71, 74–75, 81, 83, 93, 111, 140, 143, 148, 157, 161, 173, 181
hard drive, hard disk, 127, 164, 166
  see also computer

Hardt, Michael and Antonio Negri, 11, 27, 181
Hayles, N. Katherine, 2, 3, 7, 10–12, 31, 34, 40, 58–59, 65, 75, 81, 83, 88, 92, 117, 127, 130, 131, 141, 144, 148, 154, 160, 171
heart, 9, 14, 15, 25, 27, 44, 45, 55, 64, 91, 117, 153, 154, 155, 168
  artificial, 4, 5, 13, 14, 15
  clockwork, 13, 15, 42
  latidos digitales (digital heartbeats), 155
heaven, 57, 158
  see also religion
hell, 158
  see also religion
Hembros (Prado Bassi), 57
hero, 98, 127, 141
  cyborg as, 7
  hacker as antihero and, 141
heteronormative, 2, 5, 46, 169
  see also gender, heterosexual, heterotopia, nuclear family, queer
heterosexual, 59, 74, 168
  see also gender, heteronormative, heterotopia
heterotopias, 57
hierarchy, 5, 10, 11, 14, 16, 25, 59
  see also power
"Hijos" (Fuguet), 170
Historia argentina (Fresán), 153
history, 9, 27, 39, 40, 42, 50–52, 56–57, 75, 80, 98, 109, 118, 146, 150–52, 174, 179, 180
  altering, 130
  national, 110
  see also memory, past, storytelling
Hitler, Adolph, 151
Hollywood, 9, 13, 173
Holmberg, Eduardo, 1, 176
Holocaust studies
  role of television in national trauma, 182

Hombre artificial (Quiroga), 1
Hombre y engranajes (Sabato), 1
Hopenhayn, Martin, 181
Horacio Kalibang o los autómatas (Holmberg), 1
hospital, 13, 14, 24
  see also doctor, medical, surgery
How We Became Posthuman (Hayles), 10
humanist, 52
humanity, 90, 127, 143–44, 161
human rights, 24
  see also dictatorship
hybrid, hybridity, hybridization, 3, 11–12, 19, 21, 25, 27, 34, 38, 39, 41, 48, 56, 74, 97, 114, 115, 124, 127, 132, 142, 152
  see also boundary, cybernetic
hyperinflation, 113
hypertext, hypertextual, 31, 32, 180
  experience of reading, 28, 30
  machine, 42
  theory, 29, 180
  virtual, 37

iconoclastic
  cyborg, 59, 181
  hacker, 141
identity, 1–4, 10, 21, 22, 27, 31, 33, 34, 40, 41, 43–44, 50, 56, 58, 65, 72, 77–81, 83–85, 88–89, 92–93, 98, 100, 110, 117, 121, 123, 126, 132–35, 137, 142, 148–52, 158, 160, 163, 167, 175, 177, 183
  cultural, 2
  cyborg, 6, 7, 10, 11, 25, 27, 32, 34, 35, 36, 37, 39, 41, 43, 46, 48–49, 51, 59, 61, 64, 69, 75, 77–81, 110–11, 117, 142, 148, 157, 162, 176
  hybrid, 97, 151
  national, 150

identity—*Continued*
 posthuman, 3, 10, 11, 12, 24, 25, 41–42, 43, 51, 58, 59, 62, 65, 72, 74, 78–80, 90, 92, 97, 110, 115, 117–18, 123, 131–32, 137–38, 140–43, 146, 154, 158, 160–61, 169, 173–74
image, imagery, 3, 5, 15–17, 19–21, 23, 25, 27–28, 30, 32, 35, 47, 50, 56, 58, 60–69, 72–73, 77–79, 81–84, 88, 93–95, 97–98, 101, 104–05, 108, 110, 121–32, 137, 140–42, 149–50, 152, 156–60, 167, 169, 171, 173, 175–76, 179, 181
 see also camera, film, photograph
imaginary, 6, 59, 61, 63, 78, 90, 95, 97, 98, 109, 147
 Lacanian, 182
 media-based, 94, 96, 97, 103–04, 109
 posthuman, 150, 152
immigration, 1
implant, 11, 26–27, 110
 see also hybridity, prosthesis, technology
imports, 6, 115
individualism, 146
"El inmortal" (Borges), 183
insanity, 70, 124
 see also hallucinations, madness, paranoia, psychology, psychiatry
installation novel, 181
Instant Messenger, 170–71
insurgents, 6
internet, 4, 124, 125, 126, 132, 135, 170, 171, 177
 café, 138–39
 chatrooms, 132
 see also computer, email
Internet Movie Database, 170
interrogation, 24, 26–27, 35, 104
 see also dictatorship, police state, surveillance, tape recorder, torture

Jameson, Frederic, 182
Joyce, James, 24, 30
Judeo-Christian, 53
 see also religion
Jung, Carl, 165–66
 see also psychology

Kittler, Frederich, 93–94

Lacanian imaginary, 182
LaCapra, Dominick, 182
Landow, George, 29, 180
Lang, Fritz, 14
language, 2, 18, 23, 30–31, 49, 51, 53–55, 61–62, 68, 74, 108, 124, 126, 134, 140, 151, 183
 cybernetic, 27
 mechanical, 30, 61
 revolutionary potential of, 31
Las Islas (Gamerro), 6, 114–15, 182, 183
"Laws of Media" (McLuhan), 148
"The Liberator Símon Bolívar," 114
Link, Daniel, 177
Livingston, Ira, 13, 50, 140
Lóbulo (Prado), 5, 43, 58–74
López Nieves, Luis, 177
loss, 1, 13, 14, 15, 20, 22, 35, 69, 95, 99
love, 30, 32, 33, 46, 55, 66, 67, 68, 70, 72, 132
 prosthetic, 104
Lugones, Leopoldo, 36

machine, machinery, mechanical, 9, 11, 12, 13, 16–20, 21, 23, 24–30, 31–32, 34, 35, 37, 38, 40–42, 50, 53, 58, 60, 61, 64, 65, 67–69, 69, 70–71, 72, 74, 81, 83, 87, 88, 90, 94, 95, 97, 98, 101, 107–08, 110, 111, 117, 118, 121, 122, 123, 126, 130, 131, 132, 140–41, 142, 143, 144, 149, 153, 154–55, 160–61, 166, 167, 168, 174, 181

INDEX

answering, 107–08
biomechanical, 17, 29, 92, 93, 110, 176, 181, 183
intelligent, 11, 118
language, 31
story-telling/textual, 24, 48
as symbol of resistance/subversive, 31
see also prosthesis, technology
Macintosh, 125, 170–71
see also Apple computer, computer
madness, 71–72
see also insanity, paranoia, psychology
magazine, 123–24, 125, 147, 157
see also media
magic, 177
Latin America as magical (rejection of), 146
magical realism, 44, 163–64, 177
manipulation, 84, 96, 102, 105, 117, 125, 128, 130
of images, 88, 125–27, 130
Mantra (Fresán), 7, 145–47, 149, 151–57, 158
map, 150–51, 167, 168
electrical, 121
scars forming a, 121
of torture, 122
market, 31, 77, 133, 164, 165
forces, 97, 142
see also capitalism, economy, free trade
marketing, 5, 79
see also advertising, commercial, Metro 95.1
marriage, 24, 33, 35, 37, 45, 89, 104, 124, 129, 135, 169, 170, 171
see also family, relationship
Martín Barbero, Jesús, 7
Marxism, 6
Masiello, Francine, 23, 31, 114, 179, 182
mass culture, 7
see also culture, mass media

maternal, 179
see also mother
The Matrix, 64, 79, 161
McLuhan, Marshall, 7, 94, 147–48
McOndo, 146, 163–64, 173, 183
anthology, 79, 153
movement, 145, 157
see also Alberto Fuguet
meat, 96, 169
body as, 70
media, 5, 79, 83, 85, 93–94, 102–03, 147–48, 152, 182
cyborg/posthuman, 78, 85, 93
mass, 6, 44, 77, 79, 94, 147–48, 153, 157–60, 169, 181
and prosthesis, 150
see also advertising, commercial, film, magazine, news, radio, television, video
medical, 13, 25–26, 35, 62, 140, 141
medicalized cyborg, 26, 140
see also doctor, hospital, surgery
memory, 15, 33, 42, 53, 61–62, 67, 70, 108, 117, 130, 140, 148–49, 157, 159, 166, 168
collective, 163
cyborg/posthuman, 164
electronic, 162
national, 6, 109
prosthetic, 62, 105–06, 160, 168, 174
technological, 109
television and, 105, 107–09
see also history, past
Menem, Carlos, 113, 114
mentalist, 89
see also parapsychologist, psychic
mestiza, 48
metaphor, metaphorical, 1, 11, 51, 68, 69, 72, 74, 82, 84, 88, 93, 110, 133, 134, 137, 139, 141, 156, 165, 166–67, 171, 172
cyborgs, 23, 83, 92, 95, 126–28, 130, 155, 161
Metaverse, 135

Metro 95.1, 2004 marketing
campaign, 5, 77–79
see also advertising
Metropolis, 14, 179
Mexico, 2, 5, 57, 80, 147, 150, 152
Mexican popular culture, 150
Mexico City, 147, 152
Middle Earth, 151
military, 2, 6, 24, 27, 39, 99, 107,
114–15, 123, 124, 130, 181
anti-communist, 6
coups, 6
see also dictatorship
military-industrial complex, 12
see also capitalism, military
Milonga de Hackers (Garavaglia),
183
Mina Cruel (Borinsky), 44
miracle, 103–04
mockery, 22
see also resistance
modern, 16, 18, 78, 118, 150, 163
see also postmodern
money, 14, 23, 103, 113, 136
see also capitalism, economy,
market
monogamous, 168
see also family, sex
monster, 38, 59, 153, 180
cybernetic, 141
see also Frankenstein
mother, 13, 48, 50, 52, 59, 61, 62,
72–74, 80, 89, 91, 108, 176
motherhood, 75
see also family, father, maternal,
nuclear family, offspring,
pregnancy, reproduction
mourning, 42, 180
national, 42
see also pain, memory,
survivorship
Mulder, Fox, 124–25, 127–28
murder, 99, 104, 108, 115, 131,
135, 143, 181
see also death, rape, torture

music, musicians, 30, 77–79, 103,
154, 165, 168, 176, 181
myth, 5, 7, 10, 12, 52, 53, 58, 75,
81, 140, 144, 145, 146, 147,
150, 152, 153, 156, 157, 174
cyborg, 5, 23, 27, 53, 59, 74, 93,
122, 143, 144
global, 7
posthuman mythologies of Fresán
and Fuguet, 145–47, 150,
152–53, 156–57, 174
see also fable

Narrative as Virtual Reality (Ryan),
180
narrative, narrator, 1–5, 7, 9, 22,
24–25, 27–33, 36, 39, 43–44,
48–51, 55, 57, 58, 59, 60, 65,
68, 69, 71–72, 77, 80, 97, 99,
102, 104–06, 115, 123–24,
126, 129, 132, 139, 141,
145–50, 152–59, 165, 169–70,
172–74, 176, 179, 180, 181,
182
cybernetic nature of, 23
as cyborg, 29, 31
liberating potential, 29
mechanical, 5, 23, 24, 29
political, 146
televisual, 99
see also fiction, story-telling
national, 7, 17, 38, 42, 44, 100,
101, 109, 123
history, 110
identity, 150
memory, 6, 38, 109
multinational, 14–15, 136
television and consciousness,
103–04, 109, 182
see also government
nationalism, 39
see also dictatorship, police state
nature, 12, 52, 61
Ndalianis, Angela, 176
neobaroque, 176

INDEX

neoliberalism, neoliberal, 2, 3, 5, 6, 79, 101, 113–15, 118, 130–31, 137, 142–43, 145–146, 174, 176
  links between dictatorship and, 6
  policy, 2, 4, 6, 97, 114–15, 122–23, 131, 133–34, 136–37, 141, 176, 183
  prosthetics, 6, 113, 182
  rise and fall of policy, 113
Neuromancer (Gibson), 129
news, 90, 93, 95, 97–99, 101, 103–04, 110–11, 138, 156, 157, 166, 182
  as staged production, 105
  see also media
newspaper, 103, 157, 166
  see also media
Nicotina, 183
nightmares, 13
  technological, 55
  see also dreams
North America, 2, 5, 43, 129, 174
  theorists, 43, 48–49, 50, 55
  writers and critics, 129
novela del dictador, 130
La novela virtual (Sainz), 177
NSA, 131–33
nuclear family, 46, 57, 59, 62, 71, 74, 75, 140, 169
  as cause of ecological apocalypse, 52
  see also family, heteronormative

Oedipal, 12
offspring
  cyborgs as illegitimate offspring of militarism and patriarchal capitalism, 12
  see also birth, family, nuclear family, origin
Operation Condor, 137
oppression, 6, 9, 12, 14, 16, 19–20, 23, 39, 41, 56, 58, 71, 74, 123, 130, 132–33, 137, 141, 180

  see also dictatorship, repression
organ, 14, 67, 72, 74, 94, 96, 110, 138, 154, 160–63, 165, 168
  "new organs" (Laws of Media), 148
  schizophrenic's "detachable organs," 98
  see also heart, implant
organic, 1, 2, 4, 6, 13, 16, 18, 19, 20, 29, 45, 47, 59, 60, 62, 63, 70, 74, 77–78, 83, 87–88, 94–95, 97–8, 101, 102, 108, 110, 121, 137, 140, 143–44, 149, 150, 155, 157, 166–67
  body, 4, 7, 10–11, 14, 17, 18, 19, 20, 21, 38, 42, 59, 62, 64–67, 69, 70, 73–75, 79–81, 85, 87, 90, 92–93, 95, 97–99, 109, 110, 117, 120–22, 138, 140–43, 147, 149, 152, 154, 159–61, 168
  family, 12, 50–51, 55, 59
  origin, 12, 34, 36, 38–39, 50–53, 57, 63, 152, 158
  mythologies, 53, 58, 140
  rejection of in cyborg thought, 12, 38–39, 52, 140
  see also birth, Garden of Eden, genesis story, pregnancy, reproduction
Ortega, Francisco, 177
Ouija board, 157

pain, 13, 15, 21, 33–34, 38, 69
  as defining characteristic of the birth of the cybernetic organism, 34
  "objectless" state of the being in pain (Scarry), 121–22
  see also death, Elaine Scarry, torture, trauma
Palaversich, Diana, 183
Panopticon, 18, 118, 159, 167
  see also discipline, surveillance

paradox, 19–20, 31–32, 41–42, 47, 77, 81, 85, 87, 97
paranoia, 1, 26–27, 35, 72
  see also hallucinations, insanity, madness
parapsychologist, 89, 91
  see also mentalist, psychic
parents, 48, 52, 133, 136, 140, 157, 169–70
  see also birth, father, maternal, pregnancy, reproduction
party, 153–56
  animal, 154
  as cybernetic organism, 155–56
past, 15, 38–39, 52, 57, 122, 124, 130–31, 133, 149, 157, 162, 168–69, 174, 180
  as a film, 148
  forgetting, 38, 143, 149
  see also history, memory, storytelling
patriarchy, patriarchal, 2, 5, 10, 58, 73
  capitalism, 11–12
  see also father, gender, nuclear family, hierarchy, power
Paz Soldán, Edmundo, 6, 47, 113, 115, 123–37, 140–44, 145–47, 153, 164, 169, 174, 176, 182, 183
Perón, Isabela de, 9
The Pet Shop Boys, 154
phallus, 52
  prosthetic, 4, 118
  scalpel as, 13
photograph, photography, 16–17, 28, 47, 61–64, 67, 70, 104, 123, 125–30, 143, 169, 171
  alteration of, 77–8, 123–25, 127, 129–30
  cyborg/android, 47, 78
  destabilization of, 130
  symbol of resistance to dictatorship, 130
  see also camera, film, image
picana, 27, 36, 121
  as sexual prosthesis, 38
  see also cattle prod, dictatorship, Dirty War, police state, scar, torture
Piglia, Ricardo, 4–6, 10, 22–42, 43, 122, 174, 176, 180
Pinocchio, 52
Pinochet, Augusto, 157
Plata quemada (Piglia), 23
poet, poetry, 30, 36, 80, 100–01, 108
  see also literature
police state
  psychiatric clinic and, 26, 35, 37–38
  see also Argentina, dictatorship, surveillance
political, 2, 4, 12, 19, 22–25, 35, 39, 41, 48, 51, 80–81, 102, 105, 107–09, 113–14, 122–23, 128, 130–33, 144, 145–46, 173, 182, 183
  see also dictatorship, government
popular culture, 79, 151, 159, 176
  Mexican, 150
Por favor, rebobinar (Fuguet), 7, 145–46, 157–58, 162
Porush, David, 31
postdictatorship, postdictatorial, 2–7, 15, 38, 42, 43, 80, 101, 106, 109, 110, 113, 115, 130, 146, 176, 182
postfamilial (body), 13
postmodern, 11, 25, 32, 39, 86, 110
poststructuralism, 134, 175
power, 10, 12–14, 16–19, 22–23, 29, 35, 39, 41, 43, 47, 69, 100, 113, 123, 132, 155, 167, 171, 172
  cyborg's, 12, 20–21, 23, 35–36, 46, 74–75, 81, 176
  and patriarchy, 14
  solitary nature of, 40
  state, 17, 123, 132

see also corporation, government, hierarchy
PowerBook, 171
see also computer
Prado, Eugenia, 5, 43, 57–76, 169, 174, 180
pregnancy
 ectogenic, 50
 see also birth, family, origin, procreation
printer, 73–74
privatization, 113
procreation, 51, 55, 59, 74, 122, 140, 169
 see also birth, child, family, origin, pregnancy, reproduction
production, 19, 20, 61, 68, 72, 73, 74, 105, 113, 175
 cultural, 1–2, 4, 7, 32, 177
 cyborg embodiment and literary, 164
 of the visual image, 98, 160, 169
prosthesis, prosthetic, 4, 11, 13, 16–25, 34–36, 38, 40, 42, 44, 58–60, 62–63, 75, 81, 94, 121, 138, 150, 158, 160–63, 167–68, 179
 bearing testimony, 15, 22, 25, 34, 42, 74, 122, 174
 brain, 149, 161
 by-product of torture/result of violence, 36, 41, 42, 74, 122
 ears, 17, 105, 108
 eyes, 98, 101, 105, 169
 heart, 14
 love, 104
 media as prosthetic imaginary of a nation of television viewers, 103
 media as prosthetic mouth of the state, 103
 media-prosthesis, 150
 memory, 62, 105–06, 160, 168
 neoliberal, 6, 113, 182
 phallus, 4, 118
 scars as, 121–22
 sexual, 38, 45
 technological, 14, 15, 99, 110, 117–18, 121, 138, 150, 152
 telephone/booth as, 45, 65, 67, 74
 televisions and cameras as prostheses, 101, 148, 169
 see also implant, machines, technology
prostitute, 44–47, 103
 virtual, 137
protagonist, 5, 14, 59, 60, 80, 130, 148, 179
posthuman, 117
psyche, 147
 mutilated, 99
 see also consciousness
psychiatry, psychiatrist, 35, 165
 connection between psychiatric clinic and the Argentine police state, 26, 37
 see also doctor, hospital, medical, psychoanalytic, psychology
psychic, 89–93
 see also mentalist, parapsychologist
psychoanalytic, 95
 see also psychiatrist, psychology
psychology, psychological, 6, 15, 59–60, 68, 95
 conversion into cyborg, 34
 of a posthuman television viewer, 109
 television as psychological coping mechanism, 105
 see also consciousness, Jung, pain, psychoanalytic, psychiatrist, unconscious
Pubis angelical (Puig), 4, 9, 14–15, 22, 24, 122
El púgil (Reginato), 177
Puig, Manuel, 4, 5, 6, 9–10, 13–14, 23, 43, 122, 161

queer, 5
  see also family, gender, heteronormative
Quiroga, Horacio, 1

radio, 5–6, 77–78, 100, 155, 157, 167, 169
  see also media
rape, 121
  see also body, pain, torture
Rayuela (Cortázar), 1
reality, 2, 11, 22, 34, 49, 59, 68, 70, 72, 75, 79, 80, 84, 89, 92, 93, 98, 102, 105, 119, 123, 125, 130, 134–39, 143, 146, 156, 157, 160, 177
  cultural, 173
  cyborg/posthuman, 146, 165
  social, 11–12
  see also virtual
rebel, 53, 104, 146, 179
  female as, 44, 48
relations, relationship, 11, 16, 18, 25, 30, 31, 67–70, 72, 74, 121, 123, 126, 128, 133, 139, 154, 157–58, 168, 169, 170, 172
  between machine and flesh, 11, 14, 18, 58
  computer as location of, 129, 171
  and technology, 129, 138–39, 150, 153, 163, 169, 170, 173
  and television, 85, 87, 92–93, 95, 160
  see also family, parent, sex
religion, religious, 150, 159
  see also creator, genesis story, god, heaven, hell, origin
remote control, 79, 86–88, 93–94, 98, 110, 161, 181
  see also television, video, zapping
repression, repressive, 25, 54, 56, 130
  see also oppression
reproduce, reproduction, 17, 28, 50, 53, 55, 114, 157, 166, 179
  asexual, 51

  see also birth, gender, pregnancy, procreation
resist, resistance, 18–24, 49, 67, 74, 75, 107, 130, 134, 138, 143
  cyborg and, 23, 27, 58
  see also mockery
Respiración artificial (Piglia), 4, 22, 24, 33, 39, 41
revenge, 4, 20, 108
revolution, revolutionary, 11, 12, 13, 73, 135, 143, 172
  potential of the cyborg, 1, 2, 10, 12, 42, 57, 148
  potential of language, 30–31
Rivera, Diego, 176
rural, Latin America as (rejection of), 146
Russian, 25, 33–34, 37, 172
Ryan, Marie-Laure, 29, 180
Rybczynski, Witold, 110

Sabato, Ernesto, 1, 175
Sainz, Gustavo, 177
Sandoval, Chela, 48
Santiago, Chile, 57
Santo and Blue Demon films, 150
Sarlo, Beatriz, 7, 86–88, 92, 161
Scarry, Elaine, 121–22
  see also pain
scar, scarred, scarring, 4, 37, 38, 42, 46, 110, 115, 118, 121, 143, 153, 176
  as emblems of trauma/violence, 22, 34, 38, 121, 122
  forming a map, 121
  mechanical scars, 5
  see also body, flesh, pain, torture
schizophrenia, schizophrenic, 21, 58, 61, 68, 98
  see also psychiatry, psychology
science fiction, 3, 6, 9, 12, 13, 15, 23, 50, 54, 58, 59, 64, 72, 78, 122, 125, 141, 143, 156, 158, 160, 161, 173, 176–77
  the importance of for the creation of a national identity, 150

see also fiction, literature
scientific theory, 3
Scott, Ridley, 9, 14, 129
screen, 58, 79, 86, 88, 92, 94–96, 98, 125, 127, 170
   see also computer, film, television, video
seam, seamless, 11, 12, 97, 110, 118, 132, 173
   bleeding at the, 123
self, 34, 50, 62, 70, 78, 80–81, 97, 116, 122, 134–35, 137, 141, 158, 160, 175
semiotics, 74, 103
"Señales captadas en el corazón de una fiesta" (Fresán), 153, 154
Serling, Rod, 150
Serpent, 53, 71
sexism, 10
sex, sexual, sexuality, sexualize, 13, 45–46, 48, 51, 66–67, 72, 75, 139, 174
   cyber-, 137–38
   phone, 58, 69, 118
   prosthesis, 38, 45, 74, 138
   traditional sex life, 181
   virtual, 119
   see also bisexuality, erotic, heteronormative, heterosexual, heterotopia, queer, sexism
Shelley, Mary, 180
short stories, 2, 7, 80, 145, 153, 172
   see also fiction, novel
signal, 10, 34, 74, 81, 153–57
Silverman, Kaja, 7
Sisyphus, 154
skyscraper, 16
   see also building, corporation
slapstick, 102
Snow Crash (Stephenson), 135, 141
socialism, 12
social reality, 11–12
society, 3, 12, 27, 48, 50, 52, 53, 54, 55, 58, 71, 73, 75, 77, 81, 107, 109, 130, 131, 134, 137, 156

contemporary, 153
global, 153
societal construction, 12
software, 125, 134, 136
   mind functioning as, 128
   see also Adobe Photoshop, code, computer
La sonámbula, 42
The Souls of Cyberfolk (Foster), 3
Stam, Robert, 94–95, 98
Star Trek, 52
state, 3, 12, 17, 24, 26, 29–31, 35, 38, 41, 56, 113, 122, 141, 143, 174
   market-run, 31
   media functioning as prosthetic mouth of, 103
   see also dictatorship, government, police state
Stephenson, Neal, 135, 141–42
Stevenson, Robert Louis, 151
Sting, 165–66
storytelling, storyteller, 42
   altered female bodies functioning as text and, 43
   machine, 24
   technology as, 23
   see also fiction, history, memory, narrator
subaltern, 21–22
subjectivity, 3, 43, 44, 46, 48, 59, 114, 118, 143, 145, 147, 150, 158–59, 180
subversion, subversive, 10, 12, 14, 18–19, 27, 53–54, 57, 137, 141, 144, 161, 173
   subversive nature of cyborgs, 4, 22 31, 35, 38, 44, 51, 57, 74–75, 81, 141
Sueños digitales (Paz Soldán), 6, 47, 115, 123–31, 143, 182
suicide, 28, 124
surgery, surgeons, 9, 13, 99, 103
   see also doctor, hospital, medical

surveillance, 17–20, 24, 118, 137, 159, 167–68
  cyborg as emblem of resistance to, 19
  cyborg as victim of, 19–20
  and Foucault, 18
  mechanical body as agent of, 118
  software, 136
  see also control, machine, Panopticon, tape recorder
survivor, survivorship, 4, 9–10, 22, 35, 42, 100, 117, 121–22, 143, 144, 145, 153, 179
suture, 13, 80, 110, 160, 173, 177
  cinematic suture theory, 182
  cultural, 123
  cybernetic, 21, 110, 177
  television as, 109
symbol, 2, 3, 9, 19, 23, 27, 30, 34, 58–59, 78, 93, 103, 122, 130, 133, 143

Tajos (Courtoisie), 5–6, 79–102, 107, 109–11, 148
tape recorder, 16–18
  see also surveillance
technology, technological, 1–7, 11, 13–18, 23, 25, 31–32, 36, 41, 44–46, 49–51, 54–55, 57–59, 62, 64–67, 70, 72, 74–75, 78–81, 87–88, 90–94, 97–111, 115, 117–20, 122–27, 129, 131, 133–34, 136–38, 142–44, 146–50, 154–64, 166–69, 173–74, 179, 181
  anti-, 72
  appendages/prosthesis, 4, 74, 93–94, 99, 101, 102, 107–08, 110, 117, 121, 138, 150, 152
  artifacts, 3, 153
  of control, 54, 118, 123, 167–68
  dehumanizing effects of technological society, 54
  hackers and, 122, 141
  identity, 2, 4, 77, 93, 137, 158, 177
  rejection of, 141, 175
  and relationships, 129, 173
  as storyteller, 23
  of torture, 4, 118, 122
  see also technophilia, technophobia
techno-organic body, 7
  see also body, cybernetic
technophilia, 1, 79, 161
  capitalistic, 14
technophobia, 179, 181
teleology, 12
robot, 11, 160
telenovela, 106
telephone
  in *Lóbulo*, 58–59, 63–74
  in *Tajos*, 79, 85–94
tele-spectator, 94–95
television, 6–7, 26, 79–81, 85–111, 147–48, 153, 155–57, 160, 162, 182
  as the national imaginary/memory, 6, 100, 103–04, 106
  news as staged production, 105
  as political battlefield, 107
  and prosthesis, 99–101, 103, 105, 108
  as psychological coping mechanism, 105
  semi-Luddite view as cause of societies' ills, 106
  as suture, 160, 182
  see also advertising, media, news, remote control, televisual, zapping
televisual, 5, 77, 80, 85, 87, 89, 93–102, 105–06, 108–10, 160, 181, 182
  cyborgs, 98, 110, 150
  identity, 89–90, 110
  media, 6, 79
  see also television
The Terminator, 161
terror, terrorism, 15, 84, 104
  political, 130
  state, 35, 38, 122, 143

INDEX

see also torture, violence
testimony, 74
  prosthesis bearing testimony of violence, 15, 41, 144
text, 3, 10, 13, 24–25, 28–29, 31–32, 38–39, 48–49, 53, 56, 58–59, 74, 78, 80, 100, 122, 125, 127, 132, 163, 166, 175, 177, 181
  altered female bodies functioning as storyteller and, 43
  birth of child/text, 72
  cadaver as mother of, 74
  cyborg bodies as, 122, 144
  of flesh and metal subverting authoritative structures, 143–44
  textual hybridity, 39, 181
  see also fiction, hypertext, narrative, wreader
theater, 59, 158, 181
  see also art, cinema
third world, 123
  feminism, 48
  see also first world
Thomas, Douglas, 133–35, 141
Tiempo de revancha, 4, 10, 15, 18, 22, 24, 59
Tolkien, J.R.R., 151
tongue, 15, 21, 179
  prosthetic, 5, 19–22, 42, 65, 119
  see also voice
Torre, Raúl de la, 4, 9, 13
torture, 24, 27, 32, 36–37, 38, 42, 108, 121, 131, 147, 180, 181
  cyborg/prostheses as product of, 4, 36–38, 122, 174
  electroshock and, 24, 36, 118
  map of, 122
  severing the link between mind and organic body, 121
  technology of, 4, 118, 122
  see also body, cattle prod, dictatorship, Dirty War, picana, rape, scar, violence
totalitarian, 54

tradition, 2, 11, 14, 32, 37, 46, 54, 59, 62, 116, 117, 122, 130, 146, 147, 155, 160–61, 168, 170, 177, 180, 181
  cyborg's power to subvert, 12, 48, 50
transformation, 20, 23, 34, 35, 46, 63–66, 70, 92, 102–03, 155, 159
  of identity, 33, 65, 80, 133, 167
Transhumanist Society, 3
trauma, 9, 15, 19, 20, 33–35, 117, 122, 175, 182
  cyborg body/prostheses as result/testimony of, 14, 15, 20, 22, 34, 36, 37–38, 42, 121–22, 161, 174
  of dictatorship and political violence, 6, 14, 15, 22–23, 38, 108–10, 132, 144, 145–46, 176
  fictional programs as a way to understand, 105
  physical, 9, 13, 42, 99, 103, 110
  see also death, scars, surgery, torture, violence
Treasure Island, 151
Turing, Alan, 131
The Twilight Zone, 150

Ulysses, 24
unconscious, 98, 163, 165–66
  see also brain, consciousness, Jung, memory, psychology
The United States, 3, 41, 133
unity, 12, 52–53
Universal Turing Machine, 142
The Untouchables, 172
urban, 6, 77–78, 167
Uruguay, 2
utopia, utopian, 53, 55, 57
  see also dystopia

Vader, Darth, 151
Vampire, 181

La velocidad de las cosas (Fresán), 153
Venezuela, 113
victim, 4, 38, 73–74, 161, 4, 19, 38, 73, 161
  of political and economic trauma, 19–20, 84, 122
Videla Junta, 9
video, 81, 102, 104, 106, 160, 183
  see also media, technology
violence, 15, 21, 38, 41–42, 69, 80, 84, 108, 143
  governmental, political, 22, 34, 102
  see also dictatorship, Dirty War, terrorism, torture, trauma
virtual, 32, 42, 66, 70, 104, 114–15, 125, 133, 134, 136–37, 143, 175, 177
  eroticism, 119–20
  intimacy, 171
  realism, 163–64
  reality, 29, 32, 123, 126, 132, 164, 180
  sex, 119
  world, 64, 135, 136, 164
virus, 78, 115–17, 141, 142, 166–67
  see also disease
voice, 19, 20, 34, 37, 41, 46, 48, 49, 57, 58, 64, 66, 68, 69, 70, 71, 78, 87, 108, 120, 154, 156, 169
  see also tongue

Waisman, Sergio, 180
war, 9, 34, 39, 105, 108, 115, 117, 121, 182
  as a television program, 105
  see also dictatorship, Dirty War, torture, violence
weapon
  telephone functioning as technological, 181
Weiner, Norbert, 68
Welch, Raquel, 124–27
Welles, Orson, 177
wheelchair, 40–41, 103
Wilson Reginato, Mike, 177
woman, 12, 14, 15, 23–27, 28, 30, 33, 37, 44, 45, 49, 53, 61, 66, 83–84, 118–20
  body, 9, 13, 27
  challenging male hierarchies, 14
  cyborg/posthuman, 5, 11, 26–27, 32, 48, 72, 75, 118–20, 139
  cyborg women as narratives, 9–10, 43 and mentalist, 89–90
  see also body, female, feminine, feminist, maternal, mother
wreader, 29, 31, 32, 180
writing, 2, 19, 31, 35
Writing Machines (Hayles), 31

The X-Files, 128, 130

zapping, 86–88, 156, 159, 181
  see also remote control
Žižek, Slavoj, 175

GPSR Compliance
The European Union's (EU) General Product Safety Regulation (GPSR) is a set of rules that requires consumer products to be safe and our obligations to ensure this.

If you have any concerns about our products, you can contact us on

ProductSafety@springernature.com

In case Publisher is established outside the EU, the EU authorized representative is:

Springer Nature Customer Service Center GmbH
Europaplatz 3
69115 Heidelberg, Germany

www.ingramcontent.com/pod-product-compliance
Ingram Content Group UK Ltd.
Pitfield, Milton Keynes, MK11 3LW, UK
UKHW021251180426
11946UKWH00004B/87